Praise for Al

'*If You Were Here* is a moving and
life-altering dilemma' **Jill Ma**
Rumour

'It's not often that I fall in love with a book within the first few
pages, but it happened to me with this one' **The Bookbag** on
You, Me and Him

'Compelling and beautifully written' **Daisy Buchanan, journalist
and author on *If You Were Here***

'As it was favourite book of the year to date for my reader in this
field, I had to read it too… I loved it. It's character-led, warm and
sensitive' **Sarah Broadhurst, *The Bookseller* on
*Letter From my Sister***

'This is a wonderful portrait of the different dynamics within an
unusual family' **Sara Lawrence, *Daily Mail* on *The Things
We Do for Love***

'A lovely example of realistic fiction that many women will be able
to relate to' **Sun on *One Step Closer to You***

'A lovely read, tackling both light and dark material with real
assurance. I love the idea of a love triangle where one of the
characters has died, which actually makes him more of an obstacle
than if he were still alive. Also, the thought that you can find true
love twice feels a strong romantic notion – and quite true, I'm
sure' **Tom Williams, *Chalet Girl* screenwriter on *Ten Years On***

'Echoes of Jane Austen, *A Room With a View* and *Bridget Jones's
Diary*' **Robert O'Rourke on *Monday to Friday Man***

Also by Alice Peterson

THE
SATURDAY
PLACE

ALICE PETERSON

Bedford Square
Publishers

First published in the UK in 2024 by Bedford Square Publishers Ltd,
London, UK
@bedsqpublishers

ISBN 978-1-915798-52-7 (paperback)
ISBN 978-1-915798-53-4 (ebook)

2 4 6 8 10 9 7 5 3 1

Printed in Great Britain by CPI Group (UK) Ltd, Croydon CR0 4YY

Typeset using Atomik ePublisher from Easypress Technologies

To Debbie and Tracey

PROLOGUE

I stand in front of a wide-open landscape with endless miles of golden sand. The landscape is dotted with only a few people ahead of us, or perhaps it feels that way because Holkham beach is so vast and unspoilt. The sun is out. It's a warm July day. Jamie reaches for my hand, looks at me as if to say, 'I told you it was beautiful.'

'It's beautiful,' I confirm for him, as we walk towards the sea, carrying our swimming towels. The tide is out, the sea tempting us from a distance, like a gift waiting to be unwrapped. That's if I'm brave enough. I told Jamie I'd be just as happy paddling and watching him swim.

'They liked me, didn't they?' Jamie and I have been dating for six months and this weekend we travelled to his family home in Norfolk, where I met his parents for the first time.

'They thought you were *all right*.' He gives me a sideways glance.

I hit his arm playfully, before placing my hand back into his.

'Holly, they *loved* you. Mind you, I knew they would.'

I smile with him, because deep down I know it went well too. Jamie's mum exuded warmth from the moment I met her, saying how much she'd heard about me, and not to call her Mrs Roberts. 'Please, it's Pam,' she'd insisted, leading me into their kitchen which smelt of freshly baked bread and coffee. After lunch she showed me around their home and garden, pointing out her new vegetable plot, telling me with great eagerness that we could pick some runner beans for supper. Jamie's father was more reserved, but kind. I sensed he felt protective. Jamie married young, aged 23. They were childhood sweethearts, but after four years, without any warning, she packed her bags and left him for another man. I imagined his parents picked up the pieces of his broken heart. Like Jamie, his dad is a creative soul. Before retiring, he was a senior director at an insurance firm, a job he endured, but now he spends his time doing what he loves, writing, and has just had his first novel published. 'Goes to show, it's never too late,' he'd said to us over dinner.

'It's about all our friends,' Pam whispered, as if they were sitting round the table with us. 'They'll probably never speak to us again.'

Jamie teased me in bed the other night, saying I didn't need to read Dad's book before the weekend, he wasn't going to quiz me on the characters. But that's me. Always like to be prepared. 'And *please* don't read the sex scene.' Jamie had shuddered.

'You could learn a few tips from him,' I said, before Jamie grabbed the book from my hand and tossed it on to the floor, both of us laughing as he said, 'It's too weird to think Dad wrote *that*, and even weirder if you read it.'

While we've been together only for six months, I know this man is my future. I sensed it the first time we met in Milla's kitchen. Camilla, known to close family and friends as Milla, is one of my oldest school friends, and she'd commissioned Jamie to redesign her kitchen. He'd been recommended to her by one of her doctor friends, whom I will forever be indebted to.

I have a sudden vivid memory of the day we met. It was a Saturday morning. On Friday night, Milla and I had stayed out late, drinking and dancing, something we often did when her husband was away. Milla loved to let her hair down after being in hospital all week; I loved to let my hair down after enduring my boss, Clarissa Pope. I crashed over at hers, only to be rudely awoken the following morning by Milla rushing into my bedroom, saying 'Fuck! Kitchen man! Hot! Get up!'

Ten minutes later I joined Milla and Jamie downstairs. They

were sitting at the kitchen table, looking at samples of wood laid out on the floor. It was far too early to care about wood samples, I thought, until I saw his face. It was a face that made me wish I'd at least brushed my teeth. He had the most natural smile that reached his eyes. He had a manner that put people at ease. 'Holly, this is Jamie,' Milla said. I can still remember exactly what he was wearing: a loose-fitting pale pink shirt, sleeves rolled up, dark jeans and I noticed a worn leather braided bracelet around his tanned wrist. When he stood up to shake my hand, I liked how tall he was, at least six-foot. Already I was imagining we'd make a good fit, my hand in his.

As I glance at him now, I think it's too good to be true, and that any moment I'll wake up and discover it's all been a dream. Yet I don't wake up. Here I am. I squeeze Jamie's hand to make sure he's real.

It became even clearer that I wanted to spend the rest of my life with him a month ago, after he survived a weekend with my parents. I was wary about him meeting Mum. I didn't want our relationship to end overnight. Don't get me wrong, I love Mum, but she fusses and frets about everything and subtlety has never been a strong point. The moment I hinted I may have met someone special she was planning her wedding outfit. She rolled the red carpet out for Jamie's visit; anyone would have thought he was royalty. Everything had to be perfect. The house was immaculately tidy and she'd bought enough food to feed an army. I understand why she went to such lengths, despite Dad and me telling her she needs to relax, play it cool, but that's like asking her not to breathe. I'm her only child so she pins all her hopes and dreams on me. She is itching to make baby booties and cardies for her grandkids. I'd warned Jamie that she can be 'a bit much', followed by a promise I wouldn't turn into her, but, as always, he took it in his stride. When I saw him indulging her with yet another old family photograph album, an image of me, naked in the paddling pool, making both Mum and Dad laugh by saying I hadn't changed at all – that's when I knew that one day, we'd have our own family photograph album.

'It's quiet here, peaceful,' I reflect.

'I never tire of this view. When I die, I want my ashes scattered here.'

'Stop it,' I say, alarmed by his matter-of-factness.

'I mean it. When I go.'

'Don't you dare.'

'I want to rest here.'

'Jamie, stop being so morbid,' I say, not wanting to focus on his death when we have our whole life ahead of us, a life we've barely begun.

He turns to me, totally unfazed. 'Promise me, Holly.'

I realise he's being deadly serious. 'If I promise, can we change the subject?'

'I don't know why we fear death.' He shrugs. 'It's the one and only certainty we have in life.'

'I know, but you're thirty-one.'

'If we talked about it, it wouldn't be as frightening. This is my home, Holly, the beach I grew up on, so all I'm saying is when I eventually go, I want my ashes scattered in the sea.'

I nod, realising I need to grow up. 'OK. I promise.' I can't help adding, 'But please don't go any time soon. I'm kind of enjoying having you around.'

'Don't worry. I have no intention of going anywhere just yet.'

We walk past a couple flying a kite, fairly unsuccessfully since there is no breeze to speak of. It's Sunday afternoon and a few families are having picnics, an elderly couple are walking their two dogs, and yet no one has to share a patch of their sand. The sand here seems as infinite as the blue sky above. We watch a toddler, still in nappies, on her hands and knees playing in the sludgy brown mud. Before reaching the sea, there are pools of water to paddle in, but this child wants to do more than get her feet wet. She's on a mission to get her pretty smocked dress dirty and thankfully her mother doesn't seem anything like my own, positively encouraging her to have fun. I mean, what are washing machines for?

Whenever I see parents playing with their children, I long to be a mum. This feeling, this need in me, is strong. Milla doesn't get it. She can't think of anything worse than nappies and broken sleep. Yet, for me, the longing is visceral, and it's only grown stronger since meeting Jamie. I crave a child that is a part of *both* of us. Both Jamie and I are only children, and while that has had its advantages, we've also missed being part of a larger family. Jamie once told me he fantasised about having a younger brother or sister, someone he could boss around. He also knows how I longed for a sister, and that it's my fantasy to have a little girl.

'One day, we'll come here, with *our* baby girl,' Jamie says, as if reading my mind. 'Even if that means we have to have forty boys before we have our girl, so be it.'

'I'd rather we have one girl, straight off, not forty boys.'

He smiles back at me, sheepish. 'So would I. So would our bank manager. So would the environment. But you get my drift.'

'I get your drift. We could have a boy too,' I suggest, 'a younger brother.'

'Yeah. I can see them now, in the back of the car, squabbling and driving us mad.'

'They'll keep us young.' I watch the little girl giggling with her dad as he scoops her up into his arms and runs across the beach.

Finally, we're only meters from the sea. 'Feeling brave?' he asks, stripping off with confidence. One of the many reasons I fell for Jamie is he's not conscious of his weight or appearance, not that he needs to be, his job keeps him fit, but the last thing I want is a man who spends more time in the bathroom than me. He's the opposite of vain and hates the gym as much as I do. A game of tennis and a bike ride is more our thing, or a walk in the park with an ice cream. He loves to eat, drink, dance, swim in the sea… He wades into the water effortlessly, as if it's a warm bath. Bastard! But it's his fearlessness, his love of life that makes me so attracted to him. I'm more cautious, timid by nature. They say opposites attract.

I dip a toe into the water. It's ice-cold. 'Maybe I'll paddle,' I say, knowing I won't get away with it.

He throws me a look. 'Once you're in, it's beautiful.'

Come on, Holly. With renewed determination I unbutton my denim shorts and take off my T-shirt. Jamie wolf whistles as I strike a pose in my red bikini, which hasn't seen the light of day for years, and I'm now regretting that second helping of lemon meringue pie. I also wish I wasn't quite so pale. My legs are as white as stone whereas Jamie has enviable olive-toned skin.

I step in cautiously. 'Liar!' I take another tentative step towards him, knowing I need to keep moving forward, I mustn't stop or fuss or fret. I do not want to turn into my mother just yet. Be calm, cool, sexy in your little red bikini. The freezing cold water, now up to my thighs, is beginning to feel a little more bearable.

'You can do it, Holly!' he says.

There's nothing for it. I dive in, immerse myself, before coming up for air, my breath stolen from me. 'Fuck, bugger, shit!' I curse. 'Shit! Jamie! I hate you!'

He laughs.

'It's not funny!' I say, thinking my heart is about to jump out of my chest. The water stings, like needles all over my body.

'Keep moving, Holly,' Jamie urges, 'it gets easier. Follow me.' As I swim alongside him, I realise he's right. It is getting a little easier. My breath returns, the intensity of the cold recedes. I settle into the enormity of the sea, feeling free. I did it. I did it! I keep swimming, and in this moment, I realise that I couldn't be happier. Right now, this space belongs to us alone. I am in the right place, with the right person. Suddenly I can't stop smiling. I feel alive. I look up at the blue cloudless sky, the sun on my face, and quietly thank Jamie's first wife, for being foolish enough to leave him. 'I love you,' I say, not caring anymore if I'm the one who says it first. Life's too short.

'What did you say?' Jamie asks, swimming back towards me.

'I love you,' I say, knowing full well he heard, as we wrap our arms around one another.

I feel his touch, his skin, his salty lips on mine. 'I should get you into the sea more often,' he suggests with that wry smile that is becoming so familiar to me.

When he says, 'I love you too,' something inside me lights up, and stays with me, for as long as I can remember.

1

Eleven years later

'May I come in?' the policeman asks.

He refuses a cup of coffee. Or tea.

Maybe he wants a glass of water?

This can't be about Jamie. Jamie's fine. He left at five this morning. Crept out of bed without waking me up. He's working on a project in Hampshire.

No, this couldn't be about Jamie. Maybe it's Mum? Or Dad? After the policeman refuses a cup of tea, coffee or water again, 'I'm afraid I have some bad news,' he says. 'Your husband was involved in a road accident earlier this morning.'

He tells me Jamie was killed, outright, by a lorry driver, asleep behind his wheel. He wouldn't have suffered any pain, the policeman reports.

He died instantly.

And so do I.

That evening, lying in bed, I look over to the side Jamie slept in last night. My sense of not being able to live without him steals my breath from me. I sit up, gasping for air, as I say, repeatedly, 'I can't, I can't, I can't.' I hug my knees, my body shaking. 'I can't, I can't, I can't,' I say, broken and scared.

Milla rushes into my bedroom. She was one of the first people I called to tell the news. She left work immediately, before packing her bags to spend the night with me, saying she'd stay for as long as I needed. She hands me some water, encourages me to take sips, until finally my breathing returns. I am so exhausted there is no voice left inside me. It's as if my whole world has stopped and I feel scared, and so alone. Milla sleeps on Jamie's side of the bed. She places an arm around my waist, finds my hand. 'It's going to be OK,' she whispers in the darkness.

I wish I believed her.

2

Eighteen months later

Nina hands me a mug of coffee. It's half past seven, far too early to be up on a Saturday morning, but Nina told me to come to her café before mayhem kicks in. When I say café, it's Soul Food, a community café at the Pastoral Centre, next door to my local church in Hammersmith. Her dark hair is tied up in a messy ponytail, and she's wearing a chocolate-brown apron with *Food for the Soul* embroidered on to the front, over a white T-shirt and pair of dungarees. Her aqua-blue nose stud matches the colour of her eyes. Everything about her exudes youth and energy. The only things that give away that she's in her forties are the fine lines around her eyes, the reading spectacles perched on the end of her nose, and the fact that I know, from all my Googling about how Soul Food began, she has teenage children that she juggles with her career.

'So, Holly,' she says, taking a seat next to me, but the moment she sits down her mobile rings. She glances at the screen. Hesitates.

'Take it,' I insist.

'Won't be long,' she says, leaving the table.

The longer I wait, the more I lose my nerve. I steady my breathing. Keep calm, I urge myself. Don't go and have another panic attack. I look at the door. I could leave. Do I want to give up every Saturday to work in a kitchen? Breathe in, and out, in, and out. I take a sip of water. And another. I can do this. Gradually I feel my breathing returning to normal. I tell myself to stay. I have nothing to lose anymore. I think back to a few nights ago, home alone, Googling 'how to cure loneliness'. I have never experienced loneliness before, not the kind that keeps me awake at night, that stops me from wanting to go out, that makes me feel empty. Not the kind that steals my life from me. It's a loneliness that hurts my mind and heart. I didn't know loneliness like this existed until Jamie died.

One bereavement site described the simple act of sowing seeds or planting bulbs in anticipation of a more beautiful future, a future filled with hope. Another self-help page described the importance of exercise and self-care, sleep and looking after my skin. One warned against the adverse effects of alcohol and social media; another suggested getting back out there and signing up to online dating. It all made sense, but I didn't want to do any of it, especially not quitting alcohol. Often the thought of a glass of wine after work is the only thing that helps me get through the day. A glass of wine, or let's be honest, half a bottle, helps me park my problems for the night. It numbs the pain of missing Jamie. Why would I want to give that up for better skin or a healthier liver? Who cares? I realised I didn't want to endlessly think about me. I saw a therapist, Susan, for a year after Jamie died. While it was a relief not to keep burdening friends and family, I couldn't help thinking Susan must be so bored of me saying the same old thing every week. *I'm* bored of me. Yawn. I've had far too much me time, that was the whole point. As I was about to quit, I came across a website that suggested the benefits of voluntary work, quoting Winston Churchill: *We make a living by what we get, but we make a life by what we give.*

Choose something you are passionate about, the journalist suggested. People often assume voluntary work is rattling a rusty old tin outside a shop but it can help individuals find meaning in their life again. Volunteering can help us feel a deeper sense of gratitude for what we do have. Now this did make sense, so I began to think about what I used to feel passionate about and the first thing that entered my mind was cooking. I proceeded to Google voluntary work in cafés and restaurants, Hammersmith, west London, and that's when I came across the website for Soul Food, only half a mile down the road from me. Nina set this place up eighteen months ago. It's open once a week, on a Saturday. In her short biography she mentioned she'd read a book about the harsh facts on food waste, and became intent on doing something about it. 'All my life I've hated throwing anything away, let alone good food,' she wrote. 'As a child, I'd rummage in bins for bread crusts to feed the ducks. But my café isn't just about food. It's about connection. Meeting people. Food nourishes not only the body but the soul.' She mentioned she was always looking for decent cooks to help volunteer, adding she was hopeless in the kitchen herself. 'My mother was wonderful at making our clothes and toys, and she grew her own fruit and veg, but she loathed cooking. I was brought up on soggy fishfingers and carrots, I'm surprised I didn't turn orange.' This hatred of throwing anything away came from both parents, but particularly her father, who would even unbend nails so he could reuse them. After a near breakdown working in a law firm for fifteen years, she began a voluntary job for a charity that collected surplus food – food that was fresh and in-date, food that would otherwise be destined for landfill due to mislabelling, damaged packaging or over-ordering. And they distributed it to schools, homeless shelters, community lunch clubs – basically all those who were vulnerable and in need. And it was this work that gave her the idea to set up her own communal café, that offered heavily subsidised meals for anyone who wanted to come along and enjoy a bowl of nourishing soup and some conversation. She was awarded a grant and all the food she receives is donated to her by charities and supermarkets, and she has a few local friends who give food regularly. She has been overwhelmed by the support.

Instantly I wanted to find out more, so located her email address on the website's contact page and sent her a message. She responded immediately, saying it must be serendipity. One of her volunteers was about to go on maternity leave, so did I want to meet up this weekend for an interview?

After five minutes I'm still waiting. Come on, Nina, I know you do all this admirable work, but I'm getting bored now. If I have to wait any longer, I might do a runner.

A stranger plonks himself next to me.

He reeks of tobacco.

I should have made my escape.

'Hello, how are you?' he asks, drinking out of a giant mug with 'World's Best Dad' on the front.

'I'm good, thanks,' I say, in fact nursing a hangover, as Harriet and I had gone out for drinks last night. Harriet is my boss. She runs her own PR and Communications company from home. I'd told myself not to order another glass of wine, that I needed to be sharp as a pin for my interview. Instead, I knocked it back, with a packet of cheese and onion crisps.

'How are you?' I ask.

He looks as if he's nursing an equally bad hangover and hasn't had any sleep for weeks. 'Good, thanks. You waiting for Nina? She talks for England.'

I get the sense he does too. 'I'm here for an interview.'

'You must be insane. Get the hell out of here.'

'I was thinking about it.'

'There's still time. My brother, Scottie, he's the head chef here and if you think Gordon Ramsay is a diva, think again. I tell you, saucepans fly, especially with new volunteers who get in his way or don't follow his instructions.' He treats me to a generous smile, though something tells me he has little to smile about right now. 'Always feel better once I've had my pint of caffeine, don't you?' I notice the deep lines around his brown eyes. 'I'm Angus by the way. How d'you do?' He shakes my hand. I notice a crumpled cigarette packet in the front pocket of his equally crumpled denim shirt. Another thing I discovered after Googling voluntary work was how many people had met their partners through voluntary organisations. 'Belting out Mozart's *Requiem* cured not only my stress but my sex life,' one said. 'To anyone out there feeling lonely, you may even meet your Mr Right.'

Angus burps.

Luckily, I'm not looking for my Mr Right.

'I can burp the entire alphabet if you like?' he boasts. 'My children love it. Did you tell me your name?'

'Holly. Do you work here too, then?'

He nods. 'I wash up and wipe tables, important stuff like that, and for all my hard work I get a hot meal. I recommend the chicken pie. And Scottie's curries are famous round here, plus the syrup sponge is to die for.'

Angus looks like he eats a lot of syrup sponge.

'This is the result of a good life, Holly,' he says, patting his stomach affectionately, as if it's a dear friend. 'A life well lived. I couldn't care less that my blood pressure is sky high. If I die now, at least I'll die knowing I never once turned down a second helping of syrup sponge and custard.'

'Don't die,' I say without thinking, irritated he is playing Russian roulette with his life, his health. Then again, so am I.

He looks at me curiously.

I'm not fooled by Angus. This man has a story. I mean, don't we all? The tone of his voice is rich, he's well-spoken. I imagine he went to boarding school. I can see him playing cricket and rugby. Growing up he was fit and sporty, but as he's careered towards middle-age he has let himself go. Something's gone wrong. Derailed him. I decide if he brushed his hair, if he didn't stink of smoke, if he quit burping and lost at least a couple of stone… Basically, if he changed completely, he wouldn't be so bad.

'I've got a joke for you,' he says, mischief in his eyes, 'to cheer you up.'

'I don't need cheering up.'

'Trust me, you do. I don't mean to be rude but here you are, on a Saturday morning, when you could be in a million-gazillion other exciting places, like climbing a mountain.'

'I don't want to climb a mountain.' I can barely climb out of bed.

'Why not?' He looks at me as if I'm the mad one. 'Who doesn't want to be a mountain goat?'

'Me.'

He narrows his eyes, places a hand on my forehead, as if I might have a fever.

'I'm not an outdoorsy kind of person, I'm more a sit by the fire with a mug of hot chocolate reading a book.' Jamie used to make the best hot chocolate, with vanilla.

'I don't want to get to the *top* of a mountain,' he explains, 'that's the disappointing part, but the climb itself is the thrill, the act of getting there, don't you think? Slightly like dating. The chase is the best part.'

'I wouldn't know. I haven't been on a date for years.'

'Sensible. Love's not all it's cracked up to be.'

'Hmm. Anyway,' I say, not wishing to be quizzed on my love life, not that there is anything to quiz me on. That would be the shortest conversation in history. Where's Nina? 'Do you volunteer here?' I realise I've asked him this already, but never mind. He doesn't seem to notice.

He nods. 'I'm living with Scottie, rent free, providing I do my bit at the café. Have you ever slept on a futon?'

'No.'

'Kills your back. Might as well be on the floor.'

Angus looks about my age. I'm forty-four but I still think of myself in my 'early', not 'mid' forties. He could be older, maybe late forties. 'Sorry, were you trying to ask me something?' He takes another gulp of coffee. 'I have a bad habit of talking over people, butting in. My wife always said I never listened to her. Should have listened, shouldn't I?' Another smile creeps on to his face. 'Tip to self.'

I register his wedding ring, recalling he'd said he had children, before wondering why he's sleeping on his brother's futon. Has he had an affair? It's none of my business. Yet I want to know.

'I deserved it. *More* than deserved it,' he says, as if reading my mind.

'Deserved what?'

'If you knew what I did you wouldn't be talking to me right now or ever again for that matter.'

'Try me.'

'Anyway, back to my joke to cheer you up. There's a woman on the motorway,' he begins, 'she's driving and knitting at the same time, obviously something she shouldn't be doing. Naughty.' He taps his wrist. 'She hears a siren, and a copper winds down the window and tells her "Pull over!" She winds down her window, and holds up her knitting saying, "No, officer, it's a scarf!"'

His contagious laughter reminds me of Jamie's. It fills the room.

'That's better,' he says, when I laugh with him. 'My one good Samaritan deed for the day is done. By the way, on a more serious note, this place is great. You'll love Nina. Speak of the devil.'

'Sorry about that,' she says, returning to the table. 'Someone from the night-shelter is looking for work experience. That was her support worker.'

Angus gets up. 'Welcome on board,' he says, shaking my hand again, his grip strong. 'Give her the job, Nina. She's hot *and* she laughs at my jokes.'

'You are unbelievable,' gasps Nina. 'Stop cracking on to Holly and go and do something useful.' She turns round to face him. 'In fact, what are you even doing—'

'I crashed here. Was out last night, having fun, you know how it is.'

She looks at him, more like a disappointed mother than a friend.

'Anyway, lost my keys, so climbed in through the back window, the security here is shit by the way. Right, I'll leave you to it.'

'That man,' she says to me when he's out of sight. 'He's so clever, one of the brightest people I know. We're old friends, went to uni together. He's godfather to my eldest boy.' She stops. Shakes her head. Clearly, he makes her lost for words. Yet I can tell she is fond of him, protective even. I feel like he was the golden child at school who should have passed all his exams with flying colours, the world was his oyster, yet something along the way tripped him up. And that something was most likely himself. Part of me is longing to know what he did that was so bad I'd never want to speak to him again. Or was he being overly dramatic to impress me?

'He's complicated,' Nina continues. 'You could write a book about Angus and still be none the wiser by the end. Anyway, enough about him. Let's focus on *you*. So, why do you want to volunteer here?'

Because I'm dying of loneliness.

I'm drinking too much.

I'm stuck.

'I want to help others,' I say, immediately sensing she's heard that old chestnut before. 'But I do feel fortunate,' I add to the cliché. 'I have so much to be thankful for, so it's time I gave something back.' I cringe inside. I sound so dull and earnest. 'What you do here, it's amazing. It's terrible how much food goes to waste.'

'It's shocking,' she agrees, at last connecting to something I've said. 'If two hundred boxes of cornflakes are stacked together and the bottom two boxes are damaged, they will discard the whole bloody lot because it's easier to get rid of one big pile in one go. And then there are people starving on the streets, or kids sent off to school with no breakfast and rumbling stomachs. Don't get me started,' she says, as if she could talk for England about this subject. 'So, you live locally?'

'Round the corner.' That was another piece of advice. Don't choose a voluntary job that takes hours to get to. I'd only end up resenting the journey and quit after day one.

Discreetly she looks at my left hand. I still wear my wedding and engagement rings.

'And you love cooking?' she asks.

I nod. 'Especially baking. I have a sweet tooth.' I decide not to let on I've stopped cooking since Jamie died, surviving on takeaways, Pringles and Dairy Milk, washed down with a bottle of Pinot Grigio. 'Growing up, cooking was my way of entertaining myself,' I say instead. 'I was an only child, so I used to spend hours baking, pretending I was on TV – you know, *Blue Peter*, "this is one I made earlier".' Nina smiles. 'Mum didn't like cooking, well not for the family anyway. Her idea of lunch was a cheese and pickle sandwich. I mean, I love cheese and pickle sandwiches, just not every day of the school holidays.' I shrug. 'So I began to cook.'

'Amazing. What kind of things?'

'I bought this French cookery book,' I recall. 'It was a very old-fashioned one, you know, black and white with small text and no illustrations. I'm showing my age. Anyway, baking is my real passion. I started making cakes for Mum's coffee mornings.' I remember Mum's friends saying how lucky she was to have a daughter who could cook. 'Mum and I began to do cake baking competitions, Dad was the judge.' I look back, remembering those happy days, and how stupidly proud I'd feel when Dad told me how much he loved my coffee and walnut cake, that it was my best yet. 'This probably sounds stupid,' I say, thinking of Jamie now, and how I used to love him cooking for me, and equally how much I loved experimenting with new recipes for him, 'but I find cooking is a way to show love.'

'It doesn't sound stupid at all. Food *is* love. It's healing. I actually wanted to call this place "Food First" because I think food, in all its wonderful ways, is often the first step to recovery. Eating together can help us address all the other issues in our lives.'

'Why Soul Food then, and not Food First?'

'Good question. In the end, I think it made more sense. Food, as long as it's decent, is good for the soul. A lot of the people who come here, Holly, this is their first hot meal of the week, because they can actually afford it. We charge a quid for a bowl of soup, and whatever they can afford for a main and pud. And if they have nothing, we never turn them away. The only condition I have is no one gets through the door high on drugs and the faintest whiff of alcohol you're out. Visitors and volunteers, actually, we've got to feel safe. I want this place to feel like home, where people leave happy and *nourished*. Food is so much more than sticking something into your mouth. Food gives us confidence and friendship. Sorry, I'm getting carried away again,' she says, but I find her inspiring. It's no wonder she set up this place. I can see she has ambition and energy;

people would have been falling over themselves to give her a grant. In a way I envy her passion. 'I love seeing everyone here,' she goes on, 'sitting at these tables, enjoying a plate of food. Food brings us together. Mind you, I even love cooking for myself.'

I nod, but couldn't agree less. After Jamie died, the last place I wanted to be was in the kitchen. The table was too big; the space Jamie had once occupied, vast. I began to order takeaways or if I couldn't even be bothered to pick up the phone, a bowl of granola would do. When Jamie was out for the evening a bowl of cereal for supper was a treat.

'I'm so greedy,' Nina continues. 'I seriously don't understand these people who eat a bowl of cereal if their husband's away, do you?'

'No. *Crazy.*'

'I eat all the things my husband hates when he's away, like macaroni cheese. Do you have family? Children?' she asks, trying to slot together the pieces of my life.

I shake my head, somehow always feeling incomplete when asked that question. Like I'm not quite enough. I see Jamie's reflection in the bathroom mirror, before I turn to him, holding the pregnancy test kit, and he takes me into his arms, telling me not to give up hope.

'Holly?' Nina says, waking me up from my thoughts.

'Sorry.' I can feel my skin reddening. Please don't cry. 'I don't have children. It wasn't meant to be.' I fight back the tears.

Nina must clock I'm struggling. 'Are you OK?'

If only she knew Jamie's half-read paperback still sits on his bedside table. I know, after eighteen months, I should give it to a charity shop or even chuck it in the bin. I've rehomed his clothes, but that book, it's the one last piece I have of him. I glance at the door. I could leave. Fake a stomach ache. Go home now. Sink into bed. But what would Jamie think, watching me wish my life away?

'Yes, I'm fine,' I say with a smile. 'So how does your café work then?'

'Well, Scottie and his prep chefs gather here in the next half hour or so. The pudding team comes around ten. I have a pair on hot food and pudding service, a team of washer-uppers, table setters, clearer-uppers, someone who welcomes people at the door, takes their coats, introduces them to friends if they're new. I started off with four volunteers, now I have sixteen.'

'Sixteen, wow.'

'The food arrives at about nine. It comes from a local charity that delivers straight to the door which makes life a lot simpler. Then it's a mad rush to unpack before we get cooking.'

'How many do you cook for?'

'We usually have around fifty. One time ninety people turned up.'

'Ninety?' I repeat, impressed but daunted.

'I know. Makes me think about running this café on a Sunday too, but my husband wouldn't be too pleased. He says I'm married to this place.' She shrugs. 'Maybe someday I'll expand.'

'You're open once a week, right?'

'Yep, for now.'

'How do people know about you?'

'Word of mouth. Most people who come here are homeless, or they used to be. Abuse, drugs, shocking childhoods, bad life choices, I've seen and heard it all. Sometimes I hear the most harrowing stories, but you know what, it could have happened to me. What's that saying?'

'We're only one pay cheque away from being homeless.'

'Exactly.'

'It could happen to any one of us.'

'Too right. Then you get some who come here for the company. They live on their own, don't see a soul day in, day out. There's one chap, Nigel, well into his eighties, regular churchgoer, who doesn't see anyone during the week, but loves coming here every Saturday. He's part of the furniture. He told me he'd die of loneliness if it weren't for us.'

I feel moved by Nigel and instantly like him. 'What if someone like me came in? Or foodies from Chiswick?' I'm thinking of my boss, Harriet. She'd be delighted to pay a quid for a bowl of delicious soup. She'd have second helpings too.

'To be honest, if people can afford it, they always give a generous donation. Angus is good at spotting spongers too. There's nothing in the world I hate more than meanness.'

Jamie used to say that.

'The rules aren't rigid, prices aren't fixed, but somehow, it works.'

'And what do you cook?'

'We don't know until the day.'

That familiar panic rises in my chest.

'It all depends on what comes in,' Nina explains. 'On Valentine's Day last year our delivery included mackerel and black pudding. Scottie went from grumpy old sod to genius in thirty seconds and made these beautiful heart-shaped mackerel and black pudding fish cakes. We need people with imagination.'

Ninety. No recipe? Heart-shaped mackerel and black pudding fish cakes? *Fuck!* What am I letting myself in for? I remind myself I haven't said 'yes' yet.

'You don't have to cook anything too fancy, Holly, not for pudding anyway. A syrup sponge with custard puts smiles on faces. Scottie's a pro, he can always help out with ideas and sometimes we cheat and buy a few extra things. Don't ever ask this man to go to the shops for you,' she says, nodding towards Angus who approaches our table, hair damp, yet looking a whole lot better in a pale blue checked shirt with jeans. I imagine there must be a shower or bathroom somewhere in the building. 'He forgets what you asked for,' Nina warns me, 'and ends up in the pub instead.'

'Guilty,' Angus replies. 'Easily side-tracked.'

'So, when could you start? Now?' Nina stands up.

'You don't want to think about it first?' I ask, knowing it's me who needs to think about it first. I like to take my time, consider my options.

'Let's have a trial,' Nina suggests.

'Today?' *Oh shit!*

'If you burn the kitchen down I'll reconsider. What size are you?'

The room seems to be spinning. Everything is happening far too quickly. 'Fourteen,' I reply with faint shame. I used to be a size ten.

'Angus, can you grab Holly a medium apron?'

'Yes, boss.'

She turns to me. 'Unless you're busy today?'

I'm busy doing nothing. 'Um. Er.'

'We can start next weekend if you'd prefer?'

I take in a deep breath. Get on with it, Holly. You'll only fret for the whole week if you don't start today. Angus chucks an apron my way. I don't catch it in time.

'It gets hot in the kitchen, you won't need your cardy,' Nina warns me, as I pick up the apron, noticing my hand shaking, and horribly aware Angus is watching me.

'Yeah, best to wear as few clothes as possible,' he advises.

'If today goes well, there's more paperwork and forms, but let's call this a trial. Angus, can you show Holly the ropes? I need to chase the delivery guys. And where the hell's Scottie?'

'He's on his way,' says Angus, leading me into a small kitchen with cream worktops and an industrial-sized fridge and dishwasher. He places a hand on my shoulder. 'How you doing?' he asks, for a second allowing me to see a kind person behind the jokes.

'Yes, yes, I'm fine,' I say, before deflecting the attention off me. 'So, this is where it all happens.'

'Yep. Scottie cooks here.' He motions to one corner. 'Everything has to be done *just so* but don't let him bully you. And this is where you'll be stationed, Holly. At the stroke of twelve-thirty we open the doors, and take the orders.' Angus stands in front of the hatch which divides the kitchen from the dining room. 'Everyone queues up in a not-so-orderly line, I take their orders, hand the punters a wooden spoon with a letter and number on it. The tables are in alphabetical order, so the table at the far end of the room…' he points to it, 'is A, the next is funnily enough B, and so on. They take their seats, and we do our best to hand out the right food to the right people. There are a few old folk here who have dementia, they order veggies with their sausages, before telling you adamantly they ordered chips. It's best to agree with them, the customer is always right. It's a bit *Fawlty Towers* but that's half the charm.'

'How are your computer skills, Holly?' Nina asks, sticking her head round the door. Computers and I do not get on. We're like a bad marriage. I can turn one on and off and write the odd email in between and that's about the extent of our relationship.

'Great.' Why am I pretending to be a computer whizz?

'We print the menus. Angus will show you where the office is. It's upstairs. To be honest, it's more like his bedsit right now.'

'She's exaggerating. I only stay here the odd night.'

My mobile rings. It's probably Mum. Or a scam. Someone pretending to be calling from Amazon. No one else calls me this early on a weekend morning.

Angus watches me reject Mum's call. 'When you're cooking don't leave your mobile lying around,' he warns.

'OK,' I say slowly, semi-catching his drift.

'I might nick it.'

'You wouldn't. It's ancient. About as old as me.'

When Angus smiles, I notice he has a dimple, like me. He clears his throat. 'Everyone is lovely here, but occasionally things go missing if you know what I mean. Some of these guys walk in with nothing but the clothes on their backs, and things kick off. So keep your mobile and any money in your apron pocket.'

'Fine,' I say, though I'm dreaming now of being at home with no threat of being robbed.

'Oh, here comes Aleksander,' Angus says as we head out of the kitchen. Through the glass doors I can see a frail-looking man with a wispy beard, ghostly pale, walking down the narrow path towards the café, clutching a walking stick. I notice one side of his arm is covered in tattoos and he's carrying a shopping bag which looks too heavy for his withered arm. 'Polish. We call him Sander, incredible chef, far more talented than Scottie but don't tell him that. Only thirty-five,' he continues, as if reading my mind that he looks young to need a walking stick. 'In and out of prison. One word of warning.'

'What?'

His hand briefly touches my shoulder, making me almost jump out of my skin. 'It's best to keep on the right side of him,' he says, as he opens the door to let him in, and I have no idea if he's being deadly serious or not.

'Why?' I murmur.

''Cos he bakes us the most amazing cinnamon buns.'

3

I turn the key in my front door, tired from being on my feet all day, and mentally drained from trying to retain so much information: where everything was in the kitchen, how the oven worked, all the volunteers' names and what they did, attempting not to get in the way of head chef, Scottie, and then of course thinking up what to cook with my ton of ingredients. It was like a first day in the office. I didn't drink nearly enough water either and feel dehydrated.

The chaos and buzz of the café contrasts strongly with being back at home, yet for the first time I feel grateful for the peace. I drop my bag in the hallway, longing to tell Jamie all about my day. He'd be proud. As I walk into the kitchen, I notice that even if I'm tired, I'm still smiling.

'I hope we haven't scared you off?' Angus had asked as I was about to leave. Nina was standing by his side.

'Scared me off?' I repeated.

'Well, it's not exactly your average crowd.'

'Who wants *average*?' Nina challenged him. 'So, see you next week Holly?'

'Yes,' I said without hesitation this time. 'If I've passed my trial?'

'With flying colours,' Nina replied. 'Keep the apron, it's officially yours.'

And on that note, I'd smiled all the way home, like a child who had been given a gold star. And I still feel like that child. My mobile rings.

'How was it?' Milla asks immediately.

'I got it! I worked there today.'

'Today? Already? Wow! Hurry up and get here, I want to hear *all* about it. The wine's in the fridge and I'm making bolognese.'

I tell her I'll jump in the shower and be with her as soon as.

I rush upstairs to get ready, for the first time in months the solitude of home contrasting to the party going on inside my head. I realise already that I feel more grateful tonight than I did this morning. 'The guy near the back, he went to Harvard,' I replay Angus telling me, giving me a running commentary on a few of the locals standing in the lunch queue. He was referring to a red-haired man, in his fifties. 'Bad breakup and made redundant at the same time, plus no family support. Intelligent man. Loves art and woodwork. Ended up on the streets. The skinny bloke coming up, that's Craig. He volunteers here, helps clear up for a free meal. He lives outside Sainsbury's. Good Wi-Fi apparently.'

'And who's that?' I'd asked, gesturing to a slim elegant woman in her sixties, wearing a long summer skirt with a silk scarf draped over her shoulders.

'Sarah. We call her *Lady* Sarah. She's famous round here, opens her home and heart to these guys. She makes sure the likes of Sander and Craig have gloves and socks in the winter. She's a gem.'

As I step into the shower, I reason that life without Jamie is hard, but I have parents who love me. I am lucky to have a mother who fusses and frets over me. I have a roof over my head, a job that still gives me a buzz when I place an article for a client. I have Milla. Even better, her husband, Dave, is out tonight, so we can gossip and put the world to rights. And we have wine and bolognese. Sometimes it's important to remind myself how lucky I am.

Milla opens the door, wearing a white T-shirt and dark jeans. Milla's style is casual and natural. She barely wears any makeup because she doesn't need to; she has an enviable complexion in that she only has to be in the sun for five minutes before she gets an even tan. She also has a bone structure that allows her to experiment with her dark hair, and this summer she's decided to go for a pixie cut, which frames her almond-shaped brown eyes. I, on the other hand, am fair-skinned and blue eyed, with chestnut-brown hair which I've always kept long. Only once have I cut my hair short. I was thirteen, and immediately I prayed for it to grow long again. I felt naked without my locks. I imagine every single one of Milla's patients (she's a doctor) falls head over heels in love with her and thinks up various ailments as an excuse to see her. She gives me an extra-long hug and a firm kiss on both cheeks. Milla does nothing by halves.

The kitchen smells of comfort. Milla always has flowers on the island, scented candles on the go, and music in the background. Tonight, it's London Grammar, one of our favourite English indie pop bands. Basically, she's annoyingly perfect. I found myself telling my old therapist, Susan, that an ashamed part of me was insanely jealous that she had both a husband and beautiful children, and that it wasn't the first time I'd felt this way. Susan told me it was human to be jealous, and that I was allowed to express my feelings. Yet I still felt guilty begrudging Milla, someone I love like a sister, of everything I didn't have. 'The girls are longing to see you, I promised you'd say goodnight,' she says, opening the fridge to retrieve the white wine. By girls, she means her four-year-old twins, Kate and Emily.

'I'll go up now,' I tell her. 'Then we can get stuck in.'

I walk into a dimly lit bedroom, two giggly girls under the covers of the bottom bunkbed, pretending to be asleep, one fake snoring.

'Oh, if you're asleep, I'll go away,' I say loudly.

Emily sits up. 'Are you sleeping over, Auntie Holly?'

'Yes,' I reply, joining them in bed. Since Jamie died, I often stay the night. The girls wanted to give me my own, special bedroom.

'Budge over,' I say, snuggling close.

'Can you read us a story?' Kate asks.

'Why don't we do something else?' I suggest. 'Why don't you tell me something you feel grateful for, something that made you *really* happy today?'

'Strawberry ice cream!' Kate says.

Emily, my goddaughter, is more ponderous. Like Dave, she considers before she talks. 'You, Auntie Holly,' she says, melting my heart.

'Pancakes!' calls out Kate, food-obsessed.

As we carry on chatting about all the things we love, I'm reminded of how much I longed, growing up, for a younger sister, a little sidekick. The sadness for Mum was she suffered terrible postnatal depression after me, so bad she feared ever going through another pregnancy. My father had hoped for a son, but Mum came first. 'But I know you'll make up for it by giving us plenty of grandchildren,' she'd said emotionally on the morning of my wedding day. And I'd promised her, equally emotional, that I would. I didn't appreciate fully, back then, that we can make plans, we can map out our lives, but often fate has other ideas.

Milla is like the sister I never had, even if we couldn't be more different. When she first joined our school, she was independent, loud and cocksure. She seemed to know exactly what she wanted to be when she was a grown-up. Her most treasured item was her first-aid box, given to her by her parents on her tenth birthday. She used to love wrapping my arms and legs in bandages, swathing me like an Egyptian mummy, before telling me with a super grave face that my injuries would take months to heal, in fact I could die a grisly death unless she performed a miracle operation that only Professor Milla could perform. Meanwhile, my most treasured items were my books. I immersed myself in stories, devouring everything from Enid Blyton to Emily Brontë, to Jilly Cooper. I bought secondhand Mills and Boon books from charity shops, and lapped up these tales of romance, which seemed so very different from everyday life. I couldn't imagine my father kissing my mother like that. I didn't want to, either. 'We are all so lucky, aren't we, to have each other?' I say, giving them both kisses, and a goodnight hug. They smell of strawberries, bubble bath and innocence.

* * *

'Tell me everything,' Milla insists, as the mince is cooking and we're sitting at the kitchen island, perched on stools. So, I tell her exactly what the café was like, from the beginning. The delivery van dropped the food off at about nine. I was presented with a ton of oranges, grapes, watermelon, and strawberries, so I made enough fruit salad to feed an army, along with two large steamed syrup sponge puddings with a creamy citrus custard sauce, which was all eaten up. 'I couldn't do that,' Milla says, impressed. 'I have to follow a recipe.'

'I cheated,' I admit, thinking how I'd Googled the recipe.

'And what about the other volunteers?' she asks.

After my induction chat with Angus, his brother Scottie arrived, looking professional in his chef's hat and apron. He was a slimmer version than Angus, someone who looked as if he ran to the gym, not away from it. He didn't say much to me, except he hoped I knew what I was doing, that cooking in the café wasn't like throwing a dinner party for six, *darling*. Occasionally he'd finish his sentences with a dramatic sniff, as if making his point clear.

'He sounds scary.'

I shrug. 'I've had far worse bosses.'

Scottie was followed swiftly by Monika, his head prep chef, Polish, mid-thirties and an intensive care nurse. 'Puts me to shame,' Milla mutters.

'Oh, come off it, you don't have enough time to brush your teeth let alone volunteer.'

'Don't remind me.' Milla had called me the other day, saying she'd been in such a hurry to get to work that she'd forgotten to brush her teeth, plus during a meeting, when looking for her mobile in her handbag, she'd found a pair of her knickers instead. Clean, thankfully.

'I did ask her that question though. I agree. Isn't her halo shining enough?'

'Exactly. What did she say?'

'I've always had the urge to care,' I hear Monika telling me in her strong accent, 'to feel as if I am doing some good on this earth. Besides, cooking is my therapy, cooking and yoga.'

'Well, she is ten years younger than us. Makes a big difference,' Milla says. 'When you get to our age everything starts to slow down, and droop.'

I laugh, thinking how exercise is another thing I've let slip since Jamie died. Not that I ever did that much, but Jamie and I used to play tennis during the summer. We often played doubles with Milla and Dave. We won. Nothing to do with me. Jamie was a natural and could belt the ball.

I tell Milla about the volunteers who came from a local home for adults with learning disabilities, a Romanian girl called Simona, and Tom. 'Thomas, pull your trousers up,' Angus had said to him the moment he arrived, before they did a high-five and laughed together like schoolboys. Simona's job was to put flowers into vases. She did it slowly, with great pride and purpose. Tom was in charge of the cutlery, and laying the table. His job was to dip the knives, forks and spoons into warm water before drying them until they sparkled like new. I could see him working at a small table on the other side of the kitchen hatch. Yet it was hard to believe the tables were ever going to get laid, as he seemed to prefer coming into the kitchen to ask if I was married. 'Anyone who doesn't need to be in my kitchen, OUT!' Scottie bellowed in our direction, before turning to me, red-faced from the exertion of getting lunch ready by half past twelve, saying, 'For fuck's sake, don't encourage him, Holly.' I'd only let Tom lick the spoon, that's all.

Somehow, by lunch time, we were ready. Fresh flowers were on each table, the cutlery was gleaming, and it was no surprise that the smell of Scottie's Southern fried chicken breast and homemade chunky chips, along with my pudding, lured about sixty people inside. Our first punter was Nigel, the elderly chap Nina had told me about during my interview, who arrived on his scooter every Saturday, without fail. 'Nigel can never remember what he ordered but lucky for us he can remember all the words from old musicals,' Angus warned me. Angus had in fact stayed close by my side for most of the day, explaining how everything worked, and introducing me to everyone. When it came to the end of the day and I thanked him for looking after me, he said, 'Not at all, Holly. I hope I haven't put you off joining the team. We're a pretty good bunch, and Nina *needs* new volunteers. We've got to keep this café going. It's a lifeline for so many people.' I liked this side of Angus. The Angus that didn't feel he had to crack jokes all the time.

Reading my mind, Milla says, 'Angus seems nice,' clearly fishing as she tops up my glass, and her own.

'Mummy.' Emily comes into the kitchen, clutching a soft toy dog. 'I can't sleep.'

As Milla heads upstairs to settle her back into bed and I keep an eye on the mince, I reminisce about all the times Jamie, Dave, Milla and I have hung out in this kitchen. I see us enjoying breakfast with our coffees and papers before deciding what to do for the rest of the day. Maybe a bike ride and an exhibition or a lazy cinema afternoon. I see us singing and dancing like fools after a drunken evening out. I picture us playing a competitive game of Scrabble on a rainy Sunday afternoon. The amount of times Milla and I have cooked meals together. There is no better place to chat than in the kitchen, preparing food with a glass of wine. I recall turning forty was a major topic of conversation, along with children. Up until her late thirties, Milla had never wanted to be a mother. Jamie and I married when we were thirty-three. We wanted a family straightaway. When we were trying for a baby, she was incredibly supportive, but it only reinforced for her that she still had no maternal instincts. Yet, a year before her fortieth, something changed. 'I want children,' she confided to me, one evening, right here, where I'm sitting now. I recall it so vividly. She said it as if she couldn't believe it herself. Dave, who had always longed for a family, was so happy she'd changed her mind. Months later, when she told Jamie and me that she was pregnant, it wasn't an easy conversation. By that stage, Jamie and I had been trying for five years. My problem wasn't in getting pregnant. That was the easy part. I couldn't keep the baby, constantly miscarrying in the early weeks of my pregnancy. I had a series of tests; apparently, I had an irregularly shaped uterus. I didn't know this was even a thing, that some women can be born with one. I felt such a failure. Why me? Why couldn't I keep our child safe? Over time, Jamie and I more or less made peace with ourselves that it was unlikely to happen; we had no choice but to accept it. Yet it hurt so much when Milla fell pregnant practically overnight. I felt guilty for feeling so jealous. Milla felt guilty too, and would often try to tone down her happiness by not displaying her ultrasound scan on the fridge door, or by not telling me how she felt when she saw her babies, for the first time, on the monitor screen. It was the first time our friendship was tested. For so many years we'd walked side by side, but it felt as if Milla was moving on ahead, with the one thing I couldn't have. This divide wasn't anyone's fault, but the tension inevitably brewed, and for the first time in our lives, we didn't know how to deal with it. In the end, it was Milla who sat me down in this kitchen, insisting we talk. 'I know you've always wanted to be a mum, Holly, I know how cruel this is.' We hugged, we cried, and then we cried some more. Milla made me swear I'd be honest if it all got too much. Equally I made Milla swear she wouldn't censor her happiness. I knew, deep down, our friendship would always survive. If anything, it's stronger now, and I love her girls as if they were my own. Yet, only moments ago, I caught myself gazing at Milla as she took Emily's hand and led her back upstairs, to bed. It's those little moments of parenthood that I still crave. It's a yearning like no other.

'Right, where were we?' Milla says, taking over from me, tasting the mince. 'It needs more chilli,' she decides, 'and pepper. Angus. That's right. I like the sound of him.'

'Don't get excited.'

'Why not?'

Good question. 'He's not my type.'

'What's your type?'

Jamie. 'His chat-up line was he could burp the entire alphabet if I liked. I don't think romance is on his mind. I think his life's messy right now.'

'We all have baggage.'

'Mine's first class.'

'What does he do?'

'I don't think he does anything. I get the impression he was kicked out of home.'

'How come?'

I tell her how he'd slept at the café the night before and that he'd also mentioned staying with Scottie. *If you knew what I did you wouldn't be talking to me right now or ever again for that matter.*

'Affair?'

'Maybe. But to be honest, he's not looking that hot. He smelled as if he'd just crawled out of a pub.'

'Children?'

'Think so.'

'Good looking? If he didn't stink of smoke and booze?'

I have to smile. Milla can't help herself. 'Maybe, but probably because he's outgoing,' I weigh up. 'Confident. Well, he *seems* confident.'

'He sounds interesting.'

'He was kind,' I reflect, recalling him helping me prepare the fruit salad as I was running out of time. I also saw him talking to some of the older café-goers, helping them find a free seat and making sure they were comfortable. And if there was anyone who looked lost or sad or friendless, he introduced them to some of the regulars and I could see how quickly he lit up peoples' faces. Like Jamie, he's able to put people at ease, and make them smile, which is a gift.

'How old is he?'

'Late forties.'

'Perfect.'

'Milla!' I roll my eyes. 'I'm not looking for love.'

Milla doesn't want to hear that I'm not sure I'll ever be ready to meet someone else; she certainly doesn't want to be reminded how hard it is to move on.

'I know,' she says quietly, before placing the spaghetti into a large pan of boiling water.

I glance at her fridge, covered in family photographs. Milla met Dave at university. Milla is a radiologist; Dave is now an anaesthetist. They were both medics but he had the great advantage of being in the year above. Milla always joked, said she never had the chance to 'sow her wild oats' because he was her first serious boyfriend, 'and annoyingly I've never wanted to be with anyone else,' she'd said. 'How dull is that?' My eyes rest on a picture of them standing on a beach, Dave's arm around her shoulder, the two of them smiling. It's a picture of what a happy marriage should look like. Noticing how they still look at one another, after twenty-odd years, is the opposite of dull.

'But at some point, Holly, and I'm not saying with Angus,' she adds, 'you might feel ready to, you know…' She turns to me, hope in her eyes. All she wants is for me to be happy again, and I love her deeply for that.

'Maybe,' I say, to give her that hope. 'You never know.'

4

The following weekend, I arrive at the café at ten o'clock. Being on pudding duty, I don't need to start as early as Scottie and Monika. The kitchen is crowded, Scottie barking orders to Monika to hurry up with the tomatoes for the pasta. She doesn't flinch, which suggests she's used to his charming prima donna ways. I see a heap of butternut squash, spinach and cheese on the worktop, Scottie rolling out pastry on a floured surface. I slot into my space, by the hatch doors that open out into the dining room. Angus is sitting on the other side of the hatch, preparing the cutlery with Tom. He's dressed in jeans and a similar checked shirt, drinking his usual gallon of coffee. It's like déjà vu, except Tom seems morose today.

'He's cross because Scottie won't let him in the kitchen,' Angus informs me, catching my eye and smiling.

Scottie ignores Angus. 'Monika, wake me up when you're done.'

'Fuck off,' she replies in her strong Polish accent. I turn to her, impressed.

'I'm not scared of him, Holly. He's a mouse,' she sighs, just as Tom walks into the kitchen.

'Tom, out!' Scottie roars like a lion.

'I want to kill myself,' Tom mumbles as he shuffles out of the kitchen.

'Don't worry, he says that all the time,' Angus whispers in my direction.

But I am worrying. If anyone could hear our conversation. This job should come with a health warning. I scan the ingredients on the counter. Strawberries, peaches, ricotta cheese, eggs… maybe pavlova and cheesecake, and some fresh strawberries with a mint cream. 'Tom, do you like cooking?' I ask, hoping to cheer him up.

No answer. 'What's your favourite meal?'

No answer.

'Mine's roast chicken.'

'Frankfurters,' Tom says, erupting into laughter.

'Too much talking, not enough chopping!' says Nina, rushing in and out of the kitchen. 'Get to work, all of you. Especially you, Tom. I love a hot dog too,' she adds with a wink.

The café isn't as crowded as last week, about forty people come and go. There seem to be a few newcomers since I overheard Nina ask their name, and which support services they used, before asking Nigel, who always turns up on his scooter early, if he could show them the menu and tell them how the café worked. 'It's nice to be useful at my age,' he'd said to me, taking his role very seriously.

By three o'clock we've eaten lunch and cleared up. As Angus and I are finishing washing up, two women enter the building, one considerably shorter than the other, dressed in a grey tracksuit, hoody and trainers; the taller one models a navy skirt and daisy-patterned blouse, and carries a file.

'Hello Jane, and you must be Lauren!' Nina says, welcoming them inside. 'Take a seat.' She gestures to the coffee table, close to the kitchen, away from the main dining hall area. 'I'll be with you in two ticks. Would you like a tea or coffee?'

'I'd love a coffee, thanks,' replies Jane.

'Lauren?' Nina waits.

I'd need ears sharp as a pin to have heard her reply, if she made one.

'Coming up,' replies Nina, joining Angus and me in the kitchen. 'I forgot to mention this earlier,' she says quietly, 'but Lauren might do some work experience here.' She gestures to the young woman, who's sitting, head down, tapping her foot repeatedly against the floor.

'Crikey, she couldn't look *less* interested,' Angus murmurs.

'She's nervous, that's all,' Nina rebukes, taking off her apron and chucking it at him. Nina's wearing a pale grey T-shirt under dungarees, and her dark hair is tied up in a loose bun which is held together by a pencil, clearly her trademark look. 'Two coffees with milk, one with two sugars. If you have a moment, come and meet her, make her feel welcome,' she suggests.

'Your coffees are coming up,' Nina says when she returns to the table. 'We have two other keen volunteers here, Angus and Holly. Are you happy to meet them?' she asks Lauren. 'You can ask them a few questions?'

'We'll tell you the truth, the whole truth, and nothing but the truth,' Angus calls out as we assemble the mugs and a plate of custard creams on to a tray before joining them.

'We'd love to meet some of the volunteers,' Jane replies for Lauren. 'Wouldn't we? Lauren?'

'Uh-huh,' she says to the floor.

'Hi,' I say, sitting down opposite her. I imagine Lauren must be hot in a hoody, given it's a day for sunbathing. 'I've only been here for two weeks so I'm new too,' I say, hoping this might reassure her.

Nina hands Lauren her coffee with two sugars. 'I always need volunteers, so why do you want to work here?'

Angus and I glance at one another. I'm feeling the pressure for Lauren to reply, and wondering if our presence makes it even more intimidating for her.

'Tell her, Lauren,' Jane says gently, 'tell her what you said to me earlier today.'

There's another painful silence.

'I'm not surprised you're lost for words,' Angus says. 'I mean, I wouldn't want to work with *us*. I'd make a run for it, while you still can.'

She looks up at him, and I catch a glimpse of a pale face, before she looks down again.

'Lauren said her dream job was to be a chef, didn't you?' Jane continues, not sure what to make of Angus, before thanking us for the coffee.

'Yep,' she murmurs with the tiniest of nods.

She's young enough to be my daughter, yet she has no life in her. Her posture is hunched. She appears awkward, uncomfortable; I sense she wants to take up as little space as possible. The oversized hoody isn't worn for fashion or warmth; it's a blanket to hide under.

'Would you like a biscuit?' I ask.

She refuses, but Jane takes one.

'So, what kind of things do you like to cook, Lauren?' Nina asks, her tone patient, kind.

'Anything.' She shrugs, fidgeting with her pale fingers, crunching her knuckles.

'Holly needs some help in the kitchen, she makes the puddings. Do you like baking?'

She nods.

Nina proceeds to tell Lauren how the café works and why it's so important not to waste food. She doesn't appear deterred by Lauren's monosyllabic responses. On Nina goes, talking about the various volunteer roles that need filling. There are never enough people to help clear up, or she always needs a friendly face to meet and greet, which I feel is optimistic, even for Nina. 'But it sounds as if you enjoy cooking? Jane tells me you've worked in a few cafés before?' Nina pursues.

Lauren nods again.

'Do you smoke?' Angus asks her.

'Angus,' Nina says, before apologising to Jane, but Lauren's head shoots up. 'Oh yeah.' At last, I notice her dark brown eyes that contrast vividly to her pale blotchy skin that looks as if it hasn't seen any sunlight for years. Self-consciously, she tucks a strand of dyed blonde hair behind a tiny ear, pierced with a couple of studs and silver hoop earrings.

'Fancy one now?' Angus asks. 'If you don't mind?' He looks at both Nina and Jane.

'She won't go with you,' Jane replies.

Clearly, she underestimates Angus.

'Sure she will, won't you, Lauren? Come on. We can have a chat outside, get to know one another, watch the world go by.'

Jane watches in astonishment as Lauren follows Angus outside. Clearly, she underestimated her too. Lauren looks tiny alongside Angus, she can't be much taller than five foot, whereas Angus is over six foot and towers above her.

'All she does is stay in her bedroom,' Jane tells us, compassion in her voice.

Discreetly we watch them through the glass doors. Lauren produces a packet of tobacco from her tracksuit pocket and proceeds to roll up a cigarette.

'How long's she been at the night-shelter?' Nina asks.

'A week. They encourage residents to go out during the day, but Lauren has no job and she doesn't have any friends. I thought being here could give her some structure. I know it's just for one day a week, but if she enjoyed it, it might encourage her to find other work. The poor kid, she's only nineteen, but she's had enough misery to last a lifetime.'

Nina nods. 'If she can cook, I'm happy to give her a chance.'

'Thank you,' Jane says. 'I'm not sure she's going to say yes or stick at it, but let's at least give it a go.'

'Exactly. Why don't I give her a trial run, say six weeks,' suggests Nina, 'and Holly and Angus can keep a close eye on her, right? Holly, would you be happy if she gave you a hand? We usually have two people on pudding duty.'

'Yes, totally,' I say, disguising my anxiety.

'Are you sure I can't tempt you to a custard cream?' Angus asks Lauren, when they return to the table. 'Or some leftovers? Holly's pudding was delicious. What do they feed you at the shelter?'

'Lasagne. Pasta.' She turns down the biscuits and offer of leftover pudding, which is lucky as there is none left.

'What's your bedroom like?' Angus goes on.

'Fine.'

'Which night-shelter are you in?'

When Lauren tells him, Angus confides that quite a few of the regulars here have stayed at this shelter, including ex-chef and cinnamon roll baker Sander, who spent a couple of weeks there last year. 'Apparently his roommate snored like a train, his entire bed shook at night.'

'They gave me a single room,' Lauren replies, no life in her voice either.

'Lauren, I'd love you to start next weekend, what do you say?' Nina asks.

She doesn't reply.

'Lauren, Nina is a great boss,' Angus says, 'and it's worth working here for my brother's chips.'

Nina agrees about the chips. Scottie makes them with olive oil, rosemary and garlic, and they're even better dipped into ketchup. 'Why don't you get here by half past nine or at the latest ten, and how about we make you a general helper, but mainly Holly's assistant on pudding duty?'

'Yes, Chef,' she says to me, avoiding eye contact, her foot tapping against the floor.

'Oh, you don't have to call me chef!' I say, strangely moved. 'I think that's a great idea. We're going to have *such* a lovely time,' I vow, attempting to sound far more confident than I feel, but instead coming across like a desperate mother telling their child school is going to be *such* fun. Unsurprisingly she doesn't look up and agree.

5

It's Monday, two days since I met Lauren at the café, and as I grab a takeaway coffee on my way to work, a thirty-minute walk to Grove Park, in Chiswick, I notice my Monday blues aren't as bad this morning as they were a few weeks ago. For starters, I felt far less inclined to swear at my phone when the alarm went off this morning. As I showered, I thought of Lauren waking up in the night-shelter, and wondered how her day would go, what she might do, or who she might see, if anyone. I feared Monday could be no more distinguishable than Tuesday, or Wednesday, or any other day of the week for that matter, except Saturday, if she chooses to become a volunteer. A part of me hopes she does. Another feels anxious I won't know how to talk to her, but I suspect my anxiety barely touches hers, so I need to get over myself.

As I continue to walk down the Chiswick High Road, the early morning sun also lifting my mood, my mind returns to Lauren being stuck in her bedroom, alone. I know, from experience, it's a long day with only your thoughts for company. I think about Angus, who'd mentioned that while he loathed his commute into the city, work did at least give him a sense of purpose. A reason to get up. Scottie told me he used to work in finance, but was sacked, but I don't know any more than that. Again, I feel grateful that at least I'm employed, and enjoy my job.

I never planned to work in PR. I read English at Royal Holloway,

London, but had no idea what to do with my degree. But I didn't care. Moving away from my parents spelt freedom and independence. After being cooped up in my bedroom, reading, and years of being at an all-girls school, men were a novelty. I lost my virginity during freshers week, to a tall blond rugby player called Christian, who was in the same halls of residence as me. After an awkward first time, the second attempt was infinitely better, and quickly I began to see what all the fuss was about. I couldn't believe how long I'd waited to have sex. Christian and I went out for six months and after our break-up, I wasted no time finding a new boyfriend to go clubbing with and share my bed.

When I graduated, I stayed in London without a clue what I was going to do. I signed up to a temping agency, and gratefully took the first job going, working for the Royal Horticultural Society, putting together an exhibitor's brochure for the Chelsea Flower Show. I knew next to nothing about plants and flowers – my phone bill to Mum soared, and so did Mum's ego – but it turned out to be a dream job that didn't even feel like work. I loved ringing up each exhibitor to find out what they were putting on their stand and can still recall the pride in seeing my words on the page. My name, *Holly Lawrence*, in print. From that moment on, I knew, at last, I'd found something I wanted to do. Admittedly not all my jobs have been as idyllic as the first. I moved from that job to a global PR company, where I worked on London Fashion Week (fun, got to go to all the shows) before moving on to 'FMCG' – 'Fast-Moving Consumer Goods' – like sun creams, lip balms and tights. I spent my entire working day hurtling around the office like a woman possessed, attending endless meetings to discuss advertising campaigns and brand positioning, and when I wasn't in these 'brainstorming' meetings, I was busting a gut sending tons of samples of sun cream and tights to journalists and clients on time – parcel tape became my constant companion. I was on the bottom rung, working for an account manager, so I was the one given all the mundane jobs like clearing out the promotion cupboards and making the tea and coffee. Over the years I climbed the ladder to become Account Manager and then Senior Account Director. I became the person who told her assistant to clear out the promotion cupboards and make sure copy deadlines were met. But I never demanded that anyone should make me a coffee. Nor did I dream of running my own empire. I didn't want that kind of responsibility. My ambition was simply to keep working hard enough to pay my rent and go on decent holidays abroad, in the sun.

I met Harriet, who would eventually become my boss, at a press event thirteen years ago, when I was thirty-one, and Harriet must have been in her late forties, as she's sixty-two now. I was single at the time, since I had no energy beyond keeping my job, but I'd met Jamie, who'd made me realise how much I wanted a social life again. I worked for a luxury food and drinks company and at night I'd lie awake in fear, panicking about my never-ending to-do list and all the things my boss, Clarissa Pope, would reprimand me for not achieving. 'It's PR,' my mother would say to me when I turned up for a weekend out of London (they live in Oxford) looking haggard and grey, 'not saving lives, darling,' which actually annoyed me, since I loved my job, but she had a point when she said I should, at least, be able to sleep at night. 'Leave, Holly,' my dear father had said, 'Clarissa doesn't deserve you.' Thinking of Clarissa now gives me goosebumps. I see her striding into the office, dressed all in black, demanding her skinny latte, and telling me I needed to present her with a comprehensive list of my goals 'pronto!' I can still feel her heavy-breathing down my neck while I was on the phone, and then scolding me in front of the entire office for saying something 'inappropriate'. I almost had a breakdown organising a grand press event for one of our champagne brands. It was the last job I did for Clarissa. I hadn't slept for days leading up to the event as everything I did was wrong. I can still hear her screeching that the packaging for the goodie bags was too yellow in tone: 'I wanted off-white, not cream! Change it, *pronto!*' In my dreams I gave her a satisfying Jackie Collins-style slap around the face as I told her to fuck off. Yet in real life, my knees buckled, my voice dried up, and I did as I was told. On the night itself, I had no desire to socialise with anyone. I kept on disappearing to the loo to have a rest and breathe. I can recall vividly dropping my handbag on the bathroom floor. I was literally down on my hands and knees, grabbing everything off the pristine tiles, feeling desperately sorry for myself, especially when I saw my rose hand cream had lost its lid, leaving a creamy mess all over my new leather wallet, house keys and the silk lining of my favourite evening bag. Mum was right, I thought to myself tearfully. This isn't worth it.

'I think this might be yours too,' said a woman, holding a tampon towards me.

The night that just keeps on giving, I thought to myself. Yet I was too tired to care. I burst into tears before telling the poor long-suffering stranger my entire life story.

'Crikey, most people only last a week with Clarissa,' she said.

'You know her?'

'The whole industry knows her. How the hell have you survived a year?'

'I don't know. I'm either brave or spectacularly stupid.' It's funny how tiredness reveals the truth. 'Clarissa Pope makes Cruella de Vil look like a saint. I'm Holly by the way.'

'Harriet.' She handed me her card, saying she was launching her own company. 'Call me.'

Clarissa made it so very easy for me to quit my job by being particularly vile, even by her standards, the following morning. I called Harriet as soon I left the office and reclaimed my life.

That was also the day when Jamie and I kissed for the first time.

All in all, that was one of the best days of my life. It taught me that you never know what's round the corner...

'Got forty pence, lovely?' asks a woman slumped outside Turnham Green Underground Station, interrupting my thoughts. She's sitting on a piece of cardboard, her hair greasy, and she's dressed in an old tracksuit, with no shoes, dirty feet. When she smiles at me, I want to stop. I *should* stop. But what will I say? I don't have any cash on me, not even forty pence, only my credit card. Do I have time to grab her a coffee or a cup of tea? Should I tell her about Soul Food? 'Not everyone on the streets is legit,' Craig had told me when we were eating lunch. Craig is the volunteer who helps clear up in exchange for free meals. His passion is tarot cards and horoscopes. He says he's a gifted palm-reader, but I don't let him anywhere near my hand. He also knows everyone and everything about living on the streets. 'Don't be fooled, Holly, you get some real con artists, people begging when they have a four by four sitting in their drive. It makes me mad, it does.' Yet this woman doesn't look like she has a four by four. Or a drive. She doesn't even have a pair of shoes. But by the time all these questions come and go I've walked past, and it's too late to walk back. If I had, what would I have said? Besides, she doesn't want conversation, does she? She wants cash. Forty pence. That was all she wanted. And I couldn't even give her that.

'I'm back!' I call out to Harriet, after a quick trip to the shops during my lunch hour. I head towards Harriet's kitchen, my favourite room in her house because Jamie worked on it. After he'd finished Milla's kitchen, I recommended him to Harriet. I used to tease him, saying that in time most of the kitchens in west London would be designed by him. It's large and open-plan with glass doors that open out on to the garden, where Harriet grows vegetables and herbs. The walls are painted in teal, but everything else, from the shaker-style cupboards to the trio of lights hanging over the island, is white. I assemble the food on her granite-topped island and stroke Billy, her black cat, who always slinks in when he hears rustling noises in the kitchen.

'One or two?' I shout, knowing the answer as I slice four bagels in half.

'Two! And there should be some chocolate puds in the fridge. A reward for getting through Monday morning!'

As I wait for the bagels to toast, I think that what I most admire about Harriet is how she worked her way up the career ladder. Nothing was handed to her on a plate. Her mum was a housewife; her dad a mechanic. No one in her family went to university – 'Not that that's the be all and end all,' she'd said, 'it's debatable you have to go at all these days, unless you want to be a doctor or a lawyer or saddled with debt.' Anyhow, Harriet told me she was never expected or encouraged to do anything much with her life, except marry and have a family. 'Nothing wrong with that,' she'd admitted, understanding how much I wanted that for myself. But Mum was disappointed when I gave her no grandchildren. "Children are for *life*, Harriet," she used to say. "They are your future. Work is just work." Harriet claimed she was rubbish at school, didn't pass any exams, doesn't have a single A level. She wasn't thick, she explained, something I worked out for myself the moment we met. 'I'm dyslexic, but didn't know it at the time.' It makes sense, as Harriet often asks me how to spell certain words. We have an enormous well-used dictionary in our office. 'I've always been more visual, creative, I'm cack-handed with words,' she'd continued. 'My kind of hell would be a game of Scrabble.' Her mother sent her to a secretarial course instead of sixth form college, vowing shorthand would be a skill she'd always find useful, especially when she married. She could type her husband's letters, joy of joy. Yet Harriet was bottom of the class at typing. It was another failure according to her mum. 'I don't blame her, Holly, that's how it was in those days. She wanted me to be happy, and to be a mother, which probably *is* the best job of all, probably far harder than working for some of the dickheads I've come across.' Thinking of these dickheads, her first boss at the advertising firm was called Harvey. 'Think *Mad Men*, Holly. Very little work, lots of drinking,' she'd described. 'If you can believe it, I used to strut around the office in my hot pants, purple knee-high boots, striped sweaters and hipster belts. I still have all my old clothes, lurking somewhere in the back of the wardrobe, cruelly reminding me I used to be a size ten.' Harriet isn't overweight; she's *a tiny bit* plump. Like me. She sees a personal trainer every week, unlike me, and I think she looks amazing. 'Don't you dare say *for my age*,' she says whenever

I compliment her on her flawless skin and glossy hair. 'Anyway, Harvey, at the advertising firm, was in charge of the graduate training scheme. Very smooth, think Pierce Brosnan,' she said, 'but sadly far too proper, no action.' Harriet's role was to sift through CVs from students. 'I don't know what got into me, Holly, I guess I was bored, but I decided to spice things up by applying for the position myself. I thought "What the heck?" I walked into his office and planted my CV on his desk and guess what he said?' Harriet was so absorbed in telling me the story that I had no time to guess. '"Have you been to Oxford and Cambridge?"' she continued. 'So I said "No" and he says, cool as a cucumber, "Well then, you're wasting my time." So I said back, cool as a cucumber, "If you don't want me to progress, you're wasting my time too."'

And so she left, taking with her this hunger to prove him wrong and to be successful. Harriet sailed to the top of her industry, thankfully scooping me up along the way. Thank God I dropped my handbag on the floor that night.

When the last two bagels pop up from the toaster, I butter and fill them with lashings of cream cheese and smoked salmon, plus a generous squeeze of lemon juice and plenty of pepper. I carry the tray of food into our office, Radio 4 playing in the background. Our office is light, and overlooks Harriet's garden. We share a decent-sized desk, covered in paperwork, pots of pens, tubes of hand cream, two of our old coffee mugs from this morning, bottles of water, and endless leads emerging from printers, laptops and mobile chargers. It's surprising we get any work done surrounded by all the cables and mess. Yet somehow, the mess is part of our team. The room is lined with shelves, filled with glossy lifestyle, travel and fashion magazines that our clients have featured in, along with chunky coloured box files filled with our work and various contacts. Nestled among all the files are a couple of framed photographs of Harriet's parents, and a picture of Billy. By Harriet's computer is a small silver-framed black-and-white photograph of a man in his late forties, Rodney. A man Harriet loved. He died a year before I met her. He was the reason she set up her own business. She rarely talks about him. I rarely talk to her about Jamie. It's funny how we talk so little about the things that mean the most to us. People who have touched our lives in such a profound way. Instead, we chose to talk about what we're watching on Netflix, or our favourite ice cream flavour. Yet I know, without words, our loss bonds us.

'Do you give anyone money, Harriet?' I ask, towards the end of the afternoon, my mind still distracted by the woman slumped outside the Underground station, especially since it's now pouring with rain. I wish I'd bought her a drink or said 'hello'. Why didn't I? As I send another email, I reason that I don't stop and talk to the homeless mainly out of fear. What if they lash out? I know Nina would have something to say about that. She appears fearless. I wonder what could have gone so wrong with that woman's life that she ended up on the streets. Addiction? Trauma? Abuse? A bad relationship? A terrible childhood? Why didn't I have the courage to find out more? I might have learnt something instead of having so many unanswered questions inside my head. But then again, I was in a hurry. I'm paid to work for Harriet, not talk to strangers.

I tell myself to concentrate on my work, but I can't help wondering if maybe this woman simply made one bad decision, causing everything in her life to unravel. Sometimes that's all it takes. After all, we're only one pay cheque away from homelessness.

'Harriet?' I say again.

She's chewing nicotine gum as she taps furiously at her keyboard. 'Sorry, what?' She peers at me from behind her purple-rimmed glasses.

'Do you ever give people money?'

'I pay you.'

'No, I mean the homeless?'

She shakes her head. 'I hardly ever have cash on me. It would probably only go on alcohol and drugs.'

'Or a pair of shoes?'

'If I happened to be anywhere near a café I might get them a coffee or…' She stops. 'To be honest I'm always in such a hurry.'

'I know,' I concede.

'One time I bought this guy a sausage roll.' Harriet frowns, recalling the encounter. "I'm a vegetarian," he said. The cheek!'

'Maybe he was.'

'Maybe.' She's about to return to writing her email, but then swivels her chair round to face mine. She must be sensing I didn't like what she said. I tell her about the woman outside the Underground station and how I'd walked on by. That in fact, I've spent most of my life treating the homeless as if they're invisible.

'I know. I feel guilty too,' she admits. 'But remember, there are a lot of frauds out there too,' she says, echoing Craig. 'I remember a beggar coming on to our train, on crutches, saying he needed money for a life-saving operation. I gladly emptied my purse before seeing him leap out of the carriage and sprint over to the other train on the opposite platform, the crafty bugger. He could have given Usain Bolt a run for his money. He was a good actor. I'll give him that.' She turns to me. 'I'm being harsh, aren't I? I swear I get grumpier and more cynical in my old age.'

I smile. 'I don't want to get all sanctimonious.'

'Please don't.'

'They're not *all* frauds, Harriet.'

'I know. Maybe it's easier to tell myself they are. Anyway, while you were out, I forgot to mention we had a message from someone interesting, who's set up a travel company, safaris in Africa.' Harriet goes on to tell me the classic triumph over adversity story that the press love: nasty divorce and now wants to do something with her life. 'I've booked her in for a breakfast meeting next week.'

'Do you think it takes a crisis to change your life?'

'What do you mean?'

'I've done nothing since Jamie died.'

'You've kept going, that's something in itself. And now you're volunteering at this Saturday place.'

'Look at you though. When you lost Rodney, you left your job and set up your business.'

'Well, I had to. I couldn't go on working full-time and travelling twenty-four-seven. I was burnt out.' She takes off her glasses and rubs her eyes.

I think of Jamie. How his divorce pushed him into moving back to London and setting up his own company.

The phone rings but Harriet tells me to ignore it, the answer machine is on. 'Are you OK?' she asks, and for once I don't say, 'I'm fine'.

'Mum thinks I should be fine *by now*. She says it takes a year or so to grieve.' Mum was referring to a friend of hers, Marjorie, who had recently lost her husband. She was trying to be optimistic, to tell me I won't feel like this forever. 'Marjorie is feeling *so* much better,' she'd said. 'She's joined an art class and she's learning how to make honey. I've never seen her looking so well, she has her *joie de vivre* back.'

'Codswallop. I mean, good for Marjorie, but you can't label grief like you label jam jars. It might take people less time. Others might grieve for years. I had a friend who celebrated when her mother died. Equally one of my friends was far more upset about her dog dying than her husband. It is true to say she did have the most beautiful Siberian Husky.'

We smile at that.

'I'll grieve for Rodney my entire life, Holly. I don't want to get over him. He was my world, but that doesn't mean I can't have a decent life now.'

If Jamie were here, he'd be saying, 'Cry for a night or two, Holly, but then dry those tears and move on.' While I'd be miffed if he only cried a night or two for me, I know, deep down, he'd want me to live my life because his was taken away.

'I should be setting up some incredible foundation in memory of Jamie,' I suggest. 'Or go off on some *Eat Pray Love* adventure to find myself.'

'You still can,' Harriet says, 'if your boss gives you time off.'

'She won't. She's a right old dragon.'

'I always thought you came back too soon,' she says, gently.

'I did once think about going on some kind of spiritual retreat.'

'And?'

'I might find out I'm even duller than I thought.' I laugh. 'And bad at yoga. I can't even touch my toes.' I tried mindfulness once and felt so relaxed that I kept on nodding off, which I discovered, regretfully, was not the point of the exercise at all.

Harriet comes over to my side and takes my face in her hands, her bracelets jangling. 'You are young.'

'Forty-four is not young.'

'It is, compared to me. You *are* young,' she insists again, 'young, beautiful and talented.'

'Stop,' I say, wriggling free from her grasp, though secretly enjoying it.

Harriet looks me straight in the eye. 'When will you ever accept a compliment, Holly? You drive me mad at times. You can do anything you want. Though I'd rather you stay put and work for me. Do you think I'd hire someone dull and incompetent?'

Her kindness makes me feel tearful.

The trouble is, I don't know what I want. 'But the café is a start,' I say, before telling her about the characters I have met so far, including Angus and Lauren. For the past few days, I've been thinking about Lauren. Where is her family? Does she have any? Or are they the root of all her problems? I realise now how much I want to see her again, how much I hope she'll come back, even if the idea of working with her makes me apprehensive.

'You worked for Clarissa Pope,' Harriet reminds me. 'Lauren will be a pushover.'

I see Clarissa in her pinstripe suit and trademark scarlet lipstick saying to me, the morning after I'd met Harriet at the press event, 'What exactly have you done for me since you've been here, Holly? Sweet Fanny Adams. Document what you've done this week, by noon. On my desk. And get me my skinny latte, *pronto*!'

'You know what, Clarissa, have mine!' I'd said, splashing the remains of my cappuccino down the cream silk shirt of an open-mouthed Clarissa, and in front of an open-mouthed office. 'And don't even think of sacking me. I quit!'

It was like a scene in a Richard Curtis movie, where everyone cheers and claps, the baddie finally getting their comeuppance.

'I did it,' I told Jamie with pride later that day, when Milla's kitchen was almost completed. While he was working, I used to grab every moment I could to see him. Never before had I shown such a keen interest in wooden floors, ceramic tiles and paint samples.

'Crikey, remind me never to annoy you when you're drinking coffee,' Jamie had said, as I watched him pack up his tools for the night. 'The guys will be in to do the last bits and bobs, we should be finished by the end of the week,' he added, words that made me feel scared.

I looked at the pristine cupboards, the beautiful dark wooden floor, the modern lights hanging over the island, but all I could see was a room, a dark room soon to be without Jamie in it. He couldn't leave. Not when I felt so excited by a life without Clarissa, potentially a new job and a future with Jamie. So, I decided to be brave and ask him out. What did I have to lose? Weirdly I knew he wasn't going to say 'no'. There was something inevitable about Jamie and me.

'It's a date,' he'd said, resting his hand against the small of my back, and leading me out of the front door, saying he knew just the place we could go.

I can't explain how it felt when he kissed me outside my front door at two in the morning. Mum always told me that when the right man comes along 'you'll know, Holly'. I thought she was being her usual irritating self, that she'd spent far too much time reading romantic novels, until that first kiss. It was a kiss that promised more.

We slept together that night. 'Why wait when you know?' I'd said, when we lay in bed, naked beneath the sheets, limbs intertwined.

I wipe the tears from my eyes.

With Jamie I was different. I took risks. I was brave enough to be myself. He loved me. Believed in me.

It's time I believed in myself again.

The old Holly is buried inside me. Somehow, I will find her again.

6

It's my sixth weekend at the café, and I'm beginning to feel more at home. I'm determined not to feel anxious about Lauren, that's if she turns up today. It's fifty-fifty. She didn't show up last Saturday, or the Saturday before that because she had a stomach bug. 'Convenient how these bugs turn up when you need to get out of bed,' Nina had said to me, close to suggesting to Jane, her support worker, that this might not work. She needs her volunteers to be reliable.

Part of me wants Lauren to show up today. I feel this is her last chance. I can't shake off what Jane said, that while Lauren is nineteen, she's had enough misery to last her a lifetime. I want her to know that while life can deal us a shit hand of cards, there has to be a reason to carry on. I know our lives are incomparable, but perhaps I want to prove it to her, so I can prove it to myself too.

When I arrive, I'm immediately welcomed by the familiar smell of Sander's fresh cinnamon buns which are in the kitchen, by the hatch. Scottie and Monika have arrived, and Simona and her carer are arranging carnations into vases. Tom is sitting at the small table on the other side of the kitchen hatch polishing the cutlery, a job he takes seriously. He dips individual pieces of cutlery into a basin of water, before drying them off rigorously with a tea towel, and assembling them into clean pots which are placed on each table.

I head straight for the buns, no time to waste. I don't eat breakfast at home anymore, I want to save my appetite for Sander's baking.

As I take a bite, the pastry melts in my mouth, it's so warm, buttery, fluffy, with this delicious cream cheese frosting sprinkled with dark sugar. Oh my God. It's better than sex. I'm tempted to have another. While no one's looking I grab one more. I see Sander drinking a mug of tea in the dining room. He's quiet, seemingly tuned out from Tom's singing and the general bustle going on all around him. Normally he doesn't stay at the café for long. He brings the buns and leaves. I decide that for once I'm going to talk to him.

'Sander, thank you,' I say, pulling up a chair and sitting next to him. 'Your pastries are the best thing I've ever tasted.'

He shrugs. 'I can tell.' He points to the corner of his mouth, though his eyes remain on me.

I smile as I wipe my sugar-coated lips. 'You must get up at the crack of dawn to make them.' Why do I always sound like my mother when I'm nervous?

'I've never been a sleeper, Holly. I'm lucky if I get a couple of hours.'

'Two hours. You must be so tired,' I say, stating the obvious.

'I'm used to it. Prison didn't help. The lights were always on. If you think the café is noisy.' He shakes his head with another wry smile and strokes his beard. Somehow, I can't imagine he could ever commit a crime. But what does an ex-prisoner look like? A big, muscled skinhead? Sander's demeanour is soft, kind; he looks as if the slightest breeze could knock him down. I'm beginning to realise labels don't always tell the truth.

Sander has a disarming stare that makes me feel self-conscious. Does he think I'm privileged? Unworldly? Yet I sense he doesn't judge me at all. I'm the only one here worried about how I come across to him.

'You're enjoying it here, Holly?'

'Loving it. And you? It must be good to be out?' I ask tentatively.

'Sometimes I wish I was back.' He shakes his head, his aura sad, lost, confused. 'Prison felt safe. It's the outside world that's such a frightening place.'

'All right?' says Nina, rushing to our table, hair loose, a pencil resting behind one ear. She's wearing khaki combats today, with a white T-shirt and trendy trainers.

'All good,' I say, still thinking about what Sander just said.

'You can look after Lauren, right?' She hands me a medium-sized apron for her.

'She's here?' I'm jolted back to reality.

Nina gestures to the door. Lauren has arrived with Angus. She looks as if she's literally crawled out of bed, but she's here. Remember what Harriet said. I worked for Clarissa Pope. I can work with a teenager. I can do *anything*.

'Let me know how she gets on,' Nina says to me, before tapping Sander on the shoulder. 'Thanks for the buns, you're an angel.' She rushes off. It's no wonder she's slim, she barely stays in one spot for too long.

'Tom likes the cutlery to shine like the stars,' I overhear Angus saying to Lauren. 'Look, it's Holly and Sander,' Angus says, waving at us.

Lauren's wearing a baggy leopard-print T-shirt tucked into an equally baggy black tracksuit bottom.

I hand Lauren her apron, introducing her to Sander, before asking if she'd like to help me in the kitchen. It's a silly, nervous question, because what else is she going to do? She doesn't say a word, but follows closely behind me. As we enter, Scottie crashes into her by mistake. It's hard not to bump into one another in such a confined space. 'I'm sorry,' he says, darting out of her way. It seems as if he's as apprehensive as I am about having our new volunteer in the kitchen. I haven't once heard him say sorry to anyone.

'Don't worry, I'm used to it,' she mutters.

'Right, what have we got here?' I stand at our counter, my nerves still a mess. Dried cranberries. My least favourite fruit. 'D'you need a hand with your apron?'

'No.' She backs away from me quickly.

'Right. Cranberries, a lot of cranberries,' I mutter. 'White chocolate buttons. Great. It's not a children's party. Is that it?'

'We've got a ton of frozen fruit,' Nina says, rushing in and out of the kitchen like a whirlwind. 'Could do a summer pudding? They gave us loads 'cos it's close to going out of date so we want to use it today if we can,' she calls.

'Right. What do we do? What do we do?' It's hard to think with Lauren close by my side, breathing heavily. She smells of smoke and her discomfort is tangible. Think, I tell myself, come on. I'm about to ask Scottie but then remember something Mum used to make, because it was easy. 'Let's do frozen berries with a white chocolate sauce, won't take long, nice and easy, right?'

She nods.

'And cranberries? What are we going do with all these cranberries?' I hope she might offer something, even, 'I don't know' but she shuffles from side to side, crunching her knuckles.

'Garlic bread first, Holly!' calls Scottie. 'We've got masses of French bread.'

'Oh, I love garlic bread,' I say, 'we can do that, can't we Lauren?'

'Yes, Chef,' she says glumly.

'Why don't we do a white chocolate cake with cranberries? That sounds delicious, doesn't it?' I'm at it again, sounding like a mother trying to encourage her child that we can have *fun* in the kitchen. 'How about a sponge cake decorated with cranberries?' I wait in vain for her to say something.

'Garlic bread!' reminds Scottie. Nina told me he was missing Sergio, one of his prep chefs, today, so I'd need to help out with the main courses and starters too.

'Yep, got it. Lauren, can you start slicing the French bread?'

'Yes, Chef.'

'Where's the garlic?' I call out to Scottie.

'Here, Chef.' Lauren hands me a bowl of garlic bulbs.

'Thanks,' I say, about to tell her not to call me 'chef', but maybe she wants to? She feels comfortable thinking I'm in charge. Who knows? All I know is, I don't want to tell her not to say things, when it's about the only thing she does say.

'Butter is soft.' Scottie hands me some. 'Don't be mean, put loads on, and garlic.'

I swiftly chop the garlic and mash it up with the butter and seasoning, keeping one eye on Lauren cutting the French bread into even slices with great care and precision. She could speed up but I'm not about to complain. 'That's excellent,' I tell her, adding, 'we won't be kissing anyone tonight, will we?' From the blank look on Lauren's face, she thinks I'm the unfunniest person in the world. She's right too.

By half past eleven Lauren and I have finished the garlic bread; two extra-large Victoria sponges are in the oven, and we have about three quarters of an hour left to ice and decorate the cakes, make the white chocolate sauce and put the berries into bowls five minutes before serving up. Lauren pours three large tubs of double cream into a heatproof bowl, along with most of the white chocolate buttons. When no one's looking I eat a few.

'Saw that,' says Angus, joining Lauren and me.

'I only had one,' I pretend.

'Plus ten,' he says, stealing one for himself out of a half-used packet. 'What's your favourite chocolate, Lauren?' he asks, and when he places a hand on her shoulder she withdraws instantly, as if his touched burned her. 'I'm sorry,' Angus says, instinctively reaching out to her again, before she jolts away from him, this time knocking the pan off the stove, cream splattering over the floor.

'Oh for fuck's sake!' Scottie yells, entering the kitchen.

'I'm sorry, I'm sorry,' Lauren says, cowering like a wounded animal.

Angus grabs a cloth. 'That was my fault.'

'Can one of you get on with it?' Scotties raises his voice, causing Lauren to withdraw again.

'Stop shouting, Scottie,' Angus demands, adding, 'are you OK, Lauren?'

'I'm sorry, sorry,' she says, cowering again.

'No, *I'm* sorry.'

'There are too many people in the kitchen,' Scottie insists. 'Angus, you're in everyone's way.'

I see a flash of vulnerability in Angus's eyes as he throws the cloth towards the sink. It misses. 'Scottie, for once in your life, can you drop the diva act and show a bit of kindness and patience?' he says, before storming out of the kitchen.

Scottie looks confused. 'All I'm saying is we've got less than an hour to get everything ready, so we need to get a move on.'

I nod. 'Lauren, can you grab another tub of cream and one of the large pans?' I gesture to the shelf close to Scottie. Seconds later, watching her fail to reach the shelf with no success, Scottie hands it to her, saying, 'Here, and anything you can't reach, ask, Lauren.'

He apologises to Lauren for his temper, saying he's knackered and cross because Angus came home late last night, drunk, again, waking up his family. Scottie has two boys, aged ten and six.

'How come he's staying with you, Scottie?' I ask, as Nina comes into the kitchen.

'He's going through a rough patch,' she tells me. 'He'll work things out.'

'Really?' Scottie sounds dubious. 'Not sure how hard he's trying to save his marriage when he's down the pub every night.'

'Give him a break, Scott,' Nina says, leaving.

'A break? I'm giving him food and fucking shelter. Sorry Lauren.' She doesn't flinch. He turns to me. 'I'm trying. I know I get ratty, to put it mildly, Holly, but having him to stay isn't exactly helping my marriage either. I don't call six weeks temporary and I can't see him ever getting another job or moving on. I know he's been through a lot, but at some point you've got to start helping yourself, because no one else can do it for you.' Scottie looks at me beseechingly. 'You couldn't talk to him, could you? Find out if he even wants to get back with Sophie?'

'I'm not sure—'

'Please,' Scottie begs, and just as I saw a flash of vulnerability in Angus's eyes, I see it in Scottie's too.

* * *

I find Angus outside, sitting on the wall, smoking. 'How's Lauren?' he asks, staring ahead.

'She's fine. I left her with Scottie.'

'Poor girl.'

'How are *you*?' I sit down next to him.

Angus turns to me, curious.

I come clean. 'Scottie asked me to check up on you.'

'He's right to get angry. I wouldn't want to live with me right now.'

'What happened? Do you want to talk about it?'

'My wife and I, we're having a trial separation but I have no idea how long the trial is for. It could be forever.' He runs a hand through his hair. 'I'm a mess, Holly.'

'Oh Angus. If you need someone to talk to—'

'How's Lauren?' he asks again, to deflect the attention away from himself.

It doesn't work. 'Nice try.'

He raises an eyebrow.

'Lauren's fine, it's you I'm worried about right now.'

'Nina tells me I'm good with people.'

'You are.'

'I'm out of my depth. I used to work in finance for God's sake. I work with numbers, not people.'

'I work in PR. I'm not doing any better.'

Angus scratches his head. 'The moment I touched her... I managed to scare the hell out of her, didn't I? I reckon she's been hurt, really hurt.' He looks at me with fear in his eyes. He longs for reassurance that I can't give. He's right. I sense Lauren is terrified of other human beings. Even Angus and me.

'What shall we do?' he asks.

'Maybe we don't *do* anything,' I say, thinking of how friends always felt they needed to do something for me after Jamie died, when in fact all I wanted was for them to be with me. I can remember saying this to my therapist at the time, wishing people could act normal around me, whatever normal is. 'Maybe we don't try as hard,' I suggest.

'She doesn't want to be here.' Angus stares into the distance again.

I don't buy that. 'If that were true, she wouldn't have come today,' I say, even though I wonder if Angus has a point. I get the idea she does whatever she's told to do. Or else.

He rubs his eyes. 'I think she's scared of men. She'd be better off if someone else kept an eye on her. She's got you and Monika's lovely, being a nurse and all that.'

'I imagine Nina asked you for a reason,' I say, watching her approach us.

'I'm not a frigging counsellor, Holly.'

'Oh. How disappointing.' I nudge him. 'I was going to book a session with you, see if you had a spare slot later.'

Angus doesn't react.

'I did ask you for a reason,' Nina says. 'Be kind and listen to her.'

Angus shrugs. 'That'd be easy if she talked.'

'Silence speaks volumes.'

'I make things worse, Nina. Everything I touch right now—'

Nina crosses her arms. 'Oh, stop feeling so sorry for yourself, Angus.'

'Why me? Hasn't she suffered enough trauma?'

Nina grips Angus by the shoulders. 'Woe is me. You are one of my oldest friends, and I will always love you, but for such an intelligent man, you have so much to learn. I don't know what happened this morning, but if you think that was the worst thing that's ever happened to Lauren, think again. She's probably stronger than the whole lot of us put together. She might not say very much, but she's here, when most people in her position would have probably sunk.'

'What's wrong with her?' I ask, longing to understand Lauren a little more.

'I can't go into it, it's confidential. But it's not what's *wrong*

61

with her, Holly, it's what *happened* to her,' Nina puts me straight. 'Listen, I know it's a lot to ask, of both of you,' Nina says. 'You've barely begun here, Holly, and I'm throwing you in at the deep end, but I know you and Angus are going to be good for that girl,' she says, before she leaves, urging us to hurry, hungry people will be arriving any minute.

I place a hand on Angus's shoulder. Maybe Nina has a point. 'You helped me on my first day. Without you I might have made a run for it. We don't give up, OK? Everyone's probably given up on Lauren, so we can't.' He still won't look at me. 'I get life is hard right now, but you can't give up, Angus. I need you,' I say, realising how important he is not only to the café, but to me too. I can't do this without him. When he remains quiet, I walk away, before he grabs my arm and pulls me back. 'I'm sorry, I'm being an idiot.' He takes in a deep breath, as if gearing himself up to go back inside.

'It's human to be scared, or to feel sad,' I say quietly, remembering it was something Jamie used to tell me before hospital appointments, or when I had yet another miscarriage. 'I'm scared too Holly, but we can't give up,' he'd say.

He nods. Grips my hand even more tightly. 'You're right. Let's do this, together. How come you're so wise, Holly?'

'I'm not.'

He looks intently at me, as if I'm hiding something. It's unnerving. 'Your apron,' he says, eventually.

I glance down, noticing the straps have come loose.

'Come here.' Angus ties them back securely. 'There,' he says, gently touching my shoulder. 'Thanks, Holly.'

As I walk home that evening, I can't stop thinking about what Nina said, that it's not about what's wrong with us, it's what happened to us.

I see Lauren jumping like a frightened child when Angus touched her arm, and cowering when Scottie raised his voice in the kitchen.

We all have a story to tell. I fear Lauren's will be daunting to read. But I want to keep turning the pages.

I also think about Angus, and our chat, sitting on the wall. Angus took off his mask and I liked what I saw.

Maybe it's time I took mine off too.

7

It's the following weekend at Soul Food, and by one o'clock it's buzzing with all the usuals. Sarah, also known as Lady Sarah, or Lady S by Angus, is here, somehow making jeans and a T-shirt look elegant, finishing off her outfit with a pair of navy heels. She exudes warmth and genuinely loves spending her time at the café, and I've also discovered she is a prison visitor volunteer. When I asked her why she loved being here and visiting prisons she told me she couldn't explain it. 'It was never part of the plan. All I knew was I didn't want to stay at home with the television on, or spend the rest of my life feeling retired and old. I guess I wanted to do something *different*. I chanced upon this place. I was out for a walk, saw the banners outside, felt rather nosy. And hungry!' She laughed with gusto. 'I've met some of the best people here… including you, Angus,' she'd added when he'd coughed loudly in her direction. She shrugged. 'I've never looked back, and I don't think you will either, Holly.' When she met Lauren for the first time, she gave her a makeup bag filled with hand cream, lip balm, shower gel and toothpaste, along with some hand warmers she'd knitted herself, and stripy socks. Lauren didn't know how to thank her, making me wonder if she'd ever received a gift before. I've met Chris, who Angus loves to remind me went to Harvard, proving how homelessness can happen to us all, no matter our background. Chris is excited as he's been offered a space in Hackney to show his art. He's working on an exhibition to portray homelessness, called *The View from Down Here*. He has asked Nina if he can do a sketch of Soul Food café. Growing up he loved music and art but his father insisted he read a 'proper' subject at school, to get him a 'proper' job. Often, he visits Lady Sarah on a Sunday to enjoy a roast dinner. Nigel is here, as always, talking to everyone he meets, to make up for the lack of company during the week. He also has an open invitation to lunch with Lady S. I see a lot of sadness at this café, people so damaged and hurt by their past, but I also see such kindness and love.

Angus is taking orders, and Scottie and Monika are dishing up quickly before handing plates of parmesan chicken and vegetable stew to volunteers on the hot food service team. Nina told me, during my first day here, not to stand around twiddling my thumbs; there's always something to do. 'The moment people finish their food, see if they want seconds, or if someone looks lonely talk to them,' she'd urged. 'Don't hang around waiting for me to tell you what to do. And even if you're not sure what the heck you're doing you can get away with murder if you smile!'

'Lauren, see that table over there,' I say, pointing to the one in the middle, 'they need more water.' I gesture to the empty jug. 'And maybe ask them if they want seconds?' She looks terrified at the prospect of walking over to a table of strangers. Yet slowly, dutifully, she walks out of the kitchen.

Holding my breath, I watch her through the hatch. Sad as it is, during a quiet moment at work yesterday, I Googled how to be around someone who is shy (what did we do without Google?). Most of the various blogs and websites advised not to try and be their best friend overnight, forget small talk, find a subject that makes them tick. Ask questions that are more open-ended, not questions that merely require a 'yes' or 'no'. One site suggested talking about similar interests so mentally I was thinking we could at least talk about what we were going to cook. 'You're over-thinking again,' Harriet said, glancing at my screen. I knew Jamie would have said the same. 'People can sniff someone trying too hard a mile off! If there's one thing I've learned in life, we all try to bend and contort ourselves to fit in with others, but at the end of the day, it's a waste of time. I'm so relieved to be sixty-two, Holly. Finally, I've learned to be myself, and if no one else likes it, well frankly, my dear, I don't give a damn.'

I hear everyone saying hello to Lauren, before asking her if she's new, just as they did with me. I sense her increasing fear and discomfort and am tempted to rescue her from the questions. She returns with the empty jug, her breathing uneven. 'If you refill it and take it back, that would be great,' I say.

'Yes, Chef.'

I resist the urge to say 'well done' when she returns.

'Lauren, can you give Nigel his chicken?' Scottie asks. 'He's the one sitting at the far end, the one who arrived on his scooter singing.'

Lauren carefully takes the plate from Scottie and walks so slowly out of the kitchen that I'm certain by the time she reaches Nigel the chicken will be cold.

'At least she's doing it,' Scottie whispers to me. 'I'll keep an eye on her, give her stuff to do too.'

When she returns, she asks me if she can go to the loo. 'You don't need to ask, Lauren,' I say, before watching her leave, her body language dejected. I catch Scottie's eye. 'Believe me,' he says, 'I've seen this all before. She'll be OK.'

'Even Tom was shy when he arrived,' adds Monika.

As Scottie and Monika continue to dish up, I put a large bowl of cream and chocolate over a pan of gently simmering water, thinking I'm not about to lose weight any time soon, and also unable to imagine Tom being shy, especially when he walks into the kitchen and asks me to marry him. For the third time today.

'Steady on,' Angus replies, 'you haven't even been on a date yet.'

Tom suggests we could go to Greggs for our first date. 'I'll buy you a sausage roll.'

'Deal,' I reply, with a high-five.

After the visitors have come and gone, Angus, Lauren and I sit down for lunch with the remaining volunteers. After surviving the usual mayhem of the morning, starting with Scottie throwing a tantrum because the delivery van turned up ten minutes late, and Tom cross that Sander was poorly because this meant no cinnamon buns today, I realise I'm beginning to feel at home here now. Scottie's unpredictable temper no longer alarms me. As Monika said earlier, we'd find it odd if he was suddenly nice to us. 'His temper is like a suit he wears to work, Holly. Without it, he'd feel naked, exposed.'

'Who's naked?' Tom had asked hopefully, poking his head through the hatch. 'Is Holly naked?'

'That would seriously put you off your food,' I'd replied back, my heart lifting when Tom laughed, saying nothing would put him off his food, not even Angus naked. I love seeing how much this café means to Tom. He tells me he lives for Saturday, when he can come here and see Nina and his friends. 'And you, Holly. You're my friend now.'

'Friends for life,' I say.

As for Lauren, she hasn't said more than two words to me this morning, but both Angus and I have stopped trying as hard to keep the conversation going. If she doesn't want to talk, that's OK. To be honest, I did wonder if she might show up after last weekend. 'She's probably enjoying it more than we think,' Nina had said to me earlier this morning. Enjoy might be exaggerating. Yet while Lauren looks so sad, and I'm certain she's also in a fair amount of pain, as I often see her rubbing her back, maybe Nina has a point. No one is forcing her to be here. I watch her now. She certainly doesn't volunteer here for the food. She has barely eaten anything. She picks at her fruit salad like a sparrow.

'Did you ever play the game,' Angus interrupts my thoughts, 'where you spin the knife, saying, "When the knife stops, whoever it points to is going to meet…"' Angus spins the knife, before asking Lauren who she'd love to meet.

'Harry Potter,' she murmurs.

'It's going to stop at me,' Tom says, before pointing the knife at himself. He claps. 'I win. I'm going to meet him.'

'You're a rotten awful cheat, Tom,' Angus says. 'Isn't he, Lauren?' She doesn't reply.

'I haven't read any Harry Potter books,' I admit.

'None? Not even the first?' says Craig.

'No.'

'That's weird, even I've read one.'

'It's not weird,' Lauren says with surprising defiance.

'I've seen the films,' I add.

'She wrote all them books in a café didn't she?' continues Craig. 'Didn't she write them on a paper napkin?' He lifts his. 'To think, I could write a masterpiece on this scrap of paper and change my life.' Craig's skin is ravaged, his ears decimated by piercings, and he's so skinny, there's nothing of him. I want to take him home, run him a bath, give him a warm blanket and a baked potato oozing with cheese.

'I once gave writing a go,' Angus admits, 'between jobs. I fancied myself as an author, the next Dan Brown, but I didn't get beyond chapter one. Attention span of a flea, well that's what my wife, or soon to be ex-wife, said.' Scottie flinches. Nina looks disappointed, irritable. Defusing the tension, Angus continues, 'So who's your favourite Harry Potter character, Lauren?'

'Harry.'

'Oh yeah. Why?' Angus asks, careful not to touch her hand or lean in too close, but at the same time, making Lauren feel like there is no one else more important in the room than her.

'He doesn't have a mum or dad, and he lives with his aunt and uncle and cousin, and they treat him bad,' Lauren replies, deadpan.

I catch Nina's eye, thinking this is good, that she's said more around this table than she has since she arrived. Yet when I think about what she said I'm now wondering if Lauren escaped home, like Harry.

'I like Harry too,' agrees Angus. 'He's gone through a lot, but he's brave, loyal, and he'll do anything for his friends, even risk his own life.'

Lauren nods.

'What else do you read, Lauren?' I ask, not wanting to break the spell of her feeling confident enough to talk to us. I sense books are a comfort to her, as they used to be for me. After Jamie died, I stopped reading. I couldn't concentrate. I still haven't picked up a book.

'Anything,' she replies, talking to the floor.

Angus's mobile rings. I watch him grab his pack of cigarettes off the table. 'Won't be long,' he says, taking the call outside.

When he returns, we're clearing the tables and finishing the washing up. Angus begins to fold up the tables and stack the chairs at the back of the room. Noticing he's agitated, Craig rushes to help, encouraging Lauren to give them a hand too.

After the table and chairs are cleared, Craig grabs from the leftover trolley a loaf of bread and some packets of orange juice. 'Is this veggie?' He holds up a pasty, donated to Nina by a local bakery in Hammersmith.

'Take it,' Nina says.

'They think 'cos I'm homeless, Holly, I can't be picky about my food, but I don't like meat, don't like cruelty to animals.'

'It *is* veggie,' I reassure him. 'Sweet potato.'

'You're a doll.' He winks at me. 'You married? Got a fella and kids?'

That inevitable question that sometimes goes over my head, sometimes does my ego the world of good, and at other times breaks my heart. Right now, I let it go over my head, because no one here knows about Jamie, not even Angus and Nina. Though something in me wants to tell them now. 'I'm widowed,' I say.

'Oh mate, I'm sorry.' Craig looks it too.

'Thanks.'

When he doesn't know what else to add, he says, 'Stay safe,' with a wave goodbye, which feels ironic when he's the one who's going to be sleeping rough tonight.

'Craig, couldn't you stay in a night-shelter too?' I call out, thinking of him alone in the darkness, sleeping on an old piece of cardboard with only one threadbare blanket, if that.

He stops. Turns round to me. 'Nah, why would I want to do that?'

'Won't you get hungry?' is all I can come up with. One pasty, a loaf of bread and some orange juice isn't going to last him until next Saturday.

'Nah, incredible the food you can find in bins, Holly,' he says. 'People chuck out stuff that's only a day old. The trick is to know what time to go through 'em.'

'But isn't it lonely?'

'Living on the streets isn't all bad, Holly. No bills, no greedy landlords, no responsibility. I once had a house with four walls but it made me miserable, might as well have been behind bars. The only thing I miss is having a decent shower every day. Anyway love, I'll see you next Saturday. Have a good one,' he says, blowing me a kiss, before scarpering off, back into the wild.

Nina approaches me with a bunch of pink roses, the stems wrapped in foil. 'They're too good to throw away,' she says, handing them to me, but I remain lost in thought. 'If you can believe it, I see so many people, Holly, who get lumped together in social housing situations that are often even worse than sleeping on the streets.'

I can't, or perhaps I don't want to.

Nina turns to me. 'I hate it, as much as you do, and I wish I could do more. But Craig is right. To be housed isn't just four walls and a roof. He's survived the streets for years and he'll survive it for another night.' She squeezes my hand. 'I know it's hard.'

'It's not hard for me,' I say. Everyone, surely, deserves a bed and roof over their head at night? It's a basic human right, isn't it?

Nina nods, though understands there's not much more she can say to reassure me.

Instead, we turn our attention to Angus and Lauren mopping the floor, Angus at one end, Lauren at the other. Nina tells me Lauren can't return to the shelter until six; residents have to be out all day, except for Sundays, and when they return in the evening, they are breathalysed. If they're over the limit, they have until half past ten to sober up. Otherwise, they're not allowed access until the following morning. But it's a long day, so Nina wants to keep Lauren here for as long as she can, so she's not left mindlessly wandering the streets until six. 'I'm going to take her to meet Paul tonight,' she tells me. Paul is the guy who Nina meets each Friday, at Tesco's. Nina jokes, makes their meeting in the back storeroom sound naughty, when in reality all she's doing is grabbing any food they can't sell because it's close to its best-before date. 'I want her to see how the food gets here, understand how this place works.'

'That's a great idea,' I say. 'Can I come?'

'Of course! Sorry, I um, I thought you might need to get back home… to your family?'

I shake my head. 'My husband died, Nina, and I don't have children,' I say, before she can ask me the dreaded question.

'I'm so sorry, Holly,' she replies, though I sense, somehow, she's not surprised.

'He died eighteen months ago.' I tell her how it happened. Jamie was on his way to work. A driver fell asleep behind the wheel.

'Oh my God, Holly.' She places a hand on my arm. 'I can't imagine what you've been through.'

I feel close to tears. 'Well, compared to Craig or Lauren—'

'No, don't ever compare. We all have our stories. Each one is hard for a different reason.' She turns to me, looks me straight in the eye. 'How are you doing? And I mean *really* doing?'

'Some days are better than others. Some days I want to stay in bed with a year's supply of gin and Angel slices.' Nina smiles. 'Other days, it's not quite so bad. I only want to stay in bed for six months with gin and Angel slices. The café is helping,' I say, realising how much I mean it. 'I've fallen in love with baking again.'

'We all need something to get up for, don't we? I get up for this place.'

'I'm not surprised. This is your baby, Nina. I never used to get up so early on a Saturday morning.' I turn to her. 'Mind you, Sander's cinnamon buns help. I missed them today.'

'They are definitely worth getting up for.' She smiles back. 'Well, I'm loving having you here, and so's everyone else, especially Angus. I reckon he doesn't think voluntary work's quite so bad anymore with you around. Oh heck, what's he doing now?' she mutters.

I hold my breath as we watch Angus approach Lauren. He hits her mop with his own, saying, 'Your mop touched mine.'

She pulls hers away indignantly. 'No, it didn't.'

'Are you calling me a liar? Pants on fire?'

'No!' She looks up at him, and finally I get to see her face properly. It's as round as a peach, eyebrows almost meeting in the middle, and to hear her laugh like that is unbelievable. It's like a glimpse of the sun after weeks of rain.

'Take your mop and go over there. You've missed a patch.' Angus points to the other side of the room.

'That's your patch!' Her laugh is pure and childlike.

Angus places his hands on his hips. 'Excuse me?'

'You're in *my* space,' she argues. 'Your mop touched mine. I was here first.'

'Right, this is war,' Angus says and before I know it, he is chasing her around the room with his mop and I reckon it's the most fun Lauren has had in months, maybe in all her nineteen years. And judging from Angus's laugh, it's the most fun he's had in months too. 'You see,' Nina says, 'I asked him to look after Lauren for a reason.'

'He's a good bloke, isn't he?'

'The best. I tell you, Holly, you could pay a psychoanalyst a fortune for years and not hear Lauren ever laugh like that.'

* * *

Angus walks me home. It's four in the afternoon. The sun is shining, people are out shopping and dog walking, friends are sitting outside pubs enjoying either a long lazy lunch or early evening drinks. I feel as if I've been in some kind of underground world, an alternative universe, surrounded by people I'd ordinarily have never met. If it weren't for this café, I wouldn't have crossed paths with Lauren or Craig, nor Angus and Nina. I realise now how small my life had become. 'As soon as you have a routine, things don't happen by chance,' Jamie once said to me.

In the end I didn't opt to go with Nina and Lauren to meet Paul at Tesco's. I tell Angus I thought Lauren might have preferred to go on her own with Nina.

'Yeah, she's probably had enough of you too,' Angus suggests. 'I mean, she's had to put up with you all day.'

'Thanks.'

'You're welcome.'

'You were good with Lauren today.'

'Wasn't it great to hear her speak? To laugh.'

I turn to him. 'Who knew mopping a floor could be such fun? Any time you want to come over and help me clean the bathroom, let me know.'

He smiles. 'My mother always used to tell me, "Most of the things you do in life, son, are mundane, so we owe it to ourselves to make each chore fun." I can see her now, on the tractor, mowing the lawn, fag in her mouth, or hoovering the house, Dolly Parton playing at full volume.'

'Your mother sounds fun. More fun than mine, anyway.'

'Sounded. She died a year ago.'

'Oh, I'm sorry.'

'She was eighty-two, riddled with cancer. It was her time to go. "Put me down, Angus," she'd say. She was a terrible patient, furious to be old. In her young days she was a serious party girl, that is before she met my father and settled down. She despised illness, couldn't deal with it. When I was a little boy, if I so much as coughed she'd turn the other way. We weren't always close, I caused her too many headaches.' He shrugs. 'But I do miss her. I loved her. She was both insane and a wise old soul.'

'What do you mean?'

'She looked down on the "conventional type". If a mother said their son was planning on marrying and getting an accountancy job she'd say, "Doesn't it bother you how ordinary his life will be?" I remember once telling Mum there was a weirdo at school, all he did was talk about stick insects. "Life is full of dull people, Angus, so speak to this interesting boy who hunts for stick insects. Find out what he loves about them." Best lesson I ever learned is to make friends with people who are different.'

As I listen, finally it dawns on me why Angus is good with people. Sure, he puts his foot in it, but he doesn't judge or ignore anyone. He dives right in, trying to make others feel welcome. I reckon his mother did a good job. 'She doesn't sound insane,' I say.

'Oh believe me, she was, but that was partly because… well, put it this way, the sheer volume of detentions I received and visits to the headmaster's office drove her to insanity.'

'Were you *that* bad?'

'Worse.'

'You're showing off.'

He raises an eyebrow. 'I'd sit on the school roof at four in the morning, smoking. I stole the key to our housemaster's car once, just for fun. I was expelled twice. I'm not proud, but I did have a good time.'

'Why did you end up in banking?' I ask, curious, as it seems to me Angus could have done anything. We turn a corner, my house sadly in sight now.

'Good question,' he replies. 'Why did I want to sit behind a desk, doing sums and slowly dying and disappointing my mother by being so conventional?'

'I bet you didn't disappoint her, come on.'

'You're being way too nice, Holly. Mum's probably watching from above, seriously furious with me and all my fuck-ups.'

'No, she wouldn't feel that way. I mean, look at you today.'

'Nina's been asking me to volunteer ever since she set up this place, but I kept on telling her I was too busy. Now I'm doing it so I can stay with Scottie. I'm no saint, Holly.'

'We all make mistakes, but I'm sure you can put things right.' The moment I say those words I want to take them back. I have no idea what has happened in his past, and I know, more than I'd like, some things can't be fixed. Jamie will never come back.

'Nina's great, isn't she?' I reflect.

'One of a kind. We lived in a house together at uni. She was like our mother, keeping us in order. She never fitted into the world of law. What's that expression, a square peg in a round hole? A bit like me, really, I never fitted into banking. Anyway, she slots right into the world of saving food and helping others. She's helped me enough.'

I long to know more about Angus's life, but we are only a minute from my home now, and I don't want a hurried version, a whole life packed into mere seconds. 'Well, this is me.' We stand outside my front door. I open the gate. 'Would you like to come in?'

'I won't, thanks, better be getting on.' He shifts awkwardly from one foot to the other. 'What are you doing for the rest of the weekend? Will your, er, husband be home?'

I dig around for my keys in my handbag. 'No,' I tell him. 'He's dead.' I laugh nervously. 'He died.'

'Oh Holly, I'm so sorry.'

'Hopefully he's with your mother, under some cloud, having a laugh,' I suggest.

'I hope so.' He inhales deeply, and looks at me with those sad brown eyes. 'Sorry, put my foot in it again.'

'You didn't. I was going to tell you.'

'Do you miss him?'

'All the time.'

'How did it happen? Was he ill?'

I tell him the whole story, recalling opening the door to the policeman. He wouldn't have suffered any pain, he said. It was of no comfort then. It's more comfort now.

Angus tells me he doesn't know what to say. 'Except I'm glad you decided to come to the café. Kind of makes sense now, why you did.'

I feel relieved to have told both him and Nina. I don't want to hide Jamie anymore. I want him to be a part of this new chapter, a part of the café and the new friendships I'm making. I don't want to hide myself anymore. 'And you, Angus? Are you seeing your children this weekend?'

'Nope, not this weekend.'

From the way he says it, I can tell it hurts.

I sigh. 'What a pair we are.'

We both laugh at that, knowing if we didn't, we might cry.

I am taken aback by how much I want to wrap my arms around Angus, tell him, as much as myself, that everything will be all right in the end. Something draws me to him, maybe it's his humour or his vulnerability, or maybe I'm about to ask him this because I sense he's as lonely as I am. 'Angus, would you like to meet up tomorrow? Go for a walk or have something to eat?'

'Oh,' is all he says, with a little too much hesitancy.

'You don't have to if you don't want to, you can say no, I mean you're probably busy, so don't—'

'Stop right there. It's a date. Well, not a date, but—'

'I know what you mean,' I finish, noticing my heart beating faster than it should.

The following morning, I set out to the park, excited to seeing Angus again. Last night Milla had asked me more questions about my new friend, questions I didn't know half the answers to, making me realise how much I wanted to hear a few more chapters of his life, join some of the dots. I suggested eleven-thirty and then a pub lunch. 'Let's meet under the arch, by the garden centre.'

'Under the arch, by the garden centre,' he'd repeated, along with the time. 'I'll be there.'

So much for being there. It's now a quarter to twelve and no sign of Angus. I'm about to send him a message when I realise we didn't even exchange mobile numbers.

I decide to wait another ten minutes or so, but my hope is fading fast. And so is my pride. I call it quits, taking a look around the garden centre instead. I need to plant something in my window boxes, and I could treat myself to some herbs for my back garden. And I might grab some lunch from the café. The café is packed with couples and families. I notice a man holding his girlfriend's hand across the table. I order a portion of salad for one, feeling as miserable and small as the box it's in.

'Holly,' Milla says, surprised I'm calling her so soon. 'What's wrong?'

'He didn't turn up,' I say, wishing I didn't sound upset. I have no idea why I care so much.

'What? Why? No, Emily, wait. Mummy's on the phone. Hang on, Holly, I'm so sorry. Put everything back in the box, Emily! We've been playing snakes and ladders,' she explains.

'And then it's lunch. Roast chicken. Wash your hands, guys,' I overhear Dave say.

How I long, in that moment, to be in the warmth of her kitchen, playing games with the twins. My idea of doing voluntary work, to get out of my rut and meet new people, rather than escape to my parents in the country, or hang out with Milla and Dave every weekend, now feels like a bad decision.

'Maybe something came up, Holly,' Milla says, 'an emergency with his kids.'

'Mummy, I'm hungry!' I hear.

'Wait! I'm on the phone to Auntie Holly.'

'Go,' I insist. 'Honestly, I'm fine.'

'He could have called though.'

I don't have the energy to explain we hadn't exchanged numbers.

'Mummy!' I hear one of the twins calling again.

'I'll call you later. Holly?' She waits. If I talk, I'm scared I might burst into tears. 'Are you OK?'

'Uh-huh.' I bite my lip.

'You're not, are you?'

'No.' My voice crumbles.

'Come over now? Holly?'

'MUMMY!' I hear crying. Screaming.

'Dave!' Milla shouts. 'Sort them out, will you!'

'Don't worry, I'm fine,' I say, thinking I'd rather be on my own. I can't cope with the twins, not today. 'I'll call you later.'

'I love you.'

'Love you too.'

The moment the line goes dead I decide to call home. 'Mum?' I say the moment she picks up.

'Oh darling, you've called at the worst time. It's nearly lunch!'

'I know, but—'

'We have the Peacocks over, and then we're playing bridge.'

'Sure.' I fight back more tears. 'Have fun!'

'Are you all right, darling? There's nothing wrong, is there?'

'No, no, send love to Dad.'

'He's a been a good boy today, he went to the rubbish dump.' I hear a beeping sound. 'Must go, don't want the beef to burn! Bye darling. Don't be a stranger!'

'Bye, Mum,' I say, for once grateful that my mother isn't the most perceptive of people. After our call, I head into the kitchen to make myself a cup of coffee. When I open one of the cupboard doors the first thing I see is Jamie's old chipped mug, with the initial 'J' on the front. I slam the door shut before rushing upstairs to bed. I lie down under the covers and soon I can't stop crying. As I said to Nina, some days I want to stay in bed with a year's supply of gin and Angel slices. Today is one of those days. I didn't realise how exhausting it is to miss someone. It's a full-time job. A job that never ends. Loneliness makes me want to curl up in a ball, and stay like this, forever.

8

'What's for pudding?' Tom asks, poking his head through the hatch. Despite the heat, I mean it's July for goodness sake, he's wearing a thick woolly Nottingham Forest football scarf over a black chunky-knit cardigan.

'Don't know yet,' I say, staring at the ingredients, Lauren's presence distracting me. I don't have enough space to think straight, let alone cook. Since last weekend I haven't heard from Angus and he hasn't made an appearance at the café yet.

'What's for pudding?' Tom stares at me. 'Can we have chocolate cake?'

'Tom, leave poor Holly alone,' Monika calls out, as she and Scottie slice courgettes, aubergines, carrots and butternut squash. They're making a couple of roasted vegetable trays with spicy chicken thighs.

'Otherwise, there won't be any pudding, mate,' Scottie says, adding, 'Lauren, can you peel some spuds?'

'Yes, Chef.'

Tom's face drops before he shuffles off despondently, muttering, 'Why does everyone hate me?'

'No one hates you,' I call out, watching him plonk himself down at the table next to Simona, who is working on the table decorations and flowers. It's a mixture of roses, carnations and freesias today. 'Cheer up, Tom,' says Simona, thrusting some freesias towards him. Funnily enough, that doesn't cheer him up.

'Is Angus coming, Holly?' Tom asks, shooing the flowers away, causing Simona to burst into tears. Tom is asked to apologise; he refuses.

'Who knows,' Scottie answers for me, watching Lauren in awe as she peels the potatoes at lightning speed.

'Speedy Gonzales,' Scottie says. 'Wow. When I need potatoes peeling, I know who to ask.'

I notice Lauren's cheeks glowing. It's not often Scottie compliments us, so when he does, it means something.

I return to my ingredients, but remain distracted. 'How's Angus?' I ask Scottie, failing to sound casual.

Scottie turns to me. 'He was out again last night. Woke us up, and the boys.' Scottie reminds me he has a six-year-old who needs his sleep. 'I swear I'm this close to chucking him out,' he declares, pointing his knife at me. 'I know he's going through a shit time, sorry for swearing, Lauren.'

She shrugs as if nothing could shock her.

Scottie pauses, as if revising how much he should tell me in front of her. 'We're bending over backwards to help him, but he lets everyone down, *all* the time.'

I can see how worried Scottie is, especially when he says, 'I don't know what to do anymore.'

'We were supposed to meet up last weekend for lunch,' I confide.

'Sorry Holly,' he says, as if used to apologising for his brother. 'I'm sure he didn't mean to forget. He never does.'

'Can I sit down?' Lauren asks, after peeling five kilos of potatoes in record time.

I only have to look at Lauren to see she's uncomfortable. 'Is it your back?'

She nods, before Scottie quickly grabs her a chair from the dining room.

'Do you need some painkillers?' I ask.

Nina sticks her head round the door. 'Too much talking, not enough cooking going on in here. Lauren, why don't you make a start on the cutlery? You can do it sitting down. If you don't need her, Holly?'

I shake my head, relieved to be on my own. Maybe Angus didn't want to meet up? He was only being kind? Maybe he decided, after all, it was a bad idea. Perhaps he thought I meant a *date*. He thinks I fancy him and that idea is so horrifying that he's now hiding from me? No! I might have only known Angus for eight weeks but that's not his style. As Scottie said, he has a habit of letting people down. Hurting them. He never means to. But he does.

I look down at the punnets of raspberries and nectarines again; we have eggs, cream, butter, and fresh ginger. If he turns up today, I'm going to ask him straight what happened because I sense Scottie is keeping something from me. What was it Angus did that was so bad his family don't want him around and he drinks himself into oblivion most nights? I can't help thinking I'm missing a giant piece of the puzzle, the centrepiece which might help me make sense of everything. I open the cupboard door to my left which houses all the basic baking ingredients and reach for the flour, sugar and vanilla extract. I'm also thinking, to show Tom that I do love him, a vanilla sponge cake with a raspberry, cream and ginger filling. I can thinly slice some nectarines on top of the icing. One big cake won't be enough though, what else can I do? The ingredients are about as inspiring as I am today.

'What's for pudding?' Tom asks again, head poked through the hatch.

'Cake and meringues,' I announce, at last making him smile.

'Where's Angus?' Tom scans the kitchen as if Angus might be hiding in a cupboard.

'Don't know,' Scottie says with impatience and I sense a touch of envy because it seems, no matter how many times Angus messes up, everyone forgives and wants to see him again. Including me.

Lauren pours the creamy sponge mixture into two large round baking tins before I place it in the oven and set the timer for twenty-five minutes. I glance at the door. Still no sign of him.

Monika and Scottie are slicing peppers and a couple of limes for a summer curry, the kitchen now smelling of ginger, coriander and turmeric.

'Mine's szarlotka, apple tart,' Monika says to Lauren. They've been talking about their favourite food. 'I can show you one day Lauren, how to make it. And my mum used to make the best Polish coffee cake.'

'Mint choc chip ice cream,' offers Lauren.

'On the beach,' Monika adds. 'What's the hardest thing you've ever had to cook, Scottie?'

'Toast,' he replies. 'I used to work in a girls' boarding school, breakfast was the worst meal. So much bread gets wasted.'

'What do you do when you're not here?' I ask him.

'I work for a mate part time. He runs a restaurant in Covent Garden, French food. I told him right from the start I'd never give up this café though. My Saturdays are sacred. I tell you, it means more to me working here, seeing how much the food is appreciated, than being in a fancy restaurant.'

I like this side of Scottie. 'How did you get into cooking?' I ask him.

'I got bored at school, no attention span like Angus. Left at seventeen, got my first job in a pub making bacon club sarnies, but loved it. I don't know what it was about being in a kitchen but I felt calm and focused for the first time in my life. I find cooking cathartic,' he says, sticking a fork into one of his chicken thighs to see if it's done.

Monika raises an eyebrow. 'I'm glad *you* find it cathartic. Sometimes Scottie, being with you in a kitchen is more stressful than being in an intensive care ward.'

Lauren giggles as she whisks the egg whites.

'Jeez, I'm not that bad, am I?'

Lauren, Monika and my silence says it all.

'Cooking is therapeutic,' he stresses again. 'It takes my mind off things.'

'What things?' Monika asks.

'What to do about my wayward brother,' Scottie says, just as Angus appears at the door, breathless and even more dishevelled than usual.

'How's the head?' Scottie asks.

'Don't. I'm not in the mood for another lecture.'

'You're late. Most of the work's done.' Scottie's tone is clipped. Unforgiving.

'Don't,' Angus warns him again. 'I'm here now.'

'You're here now! Aren't we lucky!'

'I'm trying, Scottie.'

'Well try harder.'

When Scottie is out of earshot Angus tells me he's a sanctimonious prick.

'I heard that,' Scottie says, sticking his head through the hatch. 'Believe it or not, I love you. I might have a funny way of showing it, but I don't want to see you throw your life away.'

Angus curses under his breath. 'How are you, Lauren?'

'I'm fine.'

'Need a hand with anything, Holly?'

Ignoring Angus, I tell Lauren the only thing we have left to do is make a chocolate sauce to go with the meringues.

'Pat made hers with evaporated milk,' she says.

'Who's Pat?' Angus asks, as surprised as I am that Lauren has volunteered this information.

'I lived with her,' she replies. 'We had mint choc chip ice cream and chocolate sauce every Sunday. I used to drink it out of the jug when she wasn't looking.'

'Why don't you help me make it then?' I suggest, still avoiding eye contact with Angus. 'Let's ask Nina for some money.'

'I heard my name,' says Nina, rushing into the kitchen in her usual scruffy T-shirt under dungarees, her hair tied back in a ponytail today.

I ask her if we can have some cash for a few tins of evaporated milk.

Nina produces from her pocket a twenty-pound note. 'There's a Tesco Express round the corner,' she tells Lauren. 'They should have some.'

'I'll go, need some fags anyway,' Angus says, only to be shut down immediately by Nina.

He frowns, watching Lauren leave. 'Why is everyone in such a bad mood today?' He waits for me to say something, but I remain quiet. 'You OK?'

'I'm fine,' I say, realising I'm anything but, before rushing to the bathroom and locking the door behind me.

I lean against the wall, struggling to breathe. Why do I feel like this? Why am I crying again? *Stop crying, Holly!* He's showing no signs of even remembering we'd made a plan. Angus forgot. I'm that unimportant he forgot. I press my head into my hands, confused. I touch my letter 'H' gold pendant that Jamie gave me for my fortieth. I can't go on without you. I don't want to be here, Jamie. I sit down on the loo seat and wrap my arms around myself. Breathe, Holly, breathe. I don't want to go back out there, and pretend everything's fine. I can't face Angus. Or Lauren. I can't face anyone today. I don't want to be here. I want to be on my own.

'Holly?' Angus calls.

I freeze. Go away.

'I'm sorry,' he says through the door. 'Scottie told me. Oh Holly, I'm so sorry I forgot our lunch.'

I remain frozen.

'Look, I can hardly remember my own name at the moment. My head's scrambled. Life got in the way.'

Something inside me explodes, and before I know it, I fling open the door. 'Life's tough for everyone, Angus, not just you.'

'I know! I'm sorry,' he says again. 'My only excuse is I had another argument with Sophie.' He stops in his tracks. 'Have you been crying?'

'No.' Self-consciously I dry my eyes, not wanting him to think I've been crying over him.

'She called me that Sunday, about an hour before we were supposed to meet, saying she wouldn't let me have Benjie for a weekend, that I needed to sort my head out before she can trust me again, blah blah—'

'She's right.'

Angus looks taken aback by my tone.

'If you carry on like this, drowning your sorrows in the pub, and making excuses all the time—'

'I know. You're right. But I miss my children. It hurts not seeing them every day.'

'Well *do* something about it. At least you have a fucking family.' I raise my voice. 'You have two beautiful children. Do you know how lucky you are? Jamie and I could never have kids. He's not here anymore.'

All the colour drains from his face. 'Holly, I'm—'

'Stop saying "sorry". Your words mean nothing, Angus! Scottie's right. The only person that can help you is you, and if you keep on letting everyone down, you'll end up a sad lonely old man,' I predict, before returning to the kitchen, wondering where my courage to speak the truth came from, but realising that felt good. He needed to hear that. And I needed to say it.

As people begin to arrive, Lauren returns, breathless, with the evaporated milk. I convince her to take some painkillers, arguing she'll be on her feet all afternoon serving. I'm behind on time so Angus offers to help me slice the cake. 'Sorry, you take it,' he says, when we both reach for the knife at the same time, our hands touching. I'm acutely aware of how closely we're standing together. 'I've been thinking about what you said,' he says quietly, so no one can hear, but me. 'You were right. Can we talk later?'

I nod, before walking over to the stove to make a start on the chocolate sauce. I jump when Angus grabs me by the arm and turns me towards him. 'I'm sorry, Holly.'

I realise, from the punished look in his eyes, how sincere he is. 'It's not me you need to make it up to, Angus,' I say, gesturing to Scottie, and thinking of his family.

'I know. We need to swap numbers, so you can at least bollock me next time, if I forget, which I won't, obviously,' he stammers, 'that's if you want a next time? I wouldn't blame you if you didn't, but I like you, and I hate you thinking badly of me.'

He walks over to the hatch to take orders, a long queue forming outside the kitchen.

'You like him back, don't you?' says Lauren, who clearly heard every word. 'I mean, *really* like him.'

'Not like that, Lauren.'

'It's *always* like that.'

I turn to her, confused not only by my feelings, but by her sudden directness. 'We're just friends.'

A small smile creeps on to her face. 'Sure. Friends.'

I glance at Angus again.

'Men and women, they can't be friends,' Lauren concludes.

'One curry coming up for you, and Holly and Lauren's meringues and choc sauce,' I overhear Angus saying. 'Good choice. Take a seat.'

Lauren stirs the evaporated milk into the smooth melted chocolate and butter. 'Pat put icing sugar in too,' she says.

'Did she? I think we have icing sugar,' I say, recalling seeing it in the cupboard. I ask Lauren to keep stirring while I grab some. 'How much? We should sieve it first. Here.' I hand her the sieve. 'You do it.'

Lauren ignores the sieve, instead tipping the box upside down over the saucepan, a good deal of icing sugar going everywhere.

'You're right. Who needs a sieve?' I say, dipping a teaspoon into the mixture to have a taste. 'This tastes like heaven. Here, try some.' I hand her a clean spoon.

'Roasted veggies and meringues with Lauren's choc sauce,' Angus says, taking down another order.

'Pat's choc sauce,' Lauren puts him straight.

'Your Pat did us proud,' says Angus, as we eat our lunch after everyone has left. It's just me, Nina, Angus, Scottie, Craig and Lauren. Lauren ate a small portion of Scottie's curry with some vegetables, and is now eating some left-over fruit with her chocolate sauce. It's the first time she's eaten a main course and a pudding. It's good to see her eating vegetables and fruit, and while chocolate sauce isn't exactly healthy, at least it's putting a smile on her face.

'Who's Pat?' Nina asks, since she missed out on the earlier conversation.

'This little old lady,' Lauren replies, chocolate sauce coating the corners of her mouth.

Nina takes off her glasses, gives them a quick wipe on her shirt sleeve. 'Careful. She's probably my age.'

'And mine,' I add.

Lauren looks at Nina and then at me, a serious expression on her face as she declares, 'She was a bit older.' She stands up to stretch, before sitting down again.

'How come you lived with Pat?' Angus asks.

'My step-mum kicked me out when I was fifteen. My real mum, she died. I never knew her.'

'So Pat took you in?' I say, longing to hear how the little old lady came to the rescue.

Lauren nods.

'She had bad knees. I used to go down the shops for her, helped her in the garden too, with her pots. She used to tell me about the war, the rations, one egg a week.'

'Hang on a minute, Pat must have been *seriously* older than us,' Nina says, making us all laugh.

Lauren nods and allows herself another smile. 'Think her dad fought in the war or something. She had lots of family albums, showed me pictures of him in his uniform.'

'What happened?' I ask, praying Pat didn't die. 'How long did you live with her?'

'About a month. I was kicked out in March. Less cold at least.'

'She kicked you out?' I say, wondering how Pat could do that to a child, to someone as vulnerable as Lauren, and that it sounds so unlike this little old lady who'd previously given her warmth and kindness, and made such delicious chocolate sauce.

'Her daughter did.' Lauren looks awkward, unsure how to handle all the attention. 'I'm OK,' she murmurs. 'Living on the streets was better than living at home.' She gets up and walks away.

Angus jumps up and heads straight after her, reminding me why I like him.

'Wait,' Nina calls out. 'Leave her.'

He turns.

'Give her a few minutes on her own, Angus. She doesn't need rescuing.'

Reluctantly he returns to the table. 'Remind me never to feel sorry for myself again,' Angus mutters.

'Me too,' I say.

9

'That's a heavy rucksack you've got there, Lauren,' says Angus, as we're walking her back to the night-shelter. She brings it to the café each week and hides it in the office, behind the printer. 'Want me to carry it?'

She shakes her head.

After lunch, Nina had asked Angus and me if we could spend some time with Lauren, before dropping her back at the shelter at six. So, we ventured to a café close to Ravenscourt Park. Angus and I attempted to talk to her, but she was lost in her own world, a world which seemed dark and lonely.

'What's in there?' I can't help asking.

'This and that,' she says. 'You can go now,' she adds, when we arrive at the shelter's front door, as if we're her embarrassing parents.

A member of staff greets us by the door. He's slight in build, wearing loose jeans which reveal Calvin Klein pants and his dark hair is tied up in a short ponytail. He's called Phil. We introduce ourselves. 'Oh yeah, you're the guys she's doing work experience with,' he replies. 'Jane filled me in. Everything all right, Lauren?' he asks, as she breathes into a machine with a tube, a machine that looks exactly like the ones the police use when stopping drivers. He turns to us. 'We have to do this with everyone, even though we know Lozza doesn't touch alcohol.'

Lozza?

'Yep, all good.'

'Can we see your bedroom quickly?' I ask.

'We don't allow anyone in except residents.' He hesitates. 'Look, as you work with her, and if Lauren is cool?' Lauren nods before Phil empties the contents of Lauren's rucksack on to the table outside the office, no doubt to make sure she hasn't snuck in any drugs. Again, Phil apologises, saying he knows Lauren doesn't take drugs but he has to do his job. Angus and I can't help but stare at the packets of crisps, cheese straws, a tube of Pringles, a half-eaten chocolate bar, flapjack and a bumper pack of Jelly Babies that are tipped upon the table, along with a scruffy teddy bear with only one eye. I sense Lauren's shame as she shoves the sweets and chocolates back into her rucksack, unable to look at us. Is she comfort eating at the café? Is this why she disappears into the bathroom many times during our shifts, and has no appetite for lunch?

'You joining us for tea tonight?' Phil asks Lauren as she grabs her rucksack and heads down a narrow corridor, with closed doors on either side. The rock band Muse plays through one. We follow, walking past a store cupboard, filled with packets of cereal, tinned fruit and vegetables. Her bedroom is at the end. 'It's pasta!' he calls out.

Lauren leads us into her bedroom. It's fairly stark, a bed, a Harry Potter cushion, and a heap of clothes on one chair, but it's clean, the room carpeted, the blinds floral. 'This is cosy,' I say, wishing I could stop putting on this overly cheerful voice to overcompensate when I'm not sure what to say. Lauren lies down on her bed, crossing her arms in a way that tells me she doesn't want to talk.

'It's great,' Angus says, looking around the room. 'Well, we'll get out of your hair then. See you next weekend?' She doesn't reply. 'Bye then, Lauren. Have a good night.'

'Thanks for all your help today,' I add.

Reluctantly we close the door behind us. Angus leans against it. 'Do you think we stirred things up too much? With Pat? Too many questions?'

I'm more concerned about all the food in her rucksack. The look of mortification on her face. No wonder she wanted us to go. 'Shh,' Angus says, leaning against the door. I lean in too, our faces almost touching. Lauren is crying.

'What do we do?' he whispers.

'Lauren?' Gently I knock again. 'Lauren, are you OK?'

It's such a stupid question when I know she's not. We wait. Nothing.

'We can't leave her like this,' Angus mutters before he enters her room. She's now sitting on her bed, clutching the teddy bear with one eye. Angus sits beside her, is about to place an arm around her shoulder, but then thinks better of it. I glance at the chair, covered in clothes, so kneel on the floor beside her bed instead. I capture the protective father in Angus when he says, gently, 'Was it sad talking about Pat today? Or your step-mum? Or your mum dying?'

She shakes her head. 'I'm fine.'

'Are they treating you OK in here?' he continues. 'You're not scared of anyone?'

'No.' She rubs her thigh repeatedly with the palm of her hand. 'They're all right here. They're good.'

Angus clears his throat. 'Lauren, you can trust Holly and me, anything you say will remain between us, right Holly?'

I nod.

'I'm tired,' she confesses, still not looking at us.

'You're tired,' he repeats. 'You're not sleeping?'

She turns her face to the wall. 'The world would be better off without me.'

I catch Angus's eye. In that moment I imagine a younger version of Lauren, at home, locked in her bedroom, staring at the wall, sad, lost, scared, unsafe, with no one around her who gives a damn. A little girl who has lost her mum. Where was her dad? Why did he have to go and remarry someone unkind? 'The world wouldn't be better off,' I say, 'we wouldn't have met you.'

'Exactly,' Angus says. 'And no one would have tasted Pat's chocolate sauce.'

'Have you seen a doctor, Lauren?' I ask, thinking about her back pain too.

She shakes her head.

'When was the last time you saw one?' I press.

She stares ahead. 'I've never seen one.'

Angus and I glance at one another again. 'Right. Well, if it's OK with you,' he says, 'why don't we book you an appointment?'

'No,' she says. 'I don't want to see no one.'

'They might be able to help you sleep better,' Angus reassures her. 'Believe me, I know how low *I* feel when I don't get a proper night's kip.'

'And maybe they could give you something for your back pain too?' I suggest. 'We could come with you, Lauren, if you wanted us to?'

'Definitely,' Angus says. 'Us oldies can come along, so long as you don't mind your street cred being ruined.'

She bites her lip. 'I don't know.' Finally, she looks at us as if we're not real, or as if we must be expecting something in return. 'Why d'you want to help?'

'Because we care,' I say, meaning it.

Angus touches her shoulder, and this time she doesn't flinch. 'Sometimes there comes a time when we all need help. Hey, don't cry.'

But soon she can't stop. It's as if a tap has been turned on. Lauren is allowing herself to grieve for the fifteen-year-old who was kicked out on to the street, like a piece of rubbish, and told to look after herself with nothing but a teddy bear to her name. Where did she go? How has she survived these past four years? When I was fifteen the only thing I had to worry about was if my mother had stuck my favourite-coloured jeans into the wash, jeans that I'd wanted to wear for a party that night. I blame Lauren's father as much, if not more, than the stepmother. How can a parent abandon their child? How could he sleep at night, knowing his daughter was out in the freezing cold, alone and vulnerable? When I remember seeing Lauren arrive at the café for the first time, I feel ashamed that all I was worried about was myself, and how I was going to manage.

I can't imagine how anxious she must have felt joining a bunch of strangers in the kitchen.

When Lauren finally dries her eyes, Angus says, 'Let me or Holly book you an appointment Lauren, and if you want us to come, all you have to do is ask.'

She says nothing. So many people have let her down, including the very people who should have loved her unconditionally, so why should she trust us?

10

'Lauren Morris,' the receptionist repeats, looking at her computer screen, before glancing up at Lauren, sandwiched between Angus and me. 'That's fine, take a seat.'

That would be fine if there were any, I think, as we approach the packed waiting room, a couple of children playing with toys in the far corner, tired parents alongside. An older imperious-looking woman, with bouffant hair and scarlet lipstick, looks up from her magazine, before treating us to a stare. I'm imagining she's thinking she wouldn't be seen dead entertaining us around her dining-room table, Angus with his stubble and beer belly, gothic Lauren modelling a black tracksuit and hoody, and then me in my crumpled linen trousers, hot and sweaty after running from the office to get here on time. We are a motley crew, incongruous alongside one another. 'You sit down, Lauren,' Angus says, gesturing to the first free chair we come to.

Three quarters of an hour later, we're still waiting, but at least the room isn't so crowded, the children have gone, and we've managed to bag three seats in a row, towards the front, where we're in a good position to see the various GPs escorting patients out of their consulting rooms before calling out the next patient on their list. Lauren sits between us. She's been crunching her knuckles for the past ten minutes and tapping her foot against the floor. I offer her a piece of chewing gum, imagining she's dying for a cigarette. She accepts, shoving it in her mouth. I see a doctor walking down the corridor, towards the waiting room. *Please call out Lauren's name.* Besides, I need to get back to work. Harriet's been kind letting me take time off but I don't want to exploit her generosity. 'Mark Roland?' she says, scanning the room.

A man jumps up, sunglasses perched on the top of his head, a light beige linen jacket slung over his shoulders, a swagger in his stride. 'Doesn't seem to be a lot wrong with Mark Roland,' Angus whispers to me.

'Except perhaps dying slowly of arrogance,' I suggest, as I slump back in my seat, feeling almost as agitated as Lauren.

Angus continues to flick through a glossy wedding magazine. 'I went to see my GP the other day, Lauren.'

'What did you go for?' I ask, when Lauren doesn't.

'I have the "black cloud" from time to time. It's what Granny used to call it. It's probably not the same black cloud as yours, Lauren, but I tell you, it's not much fun when it's right over my head. So, we need to sort out this black cloud of yours, right, this cloud that says the world will be better off without you, and turn it into something else.'

'A rainbow,' Lauren mutters.

I glance over at Angus, impressed by how he talks so honestly to Lauren, and with genuine concern. Since our argument, I've seen another side to him, a side so very different from the Angus I met that first morning in the café. I've realised that if he wants to put his mind to something he is unbelievably efficient. He was determined to get Lauren an appointment as soon as possible, with a female doctor, and given that Lauren had never been to the GP surgery before, and had asked if we could come with her, there was no way he was going to let her down. There was no way he was ever going to forget, again.

'I'm sure she'll be nice,' I reassure her. *Please be nice. And take Lauren seriously.* When I was little, I used to get stabbing headaches, and our family GP asked, 'And when do these headaches come on, little Holly? When it's time to do the washing-up? Or time to do your homework?'

'I'd look good in this dress, right?' Angus shows Lauren a picture of a woman in a peach-coloured wedding gown. He's such a fool, but somehow, he makes us smile.

'Especially with your hair up?' I say, before he gathers his hair into a mock ponytail.

'Shut up,' Lauren says, with a small smile.

'Lauren Morris?' says a woman with dark hair, about my age.

Angus tosses the magazine on to the table, before the three of us approach her. 'Hello, I'm Dr Stratton. If you'd like to follow me.'

'How can I help?' Dr Stratton asks, as we take a seat in her office. She directs her attention towards Lauren.

Lauren turns to Angus, who gives her an encouraging nod, saying, 'You tell Dr Stratton what you told us.'

'I'm tired,' Lauren replies. There's a long awkward pause. Lauren turns to face Angus again. 'Is there anything else you wanted me to tell her?' Without waiting for an answer, she also turns to me.

'We were worried about you, Lauren,' I say, 'you know, how low you've been feeling, and we wanted you to get some help.'

As I'm talking, Dr Stratton must wonder who we are. She reads my mind, asking, 'It's useful for me to know who's come with a patient, so I'm aware who's helping them?'

'I'm Holly. We're friends. We work together.'

'I'm on pudding duty,' Lauren murmurs.

'Angus. We work at my friend's café. We're volunteers.'

'Good,' Dr Stratton says. 'So, Lauren, you said you were feeling tired. Have you got any other symptoms?'

Lauren chews her lip.

Dr Stratton helps her out. 'For example, is your appetite OK?'

'Fine.'

I have to fight not to say she barely eats and then binges on sweets and chocolates.

'Have you lost any weight at all?'

She shakes her head.

'Are your periods normal?'

Lauren withdraws further into her seat. Any minute now she'll be hiding under the chair.

'No other symptoms like a cough or shortness of breath, bowels and waterworks OK?' the doctor persists.

Lauren eyes the door longingly.

'She's tired, Dr Stratton,' Angus stresses.

'And you get back pain, don't you, Lauren?' I add.

Angus nods. 'We were wondering if—'

'I'm aware I'm asking lots of questions,' Dr Stratton interrupts us, 'but it's important for me to make sure there's nothing else going on. Lauren, would you be happy to have a blood test? It's routine, to make sure we don't miss anything.'

'Like?' Angus asks.

'Possibly a low blood count or thyroid problems,' she replies, trying to maintain eye contact with Lauren. 'Underactive thyroid is fairly common and can cause tiredness. I'd like to check your liver too, and a few other things, to make sure everything is all right.'

'That sounds like a good idea, doesn't it?' Angus says when Lauren remains silent.

'Are you sleeping?' Dr Stratton continues, keeping her focus on the patient.

She shakes her head.

'Is that a no, Lauren?' Dr Stratton's tone is kind but firm.

Lauren mumbles 'no'.

'I can see this is difficult for you, Lauren, but I'm here to help. Are you struggling to get to sleep or are you waking up and finding it difficult to get back to sleep?'

'Both,' Lauren replies.

'Are you worrying at night?'

'Yep.'

'Is anyone at home with you?'

'Fourteen men and me.'

The doctor looks thrown. 'Goodness.'

'It's a homeless shelter,' Lauren explains.

'Right. I imagine that's a stressful place to live.'

'It's all right, but I don't like being around men.' She turns to Angus. 'He's not bad.'

Angus and I can't help but smile. Dr Stratton's expression softens too. 'Looks like you have two good friends, Lauren.'

She shrugs as if we'll do. 'I keep my door locked at night.'

'Your home life doesn't sound easy,' Dr Stratton says with concern.

Angus leans forward in his chair. 'It's easier than maybe…' He turns to Lauren, as if realising it's not his story to tell. 'Do you want to—'

'Being homeless was fine,' she insists. 'Well, it's not fine, but… having a bed, that's what's weird. I can't lie down too long, hurts my back. I can't turn over or lie on my side 'cos it's painful.'

'Where is this pain?'

Lauren stands up. 'Here,' she jabs her back and hips, 'it aches all the time.'

'How long have you had this pain for?'

'A few years. It was better when I lived on the streets.'

Dr Stratton doesn't bat an eyelid at Lauren's past. I imagine she's seen and heard it all before. Unlike me. I hadn't considered how strange it must be for Lauren to be homeless and then suddenly have four walls around her and a bed. While it seems much safer, and you'd think more comfortable, I can imagine a mattress feels alien. 'Is the back pain worse lying down?' Dr Stratton asks.

'Yep.'

'How many hours sleep do you think you're getting?' the doctor asks.

'Two or three, four is good,' Lauren replies, seemingly warming to the attention.

'And what about your mood? If you're tired all the time, Lauren, how does that affect you?'

Lauren looks unsure.

'Have you ever struggled with your mood in the past? Is it something you've seen a doctor about before?'

'Never been to a doctor.'

Dr Stratton does appear to be struck by this. 'Never? Not even as a child?'

'Nope.'

'Do you think you could be a little depressed, Lauren?'

'Probably. Dunno. Yes, maybe.' She stares at the floor again.

Dr Stratton clears her throat. 'I need to ask a couple of questions now, to make sure you're safe. These questions might feel a little odd, but we have to ask. Have you ever had thoughts about harming yourself?'

We wait.

'Lauren?' the doctor prompts. 'This is important for us to know.'

'No,' she says finally, avoiding eye contact with any of us, and there is nothing definite about that 'no'. 'But what's the point? You know, what would happen if I wasn't here?'

Dr Stratton nods. 'Lauren, you're not alone. So many of our patients come in here feeling the same way, but what's important to us is if these are thoughts of what might happen to you, or if you feel you might do something to yourself.'

Lauren remains silent.

'Lauren?' Dr Stratton presses gently. 'I understand this is hard.'

'I won't do nothing to hurt myself.' Lauren continues to talk to the floor.

'Could I ask what stops you?'

'Don't know.'

'OK. If your thoughts ever change, will you come back and see me?'

Lauren nods.

'I'm wondering if you had any ideas what we might do for you today, Lauren?'

She shakes her head.

'So we have some options. We could wait and see how we go, but I get the feeling that you've done that for some time.'

I can tell by Dr Stratton's tone how much she wants to do something for Lauren. I sense she sees in her someone who has never considered herself important enough to be helped.

'I'm wondering if talking to someone could be an option?' Dr Stratton suggests.

'There's a counsellor down the night-shelter,' Lauren says.

'If you could talk to someone there, that would be good as the waiting lists can be a bit long here. But if you have any problems, please let me know, and I can give you the details.'

'Yeah, don't bottle it up, Lauren,' Angus reinforces. 'You can talk to Holly and me too.'

'I'd like it if you could come and see me again, so we can see how you're getting on, and get to know each other a bit better. I don't know if you've thought about taking medication for your mood?'

Lauren tells her she hasn't.

'That's worth considering, but I feel talking therapies is the best option at this point, though if things don't improve, we can think again. How does that sound, Lauren?'

I catch Angus's eye. I sense he's feeling restless too, that somehow this isn't going to be enough. I fear Dr Stratton is going to say our time is up. What about her back pain? Her comfort eating? Her smoking? I mean, she has smoked since she was a child, that's years of damage to her lungs. I want to tell the doctor Lauren can hardly walk across a room without stopping to recover her breath. And what if she self-harms? Then again, we *all* self-harm. Since Jamie's death I've numbed myself with wine and junk food. Look at Angus, doing much the same. In so many ways, we're no different from Lauren.

'Lauren, I'm wondering if you have any other strategies to help your mood?' Dr Stratton asks, increasing my restlessness. I mean, does Lauren *look* like the kind of person who would ever say the word 'strategies' let alone have them? I don't have them either, and Angus certainly doesn't. We're strategy-free.

Lauren hesitates, before finally she says, 'I eat.'

'Well, eating healthily can really help our mental health, but I imagine it's difficult managing your diet.' Dr Stratton continues, 'You probably eat what you're given?'

Lauren doesn't reply.

Dr Stratton is aware she's hearing only half the story. 'When you say you eat, I'm curious what you mean?'

'I sneak eat. Chocolate, crisps, cake.'

'It's not uncommon Lauren, don't worry, people often turn to food for comfort, but eating unhealthily probably won't help your mood in the long run, so we need to find other strategies that might help.'

Dr Stratton isn't put off by Lauren's silence. 'Another thing we can think about is exercise. Do you do any exercise, Lauren?'

'A bit.'

She doesn't do any! Mind you, nor do I. Nor does Angus. We're fine ones to talk. Here we are, pushing Lauren to see a doctor when we're hardly fine specimens of health ourselves.

'I can't say what kind of exercise might work for you, because we're all so different. I love wild swimming. My husband is never going to get into freezing cold water, he prefers gardening. It's about finding something you enjoy. I'm not about to send you off to a boot camp, don't panic.'

'Thank God for that,' says Angus. 'You'd have to pay me to do that.'

Dr Stratton smiles, clearly charmed by him. 'I could refer you to an exercise scheme, Lauren, where you get help with gym membership?'

She couldn't look less enthused. I wouldn't be too keen on the idea of entering a gym surrounded by women and teens in Lycra pants and cropped tops either.

'I'm wondering if swimming could be an option?' the doctor continues. 'It could relieve your back pain? Swimming is excellent because it doesn't put any pressure on your joints.'

Lauren doesn't respond. I feel like we're on a sinking ship.

'Well, I'll leave it with you,' Dr Stratton says. 'What I need you to do is book a time to come in for a blood test at the reception before you leave, and what do you think about the option of medi-cation, Lauren?' From the blank look on Lauren's face, I still have this nagging feeling that little, if anything, is going to change. I can see Dr Stratton can't force it but I dread Lauren returning to the night-shelter, sitting alone in her bedroom, with only her rucksack of chocolates, cigarettes and sadness for company. Maybe she'll swallow a few mind-numbing tablets with a fizzy drink, before she feels guilty, depressed and lonely again. We all need a reason to live, don't we, we all need meaning, but the hard part is how we find it. For me, any kind of meaning disappeared after Jamie died. In those early months after his funeral, my life meant nothing without him. It's still hard. Look at how I reacted after Angus didn't show up for our lunch date. Milla was taken up with her family. Even Mum didn't have time to talk. It felt as if everyone had purpose, everyone led busy, meaningful lives, except me. And it hurt.

'While I think exercise is the best option, I could prescribe you some anti-depressants for six months to see if that might take the edge off your low mood and help you put some of the things we have talked about in place,' Dr Stratton suggests.

A diet alone isn't going to change Lauren's life. Or an anti-depressant. She needs something to get up for. A purpose. And so do I. My heart is beating faster. She can prescribe anti-depressants, sleeping tablets and painkillers, but unfortunately there is no tablet that can undo the damage of Lauren's childhood. It's like a tattoo, inked in her memory, forever. There's got to be something else.

'Why don't I help?' I blurt out, wondering why I didn't think of it before. I know I want to drink less, eat better, get fit, so... 'I mean, why don't I help Lauren with an exercise programme?'

Angus turns to me.

The more I think about it the more it makes sense. 'We could do some gentle exercises in the park, Lauren, maybe a bit of walking or jogging or I could take you swimming? I *love* swimming,' I pretend, thinking the last time I went was at school, trying to master the butterfly stroke, unsuccessfully.

'I've got an even better plan,' says Angus. 'The three of us get fit together. Look at me! I'm seriously out of shape and need to quit smoking.'

'I'm not giving up smoking,' Lauren says with fierce determination and I sense Dr Stratton decides to leave that subject for today.

'We don't have to go anywhere near a gym, Lauren,' Angus goes on. 'As Holly said, we can stick to the park.'

Dr Stratton waits for Lauren to reply. I sense she is somewhat bemused by the three of us, yet at the same time I'm certain she's willing Lauren to agree. When no reply is forthcoming Dr Stratton says, 'I think this sounds a wonderful plan, don't you? I'm happy to prescribe something for you today, but exercise can have huge benefits to your health, it might improve your back pain, and it can prevent significant problems in later life, Lauren. And it's much more fun doing exercise with friends.'

'Yeah, we could make it *fun*,' Angus reinforces, trying to make himself believe it as much as Lauren. 'I mean, you should see me run. That will make you laugh.'

'We could support one another, form a WhatsApp group and everything,' I say.

'The Three Fitness Freaks,' Angus suggests.

'We can work on the name,' I add.

We all wait. 'Lauren?' Dr Stratton presses. I sense she wants her to say 'yes' almost as much as we do. 'What do you think?'

11

'Don't even *think* about it,' Ian says to Angus, leaning against Lauren's bedroom door, guarding it with his life. Ian is another resident at the night-shelter. I know, from Lauren, he's an ex-offender, in and out of prison for burglary. His bedroom is opposite Lauren's.

'Don't think about what? What's the problem?' Angus says, undeterred. 'We're only here to take her swimming.'

'Is Lauren OK?' I ask.

Ian crosses his muscled arms. I can see the veins protruding from them, they appear to be as angry as him. 'No. She had one of her attacks this morning.'

'Attacks?' Angus looks puzzled. 'What do you mean?'

'She couldn't breathe. She doesn't want to see you. She asked me to tell you she doesn't wanna go swimming today, so clear off.'

'Sure, that's fine, we don't have to go swimming, but can we at least talk to her?' Angus asks, determined not to be shooed away by Ian.

'You people…' Ian glances at me, and then back to Angus, 'with your fancy jobs.'

'I don't have a job,' Angus puts him straight.

'…and your posh voices, you think you can swan in here and sort us out, put us back together, right? But you know what? The truth is we're all broken, you, me and the rest of the fucking world. So, if Lauren says she doesn't want to see you, she doesn't want to see you, so get lost before I throw you out.' I doubt Ian would break into a bead of sweat picking Angus up and throwing him out the front door.

'Come on,' I say, defeated. 'Let's go.'

'No, Holly! Come on, Ian, we're her *friends* and you're right. We're all fucked up and need each other,' Angus insists. 'If we've upset Lauren or put too much pressure on her with this exercise programme, I want to say sorry, and then we'll clear off.'

'You humiliated her,' Ian asserts.

Angus remains as lost as me. 'How?'

'*Just piss off*,' Ian says, fast losing his patience now.

That's it. I'm going. We're going. I grab Angus by the arm, determined to leave the place in one piece.

But Angus won't budge. 'No, you piss off.'

Lauren's bedroom door swings open. 'Both of you, shut the fuck up. Ian, let them in.'

Ian obeys immediately. 'Sorry Laurie,' he mumbles, almost shrinking in size.

'And you.' Lauren points to Angus, wagging a finger at him. 'You're so bloody stubborn. I don't want to go swimming.'

I'm so stunned by her authority, there is no doubt who's the boss, that it's only when I look at her again that I notice she's dressed in the bright polka-dot orange swimming costume that we bought her from Primark last week. I took Lauren shopping last Saturday, after our shift in the café. Lauren didn't want to try it on in the shop. She'd simply grabbed the first one we saw and promised she'd pay me back when she got paid, that is, when she received her benefits allowance. My eye is drawn to her left leg, her skin blotchy and discoloured all down her thigh. 'Don't stare,' she says to all of us, her authority dissipating as she turns round and slams the door behind her.

'I'm disgusting,' she says to me. I was the only one allowed inside her bedroom. Angus didn't object, telling us he'd wait outside. And nor did Ian, who remained mortified by Lauren's disapproval.

I sit down beside her, pretending not to see the chocolate wrappers and empty crisp packets littered across the floor. 'I can't do it,' she says, shivering as she wraps her pale arms around herself. I get up, reach for the maroon dressing gown hanging on the back of her door, place it round her shoulders. I'm unsure what to say because I know I'd feel just as self-conscious if my body was covered in burn marks and scars.

'Everyone will stare,' she convinces herself.

'I understand.'

'I can't swim, Holly, never learned at school.'

'We can do something else,' I suggest, feeling ashamed that didn't even cross my mind. 'It doesn't have to be swimming.'

'I couldn't tell you and Angus I'd drown.'

'We wouldn't have minded. I mean, we would mind, if you drowned. You know what I mean.'

'You seemed all weird, excited.'

'Well, Angus was longing to show off and do a handstand in the shallow end.'

A smile creeps on to her face. 'Saddo,' she says.

'Listen, Lauren, we don't have to do anything you're uncomfortable with.' I want to touch her arm, hold her hand, but I'm unsure how welcome my touch might be. I gear myself up to ask, 'Ian said you had a panic attack this morning?'

She nods. 'Yeah.'

'I have them too. I used to have them a lot after Jamie died,' I confess, but she either doesn't hear or doesn't want to know, so I don't elaborate. 'I'm sorry for pushing you into buying a costume. I should have made sure it was what you wanted to do.'

'You was only trying to help,' she concedes, finally meeting my eye.

Every maternal bone in my body wants to take her into my arms and hold her. Yet I don't know if it might humiliate her even further.

'You were impressive with Ian and Angus,' I end up saying, 'you pulled them into line.'

She shrugs. 'Had practice with my bros.'

'You have siblings?'

'Two step-brothers, Brian and Lee. Mum died giving birth to me,' she says without blinking.

Again, I'm taken aback by her matter-of-fact tone. 'Where are they now?'

'Prison.'

'Prison?' I laugh nervously, and to my relief she laughs with me too.

'I dunno. Lee's probably behind bars. Or if he's not, he's about to be. He takes a lot of drugs. Gets into fights. It's not his fault.' She shrugs. 'He got in with the wrong crowd, you know. Easily done.'

I nod.

'Brian only wants to see me if he needs money. Not that I have any.'

In this moment, I struggle not to hate Brian.

'I could have gone the same way you know,' she says to me, defiance in her eyes. 'I got offered drugs on the streets, but I didn't take 'em.'

I wouldn't have blamed her if she had. Anything to escape the world and numb my feelings.

'I didn't beg either, Holly, not once. I could have begged, stolen, had sex to get more money for drugs, but that would have ruined my life. And I didn't want to ruin my life, Holly. My life was ruined as a kid.' She gestures to the chocolate wrappers and empty crisp packets. 'I've done this for years, sneak eat. Evil step-mum, Gail, thought it was fun feeding everyone but me. I remember one time, she cooked ravioli, it was out of a tin, everything was out of a tin, and she gave me an empty plate and laughed. As a kid I used to creep downstairs at night. If there was cake, I'd eat a tiny slice, hoping she wouldn't notice. She always did, so I had to stand outside, in the front garden, facing the main road, saying over and over, "I am disgusting." I hated not going to school, it was the only place I felt safe. I was bright, you know. Enjoyed reading and drawing and stuff.'

It's unnerving the way Lauren talks, taking me back to a time when she was starved and abused. I wonder how there can be no shred of self-pity in her voice when she describes her stepmother's cruelty. Maybe that's to protect herself from what she's experienced.

My therapist once told me my anxiety, loneliness and panic attacks were a natural response to losing Jamie. Maybe it's the same for Lauren. Her anxiety and panic attacks communicate how she feels more than words.

'I don't touch alcohol,' she continues, 'except at Chrimbo. But I'm not giving up smoking. I've smoked since I was twelve. Smoking and food, that's what helped me get by, that and not thinking or talking about it, to anyone. So if anyone tells me to give up fags—'

'They can go jump off a cliff?'

'Exactly.'

We sit in companionable silence, and I feel I've made something of a breakthrough this morning. Mainly because I've been more myself. Finally, I've got the message loud and clear not to try and cheer her up or tell her everything will be OK, but to listen. 'This scar, down my leg,' she says, gesturing to her thigh, before quickly covering it over with her dressing gown again.

I wait for her to go on. If she wants to.

'It was one Christmas. Gail used to always get me to pour the drinks and make the food, do everything basically. I forgot to turn the oven on, the turkey was raw. I'd boiled the kettle to make everyone a cup of tea. Gail came in.' She shrugs. 'You can guess what happened next. She took me to hospital, was all sweetness and light to the doctors, said I'd done it to myself.'

I don't know what to say. 'Where was your dad?'

'He didn't care. He never wanted me. Think I reminded him of Mum. Used to tell me to do as I was told and stay out the way, shut the fuck up basically. Don't worry, Holly,' Lauren says, tapping me on the arm. I look at her, realising tears are rolling down my cheeks. I never wanted to believe such cruelty could exist. 'It was normal,' she reassures me. 'You get used to it.' It both shames and warms my heart that it's Lauren comforting me, and not the other way round.

'Lauren, you never ever deserved that. No child deserves that. You shouldn't get used to it.'

She nods. 'I got away in the end.'

I look at her, wanting so much to hold her. I edge closer, I almost do, but then lose my nerve. 'Do you feel up to doing anything else today?' I ask gently instead, suspecting the answer will be no. But I want to show I'm not giving up. There is no way I'm giving up on this girl. 'You could come over to mine for some lunch? We could go for a walk, or do some baking?'

'Nah, if it's OK with you, I'll stay here, with Teddy.' She gestures to her threadbare teddy, propped up against her Harry Potter cushion, staring at me with his one and only eye. 'My nan, Mum's mum, gave him to me,' she says, picking him up and giving him a cuddle. 'I've had him since the day I was born.' When she introduces us, I see Lauren again, as a little girl, back in her bedroom at home, holding on to Teddy, her one and only friend. 'Ted slept on the streets with me, never left my side.' She gives him another cuddle. 'He's a survivor.'

I feel the tears come on again as I say, 'Like you.'

She turns to me. Instinctively I reach for her hand now and she lets me hold it. 'Yeah,' she repeats, as if thinking about what I've just said. 'Like me.'

12

I open the fridge, take out some lettuce, a tub of hummus, a packet of cold chicken, some cherry tomatoes and an avocado. I resist picking up the bottle of wine, left over from last night, even though I feel in need of a drink after hearing more about Lauren's childhood.

Ian also hit a nerve. Perhaps Angus and I are trying to swoop in and save the day. Lauren isn't some project we can throw ourselves into to distract us from our own problems. Yet at the same time, Lauren will be expecting us to give up, and I want to prove her wrong, show her that there are people out there who care, people she can trust. People like Angus and me, who want nothing in return. People who aren't going to hurt her.

'So, I think we can safely say that was a disaster,' Angus had said when I joined him outside. 'So much for our genius plan. Maybe we should call it a day, Holly.'

'No,' I replied, linking my arm through his and suggesting lunch at my place. 'We've only just begun,' which encouraged Angus to sing the song, 'We've Only Just Begun' by The Carpenters. His voice is almost as bad as mine.

'Is chicken salad OK?' I ask.

'Perfect. Anything I can do?'

'Nothing. It's literally chopping and chucking everything into a bowl.' I confide to Angus that ever since Jamie died, I've become lazy cooking for myself.

'Cooking for one can't be much fun, Holly.'

'It's not. I used to love trying out new recipes. I'd even take cook-books to bed.'

'You dirty thing.'

I smile. 'When I was a little girl, I used to bake all the time. That's why I wanted to volunteer at the café, cook for others again. How about you, Angus?'

'Me? What about me?'

When I'm with Angus, I realise I still know so little about him, except for the stark facts: unemployed and separated, two kids, Benjie and Amy, whom he sees every other weekend under strict supervision from his wife, Sophie. But there are many gaps in the middle. 'What happened? With Sophie?'

'God, where do I start?'

'The beginning?'

'You're a sucker for punishment, Holly. First Lauren, and now me.'

'Did you have an affair?'

'An affair,' he repeats, 'you think anyone would have me in this state?'

'No.'

'Thanks.' He grins back.

'So what happened?'

He sighs. 'It all started off great, it was love at first sight across the dance floor. Well, it was for me. We were at a twenty-first birthday party, black tie. Sophie was wearing this beautiful purple dress, blonde hair tied back, incredible green eyes. I remember thinking I *had* to talk to her. We danced all night. I pretended I was thirty and owned a bank, hoping I'd at least get a kiss for that.'

'Did you?'

'No such luck, but she wrote her number on the back of my hand. The following morning, I had a shower and you can work out the rest. I was inconsolable. How could I track her down now?' he says, enjoying replaying the drama. 'I was actually seeing someone else, but I was so in love with Sophie that I'd forgotten.'

'Angus! How can you forget? Lunch with me, maybe, but—'

'I told you, my head's only half screwed on. Anyway, to cut a long story short, I found out Soph's number and we started dating, and after seven years, and a lot of hints, finally I tripped up on the way home from a pub, was down on one knee, and Sophie said "yes".'

'You proposed by mistake?'

'No. Well yes, but I would have done it anyway.'

'Angus!' He is *unreal*. 'Did you come clean?'

He nods. 'The night before we married, good timing I know, but she laughed and said she'd seen me trip but was determined to grab the opportunity because I'd have happily coasted on for a few more years and she was longing to have children.'

I like her style.

'I wasn't a thinker-ahead, Holly, children hadn't even crossed my mind. When the vicar said, on our wedding day, "and may they be blessed with children" I thought what the fuck? Don't talk about sex in front of everyone. My mother's here.' Angus lets out a raucous laugh. 'Are you beginning to see why she left me?'

'Yes.' *And no.* 'Go on.'

'I guess it all started when I lost my job. In investment banking it's one mistake and you're out. I felt depressed stuck at home, doing nothing, and quite rightly Soph kicked me out.'

I can't help thinking there is more. He's not telling me the whole story.

'We hadn't been happy for some time,' he confesses. 'She'd always told me I needed to lose weight. Soph's a physio, quite medically minded. She made me go and see our GP about a year ago. I was working mad hours, constantly entertaining clients and coming home late. The doc warned me my blood glucose was high, my liver function dodgy, that I was at risk of heart disease, and on the fast track to diabetes.' He pauses. 'But I didn't care.'

'Why not?' I assemble plates and cutlery on the table, pour the dressing over the salad and give it a mix. 'I don't understand.'

'It's hard to explain.'

'Try.'

'I guess I was addicted to everything that was bad for me. After that appointment, Soph was convinced I'd quit smoking and ease up on the late nights. That I'd listen to a professional.'

'I don't get it.'

'There's not much to get, Holly. I've smoked since I was thirteen. I could have bought a Mercedes Benz with the amount of money I've spent on lighters alone. I loved it, and still do, so it pretty much boiled down to obstinacy. I hate being told what to do. If a sign reads "Don't walk on the grass", I will. Or I'll drive thirty-one miles an hour in a thirty-mile hour speed limit, just because.'

'But Angus, this is your health,' I raise my voice, 'your life.'

'I know. This is delicious. How do you make the dressing?'

'Angus.' I know him well enough now to recognise when he wants to change the subject.

'Sorry. Everything you say makes sense, Holly. I hated my job too. Sophie told me to resign, do something that made me happy. Drama and English are my real passions. And history. And photography.' He sighs.

'I don't get it. Your mum loved people who did unordinary things, and then you go into banking? I mean, fine if you loved it.'

'I wasn't brave enough to follow my dream. I never thought I'd get into drama school or earn enough doing photography. I convinced myself Mum lived in fairyland thinking everyone should be unordinary. The truth is failure terrified me, Holly. I was good at numbers so I took the easy route. I knew I could make a success of banking. Well, I thought I could. Almost killed myself in the process, but it never scared me.'

'What never scared you?'

'My health. I never believed it was going to happen to me,' he says. I still don't entirely follow so wait for him to elaborate. 'When I was in my twenties, and thirties, even my forties for that matter, I made a deal with the devil to ignore all the boring rules like eat your five-a-day and drink in moderation. *Moderation?* Don't you hate that word? To hell with *moderfuckingation*. Mum used to cook Scottie and me anything we wanted, "Eat and drink what you love" was her motto. I didn't know what a Brussels sprout was until I spent my first Christmas with Sophie's family. I spat it out across the table. Landed on Granddad's plate.'

'It didn't,' I say, laughing, beginning to realise how much Angus likes to dress up stories.

'Despite my appalling diet of pasta, pizza and beer, I was actually quite slim and fit. Believe it or not, I was the best cross-country runner at school. I could never understand why I came last in the hundred metres but first in the eight hundred. Everyone's blood sugar had run out except for mine.' He smiles. 'And I loved mountain climbing and being outdoors. I had a sense of adventure, I was up for anything, Holly. By sheer luck, after Soph and I married, I landed a job as a film locations manager, that's another story, but that was the one and only job I've ever loved. I was the man who sorted everything out. Something wrong? Go to Angus. It was non-stop-twenty-four-seven. I was on my feet or on my motorbike the whole time, checking out venues and sets. I loved it so much, no day was ever the same, but the hours were crazy. The final straw was doing a night shoot and creeping into bed at six in the morning and within half an hour Sophie's waters broke with Benjie. "Please don't have the baby now," I said, turning over and going back to sleep. Honestly, Sophie should have left me years ago, Holly.'

I'm inclined to agree.

'After Benjie was born, I quit my job. Soph, understandably, didn't want to carry on being a single mum, not with two kids. Sorry, I'm talking way too much. Are you sure I'm not boring you?'

'Go on,' I insist, helping myself to seconds of salad.

'OK. So, I went back into banking, a job with a steady salary and set hours. It was caffeine, more caffeine, carbs for lunch and zero time for exercise as I was glued to my desk. But I didn't care, Holly. Smoking and drinking were part of the territory, the culture. But Soph was right. It caught up with me. I was knackered, made a mess with figures, cost the bank a fortune, "get the fuck out" they said, escorting me off the premises.'

'And then what happened?'

'Here I am. Sitting in your kitchen.'

'She kicked you out?' I don't blame her, but why do I still feel there's something missing?

'Working in a bank is something I've always felt the need to atone for. It's kind of why I want to help Lauren,' he admits, 'but what Ian said, it hit a nerve, you know? The middle class out to save the day.'

'I know. He's right. We're all messed up.'

'I can't screw up my kids,' Angus says, to himself as much as to me. He places his head in his hands. 'I should be at home, making sure Benjie's OK.'

I imagine he mentions Benjie as he's the youngest. Perhaps he's the most vulnerable? I'm about to ask, but something stops me.

'I should be with my family.' He shakes his head. 'Sorry, I didn't mean that being here, with you…'

'Angus, I get it.'

'What you said to me the other day, at the café…'

'I didn't mean it. Well, not all of it.' I smile. 'I was having a bad day myself.'

'I needed to hear it. I've got to grow up, sort my life out. I have responsibilities. I used to be happy, Holly. I had a home, a family, an income, a modicum of pride.'

'It's not too late.'

'It is, with Soph. Things were said that can never be unsaid.'

I don't buy that. 'If this was a film, would you want to be the guy who crumples in the corner, in a heap of self-pity, or would you want to be the man who wins his family back?'

'I'd like to think I'd be in the "winning her back" camp. The knight in shining armour. The hero on the horse.'

'Good. Can you ride?'

'Nope.'

We both laugh.

Angus puts down his knife and fork, his plate clean. 'Nothing fazes you, does it?'

'Everything fazes me. I just do a good job hiding it. I should have done drama.'

'Never too late.'

'It is.'

'What do you regret?'

I decide to match his honesty. 'Not having kids. Jamie and I wanted them more than anything. We tried for years. I had one miscarriage after another.'

'I'm so sorry.'

'Eventually we reconciled it wasn't meant to be. We had each other, so…' I trail off.

'We make all these plans but life seems to love derailing them, right?'

'You're going to get your family back, Angus.'

He looks at me, affection in his eyes. 'How about you, Holly? What's in it for you? You have nothing better to do than hang out with me and Lauren?'

'Nope. Tragic isn't it?' Finally, we laugh, out of hopelessness more than anything else.

'If anyone told me I'd be forty-four, a widow, no children, and hanging out with a man called Angus…' I grab a piece of kitchen roll and wipe my eyes.

'I can't imagine how much you miss him,' Angus says, 'but you're so strong, Holly.'

It's hard to receive his compliment. If he knew how empty I feel and how I dread the long weekends, if he knew that I'd rather do anything than be at home alone, without Jamie, he wouldn't think me strong. It's like I've been trapped in a maze ever since he died, going down the same old path and never finding a way out. And I can't help thinking Angus and Lauren are going to help me find a way out.

'I miss *us*. But I don't want to throw my life away either,' I tell him, feeling it this time. 'Wanting to help Lauren, and being with you, it's not entirely selfless, you know. I need you too.'

'We're in this together,' he says, before his mobile rings. 'It's Nina.'

'Take it.'

As he talks to Nina next door, I clear the plates. When he hangs up, he returns to the kitchen. 'Nina has an idea,' he says, 'I think it's worth a go.'

13

'I don't want to,' Lauren says, veering away from me when I offer her Dolly's lead. Dolly, named after Nina's favourite singer, Dolly Parton, is Nina's pug, in need of a daily walk as much as us. Last Sunday, when Nina had called Angus to see if he could look after Dolly the following weekend, and heard about our failed attempt at swimming, she'd suggested we see if Lauren would like to walk Dolly with us. If she enjoyed it, she could offer her a regular, paid dog-walking job as Nina was becoming busier in the week running her cooking workshops for adults with complex mental health needs, in sheltered accommodation across London. Anyway, her idea made sense to Angus and me. Besides, who doesn't love dogs?

'I don't like dogs,' Lauren mumbles, 'well, not this one.'

'How can you not love Dolly, she's so pretty?' Angus says as she deposits a treat for us by the tennis courts in Ravenscourt Park. It's early August, the summer holidays, so both courts are being used, and the park is crowded.

'Seeing as you love dogs so much,' I say, handing Angus a small black bag, nudging Lauren as we watch him walk over to the scene of the crime.

As we carry on walking through the park, I tell Lauren I thought she liked dogs. 'I don't mind them. But Dolly looks like a piglet.' Lauren gestures to a Staffordshire Bull Terrier approaching us. 'He ain't too bad,' she says, before he sniffs Dolly's backside and tries to mount her.

'Men,' Angus says, shooing the dog away, 'only after one thing.'

'Always punching above their weight too,' I say. 'Dolly's far too pretty for him.'

The same dog returns and tries again.

'And they *never* get the message,' Lauren finishes.

We walk past children playing in the paddling pool area. One child is crying inconsolably because she has dropped her ice cream. I stand, transfixed, watching as her mother comforts her, stroking her back, giving her a kiss. 'One day, that will be us,' Jamie had said to me, when we'd walked around the park, newly-marrieds, watching parents with their children. Jamie had always wanted a dog too, but we didn't feel it fair when we both worked. We said the moment we retired we'd find a rescue dog. 'One day, Holly, we'll have our baby girl and boy, and a mongrel called Bruno.'

'You coming, Holly?' Angus calls. I shake the memory away, catching them up. Angus is now showing Lauren the fake crocodile, half submerged in the sand, close to the pool, a few children circling it and giggling. One pokes it in the eye before running away. It does look pretty real, lying deathly still, its stare sinister. 'I have very nearly been eaten by a crocodile four times,' claims Angus.

'Four times?' I shake my head. 'Don't believe you.'

'You can ask Sophie.'

'That's convenient, given she's not here, and I'm not about to call her.'

'It's true,' he swears.

'Nearly getting eaten once is foolish, four times is asking for it,' I reprimand, 'even if you're Bear Grylls.'

'You can't have been tasty,' Lauren says, deadpan, making us laugh again.

'Old and leathery,' Angus suggests.

We walk past a couple pulling matching suitcases on wheels behind them. 'Wonder where they're off to,' Angus says. 'Have you ever been abroad, Lauren?'

'Nope. Don't have a passport. I've only ever been on a coach and bus.'

'Where would you go, if you could go anywhere?' he continues.
She thinks. 'Bournemouth,' she ends up saying. 'I like the sea.'

'Me too. How about abroad? If you could go *anywhere*, right now?'

I sense she might feel put on the spot. It might be impossible for
her to answer this question when the likelihood of stepping on to a
plane is slim to non-existent, at least for now. Do we shut down our
hopes and dreams, when we believe them so unlikely to happen?

'Hawaii,' she says finally. 'I'd wear one of those hula skirts with a
big necklace.' She smiles at the thought. 'And I'd sip cocktails by the
sea. Maybe when I get married? I can go there on my honeymoon.'

'Sounds like a plan,' I say, noticing how good it feels to hear her
believe that maybe there is a life beyond what she has experienced
so far. That we can all have hopes and dreams, no matter how bad
our start in life.

'Want to hear my funny honeymoon story?' Angus asks.

'Go on,' I say.

'I didn't put as much planning into my honeymoon as perhaps I
should have done. It's the one and only time Soph has let me book
a surprise holiday. Anyway, we'd both dreamed of going to Jamaica
so I booked us into this incredible hotel, which Winston Churchill
and Noël Coward had apparently visited. I couldn't believe my luck,
they wanted to give us newly-weds the best double room with a sea
view, and I bagged the bargain deal of two weeks for the price of one.
Sophie is going to love me even more, I thought, buying first-class
plane tickets with the extra cash I'd saved. Anyway, it was an amazing
hotel, a lovely pool, the food was delicious, we were served martinis
by men in white gloves.'

'What went wrong?' I want us to be put out of our misery.

'I hadn't realised I'd booked us in during the hurricane season.'

I burst out laughing.

'It didn't stop raining.'

'No wonder you got such a bargain,' I say.

'Every day we were rushed into the dining room, some member
of staff saying "the wind is up" before demanding we duck under

the table because any minute now there could be flying corrugated iron which could decapitate us.'

'I should think Sophie wanted to divorce you,' I say, 'I would.'

Lauren seems quiet again, lost in her own world. Out of breath, she sits down on one of the park benches, by the pond, where Canada geese and pigeons gather in the hopes of being fed. A mother and daughter are by the padlocked gates, ready to oblige with their bags of bread. Lauren produces from her pocket her bag of tobacco, and proceeds to roll up, her gaze fixed upon a young family, with two children and a baby, eating a picnic under a tree.

'I didn't have that,' Lauren says, gazing at the family again, and in that moment, I feel even closer to her. I know the pain of wanting something or someone that was taken from you, or yearning for something that I didn't even have in the first place. When I catch Angus looking at the same family, I'm certain he's feeling a sense of loss too. He had it, he had it all, but threw it away.

Angus, Lauren and I do a few more circuits around the park, the mood subdued. Even Dolly has slowed down. 'How do you feel about what the doc said?' Angus asks Lauren, to break the silence.

'Don't know,' she murmurs.

Two teenage boys walk past. I sense, given they're not walking in a straight line, they've been drinking. One is playing music loudly from his ghetto blaster, music I'm too old to have heard of. They catch a glimpse of Lauren in her red Incredible Hulk T-shirt tucked into black trousers. I wish I had the courage to tell them to stop staring.

Angus distracts Lauren by showing her the pedometer app he downloaded on to his mobile. He suggests the three of us aim to do 5,000 steps a day. 'We've already done it this afternoon.' He shows Lauren the number. 'We could do a morning walk.'

'I have breakfast from seven to eight,' Lauren says mechanically. 'I eat a bowl of Shreddies.'

'Well, we could pick you up after breakfast. We could stop outside the night-shelter just after eight, and wait for you?' It has been agreed with the staff that Angus and I can only go inside the shelter to see Lauren if she needs us. 'And then we walk for an hour or so, before Holly has to go to work. What do you think?'

Lauren shrugs.

Angus looks at me helplessly. Perhaps there was an arrogant part of us that truly thought Lauren might be grateful for the efforts we're going to, for our persistence and company, but I'm wondering if it's making her feel increasingly anxious and uncomfortable being the centre of attention. Occasionally she joins in, as if allowing herself to enjoy our company, but most of the time, I sense she wants to push us, and our attention, away. I'm no shrink, but maybe any kind of relationship feels threatening for her since there is too much to lose? Someone will only go and hurt her again? What's familiar for Lauren is being left on her own, to fend for herself. 'Lauren,' I venture with caution, 'I don't want you to feel this is all about you. Angus and I are going to do this anyway, we need to get fit, but there's no pressure for you to join us. If you don't want to, we'd understand.'

Please join us.

'Exactly. It's your choice,' Angus echoes.

'But we'd love it if you did,' I say, fearing she will opt out if I show her the exit door, 'because I enjoy spending time with you.'

'I want to,' she says, face down.

Ahead of us, by the basketball courts, are a group of women exercising on their mats, doing some kind of yoga. 'Reach up! Inhale… and exhale,' instructs a young woman, dressed top to toe in black, also down on her hands and knees, leading the class. 'And into the spine,' she says, counting, 'Five, four, three, two, one! Now sit back into child's pose. That's right, Debbie! I want to see a nice deep stretch into the back! You know what they say about stretching? It's good for your mental health. We all need to do it, every day. Good! Five, four, three, two, one.'

In the next minute they're being told to divide into pairs and run around the park, to the tennis courts and back. 'We're doing the four-minute circuit, you know the drill! Grab a partner and go! All of you! What are you waiting for?' There's lots of laughter as they pair off and even Dolly seems to wake up from her slumber and wants to join in too. I leave Angus and Lauren walking on as I rush back to grab her, apologising profusely. 'Don't worry,' the woman says with a beaming smile. 'We get dogs joining in all the time.'

I put Dolly on the lead and am about to walk away, but something tells me to stay. I like this woman. Maybe partly because she doesn't conform to the stereotypical personal trainer. Firstly, she's no stick insect. While fit and toned, she's a generous size, which makes her far less intimidating to approach. 'Do you run classes every day?'

'Yep, most days.'

'For beginners?' I gesture towards Angus and Lauren, who are in the distance, leaning over the bridge overlooking the pond. Angus catches my eye and waves. 'For men?' I ask.

'Sure. Some of my clients have run marathons, others haven't stepped inside a gym. I get the odd guy signing up.'

'What time are your morning classes?'

'Seven o'clock is for the serious.'

'And the not-so-serious?'

She laughs. 'Nine-thirty is for the parents who've dropped their kids off at school, and mid-morning is for my slightly *older* clients, let's say.'

'About my age, you mean.'

'Retirement age.'

'Would you have time to do a class for the three of us?' I ask, imagining Lauren might be too shy to join a group.

'It's better in a group.' Her eyes follow my gaze again. 'Is she your daughter?'

'Friend. They're both friends. We volunteer together.'

'I could do an initial class with you all,' she suggests, 'find out what everyone wants, and set up individual programmes? Then maybe, when you feel ready, you can join the class later?'

I hesitate.

'Listen, think about it. I'm always here, in this spot, every morning, unless it's bucketing down. Then we go under the arch, by the railway. I'm Angel, by the way.' She shakes my hand.

'Holly. Have you got a card?'

'Google Angel's Classes, fun and friendly fitness for all.'

'Not so sure about the fun part,' says one of the women, returning from the tennis courts and now doing press-ups on her mat. 'Don't be fooled. Angel's all smiles and then she gets us to do all these terrible exercises.'

Angel grins. 'They call me "the Smiling Assassin".'

'Come on, Holly!' Angus calls.

I wonder how much it costs. Is this a good idea? 'We need a lot of help,' I say, testing her.

Angel doesn't appear put off. 'Don't we all,' she says.

As I walk away with Dolly, I glance over my shoulder and see Angel back in her position, marching up and down with her stopwatch. 'That's so good, Debbie, keep going!' she encourages. 'Well done, Mary, you've *got* this!'

'What was all that about?' Angus says, as I catch up with them, though I think he's cottoned on to my idea and by the look on his face, I can tell he's willing to give anything a go. I decide to tell them that I'd like Angel to train the three of us. Lauren remains quiet and I don't force it. Nor does Angus. There's only so much we can do. I simply tell her that the offer is there. I'm going to sign up. The rest is up to Lauren.

14

Angus and I are with Angel, by the basketball courts, as her first class are rolling up their mats and leaving, some on foot, others cycling. After bumping into Angel just over a week ago, I got in touch via email, and she agreed to slot Lauren, Angus and me in between her classes, at eight o'clock, telling me it was no problem, that she'd have her coffee and breakfast on the go. Today is a trial run, she said, no charge, and again, no problem. Angel has that kind of demeanour where nothing feels like a problem, or at least there is no problem that can't be solved. She is kitted out in black again, only this time she's wearing a black cap and lightweight jacket with an orange zip, as the sky is an ominous grey. 'Shall we wait for Lauren?' she asks, sipping her coffee from a flask.

'She should be here any minute now,' I say, scanning the park again.

Angus and I devised a new approach: not to mother her. We felt, after our dog walk on Sunday, that the last part was like dragging a teenager round the park. She's nineteen. Maybe the last thing she wants to do is hang out with us? 'She's survived living on the streets,' I said to Angus, 'so she can make her way from the shelter to the park if she wants to.'

Angus agreed. 'Also means we don't have to bump into her bodyguard.'

Angel peers at the sky. 'We could make a start?' she suggests as it begins to drizzle. 'What I want to do today is have a general chat, see what you enjoy doing, what you hate doing, how much time you can put into a programme.'

I'm still scanning the park from every angle. Maybe she forgot? I did remind her at the café on Saturday but should I send her another text?

'While we wait, have either of you got any injuries I need to be aware of?' Angel asks.

'No injuries,' Angus declares, 'just a dodgy liver, pair of knackered lungs, and a lot of excess fat to keep me warm. I've avoided the gym for years. You have no idea what you've signed up to Angel.'

'I was a late starter,' she replies.

'Can't have been as late as me,' Angus says.

'When I moved over here, my home's Ghana, I'd never felt different until people treated me like I was. I was overweight at school, got called every name under the sun. The colour of my skin didn't help either. I spent most of my time in my bedroom, hiding, and hating myself. I never did any exercise until my thirties.'

Angus looks impressed by her honesty. 'I'm trying to quit the booze and fags. I haven't smoked or had a beer for a week.'

'That's a lot to give up all at once,' Angel considers. 'How about reducing—'

'I'm an all-or-nothing man. I don't want to abuse my body anymore. Full-stop.'

'OK. Well, keep going, and think of all the money you're saving,' Angel says, as the rain steadily worsens. 'Guys, I think we should go to the café. Today is mostly talking, with a few exercises at the end.' Angel clocks me checking my mobile. 'Nothing from Lauren?'

'Can we wait a few minutes longer?' I urge, thinking perhaps we should have picked her up. I hate the idea of her being stuck in her bedroom, hiding and hating herself. Maybe she felt too anxious to meet Angel. She could have had another one of her attacks. *Please come, Lauren.*

It's so easy to slip into 'rescuing mother' mode again.

Angus nudges me. 'Holly.'

'I'm just texting her.'

'Lauren!' He swipes my phone from me. 'Over here!' He waves.

When I see a familiar figure walking towards us, in her Harry Potter T-shirt tucked into old black leggings, I want to dance with joy. We haven't even begun, yet this feels like the biggest victory.

Angel, Lauren, Angus and I are at the W6 Café, attached to the garden centre at Ravenscourt Park. Jamie and I used to love this café. It was one of our rituals to come here for breakfast, whenever we needed cheering up, or the house felt too quiet, if we'd run out of milk or needed a sugar fix. Jamie called this café his oasis of calm, which it is, nestled under the railway arch. Somehow, we found it comforting, rather than distracting, hearing the Underground trains rattling above us as we ate breakfast together. 'W6?' was all I needed to say, and he'd be grabbing his coat and keys. I see us now, sitting at this table, as if it were yesterday. He reaches for my hand, saying tentatively, 'Maybe we have to be realistic, Holly.'

I fought back the tears, knowing he was right. I couldn't experience another miscarriage, the pain, the disappointment, the hope followed by the all-consuming loss. It was exhausting. 'Maybe we should stay in London?' he suggested. 'Milla and Dave are here. We have good jobs. We have this park. This café on our doorstep that serves the best mushrooms on toast and chocolate brownies.' He was talking quickly, and when he talked quickly, I knew he was feeling anxious. 'I know we expected to move out Holly, get a house in the country, with a garden for our kids, but we can build a life here, a different one.'

'I agree,' I said, realising how much I wanted to stay in London too.

'You do?' Jamie had looked at me with surprise, as if he'd been expecting resistance. Maybe he'd expected me to say I wanted to try and get pregnant once more. But we'd been trying for seven years. I was forty-one. All our married life had been dominated by trying to have a family. We'd agonised over adoption, but in the end had decided to let fate decide. If we were meant to have children, it would happen. It was time to let go.

The idea of our future had been hanging over us for so long. I'd reached the point where I couldn't feel sad about it anymore. I was all cried out. Fed up of waiting, hoping, anticipating... and then feeling like a colossal failure, even though Jamie told me time and time again it wasn't my fault. I wanted to start living again. 'We can travel,' I suggested. 'Fall in love with London again.'

Jamie agreed.

'See some art, go to the theatre, spend our money on things that make us happy. We can be the best godparents to Emily and Kate. We don't even have to do Christmas.'

He laughed in that bittersweet way. 'Now that *is* a relief. We will never have to tell our children Father Christmas doesn't exist.'

'We can do whatever we like, Jamie.'

'Exactly. We've got each other.' Like me, he was close to tears. I knew how much he'd always tried to be strong for me, for us. His role had been to hold it together, when I couldn't.

'We've got each other,' I said, handing him my paper napkin. 'You are more than enough for me.' I leaned across the table, ran a hand through his hair, gently wiped a tear from his eye. 'It's you and me. We're in this, together.' He rested his cheek against the palm of my hand. 'It's time to start living again,' I said. 'Deal?'

'Deal.'

Jamie died less than a year later.

'Holly?' Angus touches my shoulder, bringing me back to the group. 'You were miles away.' He hands me a paper napkin. 'You're...' He gestures to my eyes.

'Sorry, sorry,' I say, disorientated, relieved attention on me is deflected when our coffees arrive, though aware Angus is watching me.

We spend the next fifteen minutes going through injuries (none yet), medication ('Anti-depressants,' confides Angus), have I hit the menopause (not yet, got that treat to look forward to), how much time do we all have ('Too much,' Angus replies) and the exercise we've done in the past ('Not a lot,' Angus and I admit, 'None ,'Lauren mumbles). Angel is clever, not singling out Lauren as the most challenged with her smoking and chronic back pain, along with her living circumstances. Nor does she make her feel the odd one out for not having done any exercise since games lessons at school, when Jamie and I used to play tennis and cycle, and Angus has climbed mountains and excelled at cross-country running. Angel is now making it clear that exercising in your late forties and fifties has a different set of challenges from Lauren's. For Angus, testosterone levels decrease from your early thirties. For me, my levels of oestrogen are falling, which impacts fat distribution, she tells me. Basically, I've become more attached to the fat around my thighs and belly. Angel also points out that some of her mid-life clients can feel more risk-adverse, thinking mid-life is a journey towards the mundane and the menopause. 'But it doesn't have to be,' Angel enthuses. 'It's never too late to start,' she says to us all. 'Leaving the house today was the biggest mental challenge. You've made a choice to be here. You've all done brilliantly.'

Lauren doesn't react; I find it hard to know how much she takes in, but I like Angel for saying it.

'Which leads me to my final question, guys,' Angel says.

Angus makes the sound of a drum roll.

'I want you to think about *why* you want to get fit,' she says.

'Isn't that obvious?' Angus says. 'I've let myself go. I want to be able to get out of a chair without an Olympian effort.'

'I don't fit into half my clothes anymore,' I say. 'I want to go back to my normal dress size.'

'Oh yeah, me too,' says Angus, making us laugh.

'I don't want to be too thin,' Lauren replies. 'I'm a size sixteen. I don't want to look as if I haven't eaten for six years.'

We smile at that.

'But I wouldn't mind not losing my breath all the time,' she points out earnestly.

'That's all good,' Angel says, yet I sense there's a 'but'. 'For me, guys, as you can probably tell, I'm not your average-sized personal trainer. I'm a size sixteen too Lauren, and proud of it, right. But never, in my wildest dreams, did I think this is what I'd end up doing. I was fresh from uni, with a sparkling degree, I landed a great job, enjoyed it for years, but then along came a colleague who destroyed my confidence. I began withdrawing, binge-eating, staying at home. There were some days when I didn't even want to get out of bed.'

Angel seems the least likely person not to want to get out of bed.

'I didn't have the confidence to resign. Carried on working there for far too long, my mental health deteriorating. In the end I quit.'

'I'm sorry,' Lauren mumbles, chewing her thumbnail.

'Don't be! It was the best decision I ever made. Should have done it a lot sooner. Anyway, the story has a happy ending, guys! So my GP gave me some meds for anxiety,' she continues, 'but she also prescribed exercise. I began running, and became hooked. When a friend suggested I do this as a job, saying how good I was at motivating her to get fit, I thought she must be joking because I was convinced I needed to look a certain way or be a certain type. In fact, all my life I've believed I need to be slimmer and brighter and stronger to do anything. I realise now, it's all a load of bollocks. I am who I am. So, this is my question to you. I exercise for my mental health. I exercise to feel *well*, not to be thinner, Holly, and not to be a certain dress size, *Angus*.'

'Wow, how do I beat that?' he reflects. 'Although I seriously wouldn't mind shedding a few stone for my physical health, to keep my heart ticking and diabetes at bay. That has to be a good enough reason.'

She nods. 'Sure, it's a great reason, and that will happen, the weight will come off in time.' She pauses, trying to work out what it is she's trying to explain. 'Put it this way, I know, from experience, all of you are going to dip at some point, you're going to want to sleep that extra half hour in bed, especially on a miserable wet day like today, so that's why I always ask my clients *why* they want to do this. Whenever you decide you want to change something in your life, you meet resistance. Subconsciously we all want to stay in that comfortable, safe, familiar place, particularly as we get older.'

I shift in my seat.

'This isn't just about losing inches around our waist. I've been lucky enough to see, with all my clients, that when they feel better their relationships and their sex lives improve.'

'A two-in-one treat,' mutters Angus, before adding, 'That would be a miracle. Mind you, my non-existent sex-life can't exactly get any worse.'

'Mine's non-existent too,' I say.

I haven't been on a single date since Jamie died. I can't remember the last time I was touched. I feel starved of human connection, skin on skin.

'Me too,' Lauren agrees. 'Ian keeps on hinting, but I'd rather knit than have sex.'

Unperturbed by the three of us, Angel continues, 'Just you wait guys. I can see, by the way a client walks into my class and places their mat at the front, instead of hiding at the back, that they feel more confident. For me, my "why" is I don't want to go back to the person I was, crippled by anxiety, who used to cry in shops for no reason, and have panic attacks at night.'

Lauren nods, as if she can relate on some level.

'I still have dips,' Angel continues, 'but remembering my reason to exercise helps me get through them.' She stops and waits for one of us to revise our reasons but instead there is a deathly silence.

Angus is the first to break it. 'I can't remember the last time I woke up and felt...' He tries to think of the right word. 'Felt good about myself,' he admits, and I catch the look of surprise on Lauren's face, as if it's hard for her to imagine someone like Angus feeling bad about himself.

'Are you saying you want to feel more like your old self maybe?' Angel asks.

'God no, I don't want to go back to an old version of me,' he says, as if that idea is abhorrent. 'I want to be a better person, a better father.' Angus explains to Angel he is separated. 'At times I was so impatient with my kids, I was knackered all the time, I wasn't nice to be around,' he reflects. 'Yeah, I want to clean up my act and be a kinder person. I want to stop hurting everyone around me.'

'You're getting it now. That's a strong why, Angus,' Angel says.

'I don't want my anxiety no more,' Lauren follows, tapping her foot up and down, up and down. 'Or my back pain. I'd like to sleep better and stop hearing voices in my head.'

'What do the voices say?' Angel asks.

'You can't do this, stay in bed, stay indoors, you're not worth anything, you don't deserve friends. That's what they said to me this morning.'

'Oh Lauren. But you did, you got up, you're here, with us, now. You've done so well already. I'm wondering, what helps you deal with these voices, what relieves your anxiety?'

'Chocolate.' She laughs. 'And fizzy drinks. Sugar makes me more hyperactive so the voices quieten down, they kind of go to the back of my head.'

'It sounds like exercise could be a good way to reduce your anxiety, as well as help your back pain, maybe even help quieten the voices too?'

Lauren nods. 'When I was homeless, I didn't walk anywhere. Didn't want to lose my spot or leave behind my blanket and tent, 'cos it would only get nicked. I sat in my spot pretty much all day long, smoking and eating to keep warm. And covering up, 'cos I didn't want attention. Didn't like myself. Still don't,' she says, avoiding eye contact with all of us.

'And it hurts, right?' says Angel, visibly moved. 'We want you to walk down the street with your head held up high, right?'

'I want to walk without having to stop so much,' Lauren states. 'Without having to catch my breath.'

'We can definitely work on that, Lauren. I want you to feel proud of who you are, and what you've been through. Anything can happen once you feel more comfortable in your own skin, take it from me.'

And the thing is, we can.

'I'm lonely,' I say, thinking it's about time I showed Angus and Lauren the part of me I've tried to hide. 'I miss Jamie so much but if I spend another weekend at home, alone, I'll go insane.' Lauren looks at me as if I've said I'm slowly dying, as if I couldn't possibly be lonely like her, but then I guess she doesn't know about Jamie, or the life I had before, or how most of my friends have moved out of London with their families, children I yearned for. She doesn't know me at all.

'I know I'm grieving. My therapist once told me it's a process, it takes time, but I can't help thinking there has to be more to life than this. Jamie wouldn't want me to live like this. We made a deal. We sat here. At this table. We made a deal to start living again. And I'm failing. If it wasn't for you two...' Angus and Lauren don't know what to say. Lauren hands me her paper napkin. 'I don't know if feeling lonely is a strong enough reason why, I mean exercise isn't going to bring Jamie back, but—'

'Exercise is a great way to fight loneliness, Holly,' Angel says with such kindness, as if she truly understands. 'The four of us get to hang out together, and being outdoors, even in the wind and the rain, being in nature combats loneliness,' she says, as if she's experienced the benefits herself. 'I can't imagine the grief, Holly, I haven't lost someone I love. But I know what loneliness feels like. I miss my parents like mad. I only get to see them once a year, if I'm lucky.' She stops, grabs one of the paper napkins and blows her nose. 'I kind of wish I'd bought some tissues this morning guys. I've got to say, I've never trained a group like you before, and I mean that in a positive way,' she hastens to add. 'Sorry, ignore me.' I hand her my clean napkin, and she wipes a few tears from her eyes. 'Right, the rain's stopped,' she says, getting up from the table. 'We've got about ten minutes left. Now we know *exactly* why we want to do this, how about—'

'I never want to put my son's life at risk again,' Angus interrupts, staying firmly seated.

Angel sits down again. Lauren and I wait for him to go on.

'I haven't been entirely honest with you,' he says, aiming it mainly in my direction. 'Benjie nearly died because of me. I nearly killed my son.'

15

'How did it go?' asks Harriet, when I arrive at the office.

How do I begin to tell her about this morning? We didn't do any exercise. After Angus's revelation, there was no time at the end, or inclination. Little did Angel know that her question would lead to a confessional. We should be paying her for therapy.

'It was interesting,' I say, taking a seat.

'Did Lauren show up?'

I can't ever hurt my children again, Angus had said to me, five minutes ago, as he walked me to my office.

'Holly?'

'Sorry?'

'Lauren?'

'Oh yes, she came.'

'So is Angel going to train the three of you?'

'Um. Yes.'

You should have seen the way Sophie looked at me.

'That's great. When are you going to start?'

The disappointment in her eyes.

I stare at my inbox, over one hundred emails unread. 'This Friday.'

'Let's do every Monday and Friday, for six weeks, eight o'clock in the park,' Angel had said, at the end of our session. 'And let's set up a WhatsApp group to motivate each other, OK?'

'Good for you. How much does she charge? Holly?'

'Sorry?'

'How much does she charge?' She waits. 'Holly?'

'Yeah. Um, she's giving us a special deal.' Angus and I had discussed fees with Angel. We didn't even have to explain Lauren's circumstances; Angel simply suggested she contribute what she can, to help her feel invested and independent.

Can we meet up tonight?

I can still see the shock on Lauren's face. Until this morning, I'm not sure she'd seen Angus and me as anything other than two people who worked at the café, the two oldies nagging her to exercise and dragging her to the doctors. What must she think of us now?

I'd like to explain.

'Holly?'

'Yes?'

'Is everything all right?'

I turn round to face Harriet in my chair, determined to put this morning out of my mind until I've spoken to Angus tonight. I don't want to tell Harriet. Not yet. I don't want to break his confidence. Besides, I don't want to think about it again, not until I know more. I need to let the shock settle.

'Sorry, Harriet, I'm knackered, but it's all good,' I say, relieved to have the distraction of work, and even more relieved when Harriet needs to take a call.

16

Angus and I meet in a pub halfway between my office and home, on the Chiswick High Road. He'd called me earlier at work, suggesting we meet somewhere neutral tonight, 'in case you decide you want nothing more to do with me, you can make a run for it,' he'd said, his laugh hollow. I sense it's become habitual for Angus to laugh; it almost sounds as if he's throwing his feelings away, yet ironically, for me anyway, his laughter often only heightens his sadness and fear.

'What a day,' he says, as a waiter brings over some water, along with our non-alcoholic beers.

I glance at the menu. I'm not hungry. I still don't know how I feel, or what to say to him. 'I'm sorry I didn't tell you before.' Angus attempts to ease the tension. He's made an effort tonight, in a clean and ironed white shirt, and he's definitely washed his hair since this morning. But his body language is as awkward as mine.

I put the menu down. 'When you had lunch with me the other week, when I asked you what happened?'

'I guess I was in denial. I felt so ashamed. I still feel ashamed,' he says, unable to meet my eye. 'I carry this guilt with me, wherever I go. It doesn't go away. If anything, it gets worse because Soph can't forgive me, and I can't forgive myself.'

The anguish in his eyes tells me how sorry he is, how tormented he is by his mistake. 'The more time I've spent with you,' he continues, 'the more I've longed to say something, but I didn't know how.' He takes a swig of beer. 'You and Lauren, you were both being so honest. I couldn't hold it in any longer. I realised in that moment my marriage is over, but I have to gain Sophie's respect again, and my children's. It's not enough saying how sorry I am all the time, or that I'm going to do something, is it? Scottie's right, you were right. My words mean nothing. I used to tell Soph all the time I was going to make changes, quit smoking, look after myself more, but that was just to shut her up. She told me my words were empty, all I ever did was make excuses. I have to show them how sorry I am for letting them down.' He exhales deeply. 'The damage is done. It's what happens now, right?' Angus longs for reassurance and support, which I want to give, but something holds me back.

'I'm glad you told me, *us*,' I say, unsure how to go on. I realise that there is a part of me that still feels angry, and that my anger has been brewing all day. He has a son with anaphylaxis, a son who is allergic to nuts, milk and eggs, and if he eats any one of those things, his life is in danger. Angus had described to Angel, Lauren and me how he'd picked Benjie up from school on a Friday afternoon, driven him and his friend, Toby, home; he'd decided to have a drink, which led to another, and another. He'd left Benjie and Toby to fix something to eat for themselves, helping himself to another beer, and ignoring Sophie's phone call at the same time. She was always checking up on him, he thought, making sure he was looking after the children. Had he done this, had he done that, nag, nag, nag. That night, Amy was having a sleepover with friends, so she was probably reminding him about that, treating him like her third child, and quite frankly, it was dull. It was no wonder they had no sex life. She didn't turn him on anymore with all her nagging. As Angus had said this to the three of us, his face had clouded over with shame once again. Ever since he'd lost his job, his mental health had declined, his depression returned with a vengeance, he was constantly tired and bored out of his senses being a house dad, but he accepted nothing could excuse his behaviour that day, that night. Sophie had written him a shopping list, explaining what to cook Toby and Benjie for dinner. He should have been to the supermarket, but he hadn't even tidied up the breakfast plates, dirty coffee mugs and old cereal bowls left accumulating by the sink. Sophie used to complain, saying the least he could do was wash up. Anyway, before he knew it, he'd crashed out on the sofa, only to be woken an hour later by Toby, screaming and shaking him by the shoulders, saying he couldn't find Benjie's EpiPen. Angus, fired up with adrenaline, rushed into the kitchen, took one look at Benjie, covered head to toe in a red rash. He could see all the familiar signs; his mouth and tongue were swollen, his chest had tightened, his throat had closed up, he was blue around the mouth, he couldn't breathe.

'We were hungry,' Toby said, shaking. 'I shared my chocolate bar with Benjie, we didn't think it had any nuts in it. We checked on the packet. He only had one bite.'

'You hate me, don't you?' Angus says, interrupting my thoughts.

'I don't hate you. I could never hate you.'

'I haven't seen Toby since. The poor kid. I blamed him. I need to tell him how sorry I am. Holly, you have every right to be angry. I should have told you sooner, and if it makes you feel any better, I hate myself too.'

'It doesn't,' I say, not wanting to judge him anymore, because he's already his own worst critic. 'I can't imagine how frightening that must have been, to see Benjie like that.'

'It's the worst thing in the world seeing someone you love not being able to breathe.'

'Are you ready to order?' asks a waiter.

'Can you give us a little longer?' Angus says, since neither of us have looked at the menu yet. 'It's happened before. He had his first anaphylactic shock at a parents' evening when he was about seven. They were handing round food and he ate something that didn't agree with him. He was rushed into hospital with Soph. After that, he had terrible separation anxiety, we all did. He slept in our bedroom. I can remember him saying, in the darkness, "I thought I was going to die, Mum," and we promised him nothing like that would *ever* happen again.' Angus is close to tears.

'What happened that night, after Toby called the ambulance?' I ask.

'Soph arrived as it pulled up outside our drive. Even if I'd been sober enough to drive, Benjie needed oxygen immediately. His hands…' Angus looks down at his own. 'They were blue. I honestly thought he was going to die.' He clears his throat, as if his words are impossible to swallow. 'I thought I'd killed him. I'd killed my son. Because it would have been my fault. Soph and I, we've always had a policy to check everything he eats at home and never to become complacent because we can't afford to be. Benjie was born with eczema and asthma too, the two often go together with allergies,' he explains. 'As if he didn't have enough.' Angus presses his face into his hands. 'All his life he's been in and out of hospital needing emergency treatment for his asthma. As a toddler he always had a cough and cold, and hay fever in the summer. Whenever we went away as a family Soph and I would have to think, "Are we in a safe place? Is there a hospital close by?" An attack could escalate so quickly. One moment he'd be fine, the next dire, and we'd have to get him to hospital asap. It was far worse for Soph. She was the one looking after him full-time, but when she called me at the office at an odd time, my heart would literally stop. Benjie has to be careful about *everything* Holly, not just what he eats, and if I could give him one gift, forget cash or a new phone, I'd give him freedom. The freedom to do what he wants, play rugby with the boys without fearing he's going to overdo it, eat a slice of fucking pizza at a kid's birthday party or enjoy a chocolate bar without ending up at A&E.'

Angus is talking quickly, hurriedly, anxiously, as if he needs to get it all out.

'But what hurts, what keeps me awake at night, is knowing the one person he should have been able to count on, let him down. He doesn't blame me. He asks me when I'm coming home. He thinks Mum and Dad's breakup is his fault. Benjie's the kind of kid who'll steal from you to buy you a present. He once nicked a fiver out of my pocket, bought his mum a bunch of flowers from the market. Basically, he's impossible to get cross with, has no mean bone in his body. He doesn't blame me or anyone. He gets frustrated, sure, he gets low and occasionally angry, who wouldn't, but he'd never blame anyone, especially me. "It's all right, Dad," he said, when I told him how sorry I was. But it's not. Home is the one place Benjie should feel safe. That night, when the ambulance parked outside our home, Soph figured out pretty quickly what had happened. She wouldn't let me go with them. "You've done enough," she said. You should have seen her face. I'm not a religious man, Holly, but when I saw the ambulance drive off, siren blasting, I made a deal with God. I begged him to take me instead. It was honestly the worst night of my life. I still have nightmares about it. It's why I hate going to bed. I hate closing my eyes.'

I reach over and he takes my hand into his, grips it tightly. 'When Sophie called me in the early hours of the morning to say Benjie was going to be OK, I was sick, so sick I had to call her back. He needed to be monitored, she said, she was going to sleep at the hospital. They came home the following day, in the afternoon. Soph couldn't look at me, wouldn't talk to me, unless asking me to do something. She told me to pick Amy up from her sleepover, and that it was my job to tell her what had happened. That night Benjie asked if he could sleep in our bedroom. "Of course you can," Soph replied. "I won't ever let anything happen to you again." That's when I knew it was over. It had always been, "We won't ever let anything happen to you." We were a team. At restaurants I'd be the one grabbing the waiter's attention, demanding more information about the menu, saying it wasn't enough to say that there might be traces of peanut, that the chef clearly didn't quite understand that this was about life and death, not about fussy middle-class parents. In so many ways, Benjie's troubles had brought us closer together. Later that night, when Benjie and Amy were both in bed, I told her I'd move into the spare room. She still wouldn't look at me. All she said was "I want you to leave. Pack your bags and go." I begged her for another chance. I cried. She cried. I remember feeling a tiny glimmer of hope when she let me hold her. I promised I'd change, that I meant it this time, that I'd go to the doctors, that I'd do *anything* to earn her trust again.' Tears now stream down Angus's cheeks, his body is shaking, as if reliving the trauma.

'Are you ready to order?' the waiter asks.

'Can you give us another five minutes?' I say to an increasingly disgruntled waiter. 'Do you want to get out of here, Angus?'

Angus and I end up walking down Chiswick Mall, a street on the north bank of the River Thames. 'Jamie and I always used to say that if we won the lottery, not that we played it, we'd move here,' I say. 'We'd rattle around in one of these grand houses.' I gesture to the Georgian house on my left, the front door flanked by a statue of a lion. 'We always dreamed of waking up by the sea or being close to water. But when it became clear we couldn't have children, we decided to stay in London.'

'Tell me more about him,' Angus says.

'He was the opposite of me.'

'In what way?'

'I remember us packing for a holiday. He'd chuck in a pair of boxers, some swimming trunks and a toothbrush, and that's about it.'

Angus laughs. 'Sounds suspiciously like me.'

'I'd pack for every single kind of eventuality, leaving nothing to chance. I remember Jamie and I going off on our first mini break together, to Cardiff. He couldn't believe how much I'd packed. "Anyone would think you were going for a year, not a weekend," he said, heaving the suitcase into the boot of his car. He drove us in his old battered Golf, car roof down, me belting out Belinda Carlisle's "Live Your Life Be Free". He thought I was so funny, until he realised I was tone deaf.'

It feels good to laugh with Angus after the intense evening we've had.

'I used to love dancing and karaoke,' I say, unable to remember the last time I did either. 'Jamie had two left feet, but he didn't mind getting on the dance floor. He didn't care what others thought of him, actually. I think that's what I loved most about him. He wasn't an extrovert, was equally as happy staying in as going out. If we were going out, I usually had to make him put on a clean shirt. Jamie would have happily turned up at a party in one of his old jumpers that he'd been working in that day.' I smile. 'But once he was there, he enjoyed seeing people. He was tall like you, and had this laugh.' In so many ways, Angus's laugh reminds me of Jamie's. 'It was contagious. He managed to put everyone at ease without trying... I don't know, this probably sounds clichéd, but he lit up a room.'

'He sounds—'

'Jamie wasn't a fan of routine,' I continue, realising how much I'm enjoying talking about him now. He used to say, "As soon as you have a routine, Holly, things don't happen by chance." I liked to make plans for the weekend or for the following summer. "Who knows what will happen tomorrow, let alone next month or year?" he'd say. I guess he was right but my attitude was if you make no plans, you don't have anything to look forward to. If it was his birthday, I would be dying to plan a party for him, any excuse, whereas Jamie would knock on a friend's door to see if they were around.'

'How did you two meet?'

I tell Angus I was thirty-one and beginning to doubt ever meeting anyone or falling in love, until I met Jamie at Milla's house. I recall how his smile instantly cured my hangover. 'Gather you had a late night,' Jamie had said, humour laced in his voice, a dimple appearing in one cheek. I had to force myself to stop gazing at him.

'We should know better, right?' I said, pouring myself a cup of coffee.

'No, never grow up,' he replied. 'What's that phrase by Oscar Wilde?'

'*Only dull people are brilliant at breakfast*,' we both said at the same time, before laughing self-consciously. Milla caught my eye, instantly catching the mood in the air. I loved how she could read me so easily, because in the next moment she was suggesting Jamie stay for breakfast. He looked from me to Milla. 'I don't want to intrude. I can quickly show you the plans I drew up or leave them here.'

'No!' I insisted, a little too strongly. 'I mean stay, if you're not in a hurry?'

'Holly is the best cook,' Milla enthused. 'You don't want to miss out on her fry-ups.'

I tell Angus that over breakfast Milla and I discovered Jamie had moved back to London six months ago, after splitting up from his wife. He was in the process of a divorce. 'Oh, I'm sorry,' I'd said, trying my best to sound it.

'When in fact you wanted to dance around the kitchen table?' Angus suggests. 'And sing hallelujah.'

'Exactly,' I say, realising Angus is getting to know me well. 'I was so relieved Milla was there because she could ask all the questions I wanted to, like did he have any children, and was he single?'

I go on to describe how Jamie had told us he and his ex-wife, Fran, short for Francesca, had met at school, and went to college together – he was doing a furniture design diploma, he'd always loved woodwork and carpentry. Fran was studying art. They'd married in their early twenties before moving to a remote part of Ireland, where his wife's family lived. He told us they were like Barbara and Tom from *The Good Life* – they grew their own vegetables, he designed and made all their furniture, they lived life as simply as possible. 'What happened?' I'd asked him.

'My hair,' he replied with a hint of a smile.

'Your hair?' I repeated. His hair was short, in fact exceedingly short, accentuating his bone structure and dark eyes.

'It used to be down to my waist. I was a right old hippy. Still am, inside.'

I'd laughed at that.

'Anyway, one night I felt in need of a change so I shaved the whole lot off. The following morning, she took one look at my bald head and said, "I'm leaving you."'

'She didn't,' Milla said.

He put his knife and fork down. 'No, she didn't.' He'd smiled, but I could see the hurt in his eyes. 'She left me, out of the blue, for another man.'

'I'm so sorry,' Milla said.

'What a fool,' I added.

For the rest of the morning, we looked at his plans to redesign Milla and Dave's kitchen. They had recently moved into a five-bedroom house in Shepherd's Bush. It seemed so grown-up, a house on three floors, with a kitchen as large as my entire ground floor combined, but it was a kitchen that needed a lot of work. It was painted in a vile mustard yellow and the cupboards were a sludgy manure brown. Jamie talked passionately about his ideas to knock everything down, 'That's the fun part,' he'd said, 'demolition. Therapeutic. Much cheaper than going to counselling.' I attempted to be interested in wood samples and paint finishes, and the best place for Milla to put her washing machine and tumble dryer, but instead was hopelessly distracted by the rapid beating of my heart, especially when Jamie leant across me to reach for his paperwork, our hands touching.

I tell Angus how over the next few weeks, I found myself rushing over to Milla and Dave's after work, on the pretext that I wanted to see how 'the kitchen' was coming on. It was during the summer, so Jamie often worked late, giving us at least half an hour to chat, Milla discreetly saying she needed to make a phone call or have a shower after work. Left alone, we talked about everything, from his school days to his dream job: making props for film. As a boy he'd loved film and television. 'That's why I chose to come back to London. Not many opportunities in the middle of nowhere. But it's been harder than I thought,' he said. 'I've got no idea how to open that door.'

'Did he ever work in film?' Angus asks.

'In the end, no. His business expanded and became so successful, and besides, he loved his job.'

'Carry on,' Angus encourages me. 'I want to know how you got together.'

I tell Angus about my boss, Clarissa, and how I'd confided to Jamie, one night, how she reduced me to a nervous wreck. 'I recall him vividly stopping what he was doing, saying, "Quit, Holly, no job is worth it."'

'That's what Soph used to say to me,' Angus says. 'So come on, what happened next? I want to get to the juicy part.'

'"Ask him out," Milla said to me one evening, after Jamie had left. But I couldn't. I had to hope that my visits and gifts of chocolate were enough to get the message through. "Boys don't get the message," Milla insisted. "I had to practically throw myself on Dave."'

Angus nods. 'We can be slow on the uptake.'

'Milla was desperate,' I admit. '"Ask him out and then the two of you can hang out at *your* place, and I'll finally have a kettle where it should be,"' she'd said, gesturing to hers, perched on top of the television, surrounded by mess.

'In the end I took both their advice. "I quit!" I told Jamie with pride, when the kitchen was almost completed, some three weeks later. He seemed particularly impressed when I told him I'd thrown coffee down my boss's silk shirt. "Crikey, remind me never to get on the wrong side of you," he'd said, as I watched him pack up his tools for the night, telling me he'd almost finished the job.

'I wanted to celebrate the end of Clarissa, and the beginning of me. A new me who had already called Harriet and had an interview the following day. "Will you come out with me tonight and get drunk?" I asked.

"'How drunk?'"

'I recalled Milla's warning that boys don't get the message unless you spell it out. "So drunk you can take advantage of me?"'

'You go girl,' Angus says, as we approach a bench overlooking the river and decide to sit down. 'That took guts.'

'We got blindingly drunk on tequilas. I have never laughed so much as that night. I can remember him walking me home, it was miles across London. Probably the most exercise I've ever done in my life. But I don't think either of us wanted the evening to end. We reached my front door at about three in the morning. I didn't even ask if he wanted to come inside. We slept together that night. I know I should have been more...' I shrug. 'I know men love the chase,' I say, reminded of what Angus said to me when we first met.

'Chasing is overrated.'

'The following morning, he made me a hot chocolate.' I see him now, in our kitchen. 'The secret is vanilla extract,' Jamie had said, my arms draped around his waist. 'We spent the whole day in bed, drinking hot chocolate, and, you know.'

'Doing the crossword.'

I smile. 'Exactly.'

'It feels good, doesn't it? Falling in love is like a drug.'

'He wasn't perfect, Angus,' I go on. 'I'm probably making out that he was, but he rarely tidied up after himself, socks had a habit of being left on the landing, and he was good at fixing and designing everything for other people, but he never made us our own wardrobe, which he'd promised me for years. He didn't buy into the commercialism of Valentine's Day so never apologised for the absence of flowers and chocolates.'

But who am I fooling? He was perfectly imperfect. He bought me flowers on days when I wasn't expecting flowers.

'He brought out a certain strength in me. He made me believe in myself,' I confide.

'I believe in you,' Angus says quietly. 'I don't know if that means anything, coming from someone like me.'

I turn to him. 'It means a lot.'

'Holly, you're the reason Lauren showed up this morning. You're the reason I'm not drowning my sorrows in the pub right now. You've made me see how much I want and need to change. You are one of the best people I know. I can't imagine what you've been through, it's not fucking fair. Life is not fair.'

Relief overwhelms me. It feels so good when people don't trot out those tired old clichés like 'time heals'. 'I don't want to get over him,' I reflect. 'Why would anyone want to get over someone they loved? But I want to feel my heart skip a few beats again. I want to feel passionate about something, or someone. I want to feel the way I did when Jamie and I set off to Bristol in his car. I was so excited. I want to feel life has some kind of meaning again. Does that make sense?'

'Perfect sense.'

'I still haven't scattered Jamie's ashes. They're in a box, at the back of our wardrobe. It feels odd. He's there, but he's not.' I rest my head on Angus's shoulders. 'I always believed we'd grow old together.'

He draws me close, wrapping his arms around me. 'When the time feels right you will. You're stronger than you realise, Holly.'

Minutes go by, the two of us comfortable in the silence, and I notice I'm liking his touch probably more than I should be. I'm forced to move when Angus reaches into his pocket for his mobile and headphones.

I sit up. 'What are you doing?'

'Trust me.' He hands me one earplug, puts the other one in his left ear.

'Live Your Life Be Free' blasts into my ear. Angus stands up, gives me his hand, and we dance by the river, with the night lights of Hammersmith Bridge twinkling in the distance, not caring who walks by and sees us, or what anyone thinks when I laugh and cry, and soon I'm thirty-one, sitting in the passenger seat, alongside Jamie, the car roof down, the sunshine warm against my face, my hair blowing in the breeze, and I'm singing my heart out, feeling young and full of hope for my future, once again.

17

As I'm walking through Ravenscourt Park, towards the basketball courts, my phone pings. Thank God it's Friday, Angus texts our *Fitness Buddies* WhatsApp group. But I've made it through another whole week without smoking and drinking ☺ Sorry if I sound smug. Everyone ready for our first session?

'Yes,' I text back, before seeing him in the distance, jogging up and down on the spot, sporting an old blue tracksuit and Nike T-shirt. Thankfully the sun has decided to join us this morning too.

'You're keen,' I call out, approaching him, putting my mobile back in my bag.

He places a sweaty hand on my shoulder to steady himself, his breathing that of a heavy, unfit smoker. 'Feel like I've already done my workout getting here on time.'

Our phones ping again. 'I'm five minutes late,' says Lauren. Never mind she's late, it's enough to know she's coming. Yet weirdly I didn't doubt it this morning. Angus, Lauren and I have been in touch all week on WhatsApp and nothing suggested to me that Lauren wasn't going to turn up. While she hasn't mentioned the morning when we confided our problems it does feel as if something has changed. It's as if we're all in this together now.

'You look sporty,' Angus says, gesturing to my long hair tied up in a ponytail, and I'm wearing a brand-new turquoise T-shirt with a pair of equally new leggings that I bought at least a year ago, with good intentions to join a Pilates class.

'I went once,' I confess.

Why is Angus staring at me?

'What's wrong?' I check my hair, my face.

He comes over, tucks the price tag back inside my top.

'Pull it out!' I urge, laughing as Angel approaches us, carrying a bulky gym bag over her shoulders. He gives the price tag a yank.

'Wow, you're a bargain,' he says.

Angus, Lauren and I are working out in our own space, Angel giving us different exercises to do so we're not comparing ourselves with one another. I can't remember the last time I did a press-up. It feels harder than Angel made it look. 'That's so good, Holly,' she says, 'fifteen seconds left!' I swear time goes slower when you're doing press-ups.

'This might not look much, but it's hard work,' I overhear Angel say to Lauren. She's wearing what looks like one of Ian's shirts tucked into a pair of old grey leggings which contrast strongly with her new white trainers, which we found at the shelter, in the room filled with donated clothes and shoes. 'Right, I want you to do some squats, but we're going to do it with the support of the chair first, to put less pressure on your back and to get you used to pushing through your legs. It works your thighs and core. Yes Lauren! That's it, and another, that's awesome, try and do ten if you can in forty-five seconds. Go! Holly, sit-ups. Angus, why have you stopped? Lauren, you've *got* this, well done.'

'Teacher's pet,' calls out Angus, making us laugh.

Soon we're all engrossed in our different exercises but Angel gives us plenty of mini-breaks, impressing upon us the need to drink plenty of water. I try not to stare when I see Lauren lying on the grass, wheezing, unable to sit up. 'Don't worry,' Angel says, kneeling beside her. 'It's hard, take a deep breath. There's no hurry, we can have as many breaks as you need. You haven't done this before, but believe me, one day you'll be able to, I promise. We can do this.' When I watch them high-five, I feel someone, up there, in the sky, was looking out for us on the day I met Angel. She truly was sent to our funny little trio.

'Keep going everyone!' Angel calls out towards the end of our sixth session, on Monday. After our initial taster on Friday, two and a half weeks ago, Angel created individual training circuits for us which include sit-ups, press-ups, squats, star jumps, step-ups, planks, lunges and running, although Angel told Lauren she didn't want her to run immediately. She wanted to spend more time with her doing gentle stretching exercises for her back, that felt like more of a priority. 'I don't want to rush you,' she'd confided. 'It's important we take this slow and safely, OK?' Lauren didn't seem to mind or appear to feel left out. Angel has a magic way with words, a gift of making her feel special rather than the most vulnerable. Angel had said quietly to Angus and me, after our second session, that physically Lauren would be able to run, but emotionally she might struggle with doing too much too quickly. She'd seen this happen before. 'You know best,' Angus had said, both of us thankful for her guidance. As Angus and I are returning from our second lap to the tennis courts and back, he calls out, 'Why isn't running as much fun as coffee and a fag?'

'Or a glass of rosé,' I say.

'Or one of Sander's buns,' Lauren suggests.

'What are we all running towards, guys? Visualise something or someone amazing, makes you go faster!'

'Chris Hemsworth,' I say, my pace picking up.

Angel agrees. 'Why aren't you sprinting?'

'Debbie Harry,' Angus says breathlessly, adding, 'My feet hurt.'

'Oh, you poor little boy,' I say.

'It's the trainers. Scott's feet are smaller than mine.'

Angel isn't impressed. 'Come on big feet, don't whinge, or get your own shoes.' Angel turns to Lauren, who is jogging up and down on the spot.

'Who's Debbie Harry?' Lauren asks, making Angus and me feel even more our age.

'She's Blondie, a famous singer. How about you, Lauren? What or who are you running towards?'

'Food.'

'If you could have one last meal, what would it be? Keep going everyone!'

'Cheeseburger,' Angus says, now doing press-ups for a minute. I'm doing star jumps, though my legs feel like jelly. I don't know if I can keep going. My heart is pounding in my chest and my body wants to go on strike.

'Keep going,' Angel instructs, 'only three minutes to go. I'd have a buffet, French cheeses, good-quality butter and a fresh crusty baguette. Delicious!' Lauren is now going up and down on her folding step stool. 'One, two, that's it, keep marching, up, down, but if you need a break Lauren, stop.'

'Teacher's pet,' Angus says again.

'Thirty seconds left! You've *got* this, everyone.'

As we're nearing the end of our session, Angus is doing sit-ups and making a lot of noise about it, I'm skipping and Lauren is doing star jumps. 'If you get tired, Lauren, do regressive ones, remember?' Angel waves her arms above her head. 'One leg at a time. Great, Angus, you're doing *so* well.'

Angus doesn't have the energy to answer back.

My legs want to die now, but watching Lauren keeps me going. 'Reach for the stars, Lauren,' Angel says as they complete a third, and a fourth. In session one she could only do regressive ones because she lost her breath so quickly. 'Amazing improvement already, Lauren,' Angel says. 'All of you. Good job.'

'It'll be the Olympics next?' suggests Angus.

'I'm good, but not that good,' Angel says, making us laugh.

'OK guys,' Angel says, as we roll up our mats and have another drink of water. 'You're doing brilliantly, but what I want you to think about are the days in-between our sessions now. You don't need to keep fit in a gym or park. You don't need the Smiling Assassin standing over you, barking orders.'

'But you have such a lovely bark,' says Angus.

She tuts at him. 'You can keep moving *everywhere*. Take a day off and get out of London. Go to the beach and run across the sand, play music, dance in your kitchen, or in your bedroom,' she says. 'Dance while you're peeling spuds at the café, dance when you brush your teeth. Stretch before you go to bed. Walk home when you might have taken the bus, take the stairs instead of the lift. Be creative. Every time you hear the word "run" in a song, get up, move your feet, get those steps up every day. You don't have to run or jog, walking is just as good, so long as we do it regularly. And finally, I'm giving you all presents. You can take these home and practise, but I want you to bring them back each time, to show me how much you're improving.' She hands us each a bright pink fitness hoop. 'Remember these in the school yard? Who could keep their hoop going the longest?' Angel puts one around her waist, and we all copy. In that moment I feel such affection for Angus. He doesn't care about his street cred, his image. In so many ways he reminds me of Jamie. 'They're weighted,' Angel tells us. 'To make it harder for you.'

'You're so kind,' Angus says. 'You think of everything.'

'You're welcome. Works the hips, waist and your balance.' Angel shows us in style.

'Lauren, imagine you're in Hawaii,' I say, before my hoop falls on to the ground.

'On the beach, hula hula,' she says, laughing, much to the amusement of a few dog walkers, who clap and cheer as they walk on by.

As we all imagine we're in Hawaii, I realise, for the first time in months, I feel happy. Angel was right. Being here and working out with my friends does help the loneliness. We are in this together. We have goals. A sense of purpose. Everyone needs somebody. I have Angus and Lauren, reminding me I'm not alone. I'm part of a team.

18

'I need someone to print out the menus, quick,' Nina says, rushing into the kitchen, her hair tied back, strands falling loose, a pen tucked behind one ear to complete her trademark look.

'I'll do it,' Lauren says, putting her hand up.

Surprise flashes across Nina's face, before she says, 'Great, thanks.'

Lauren leaves the kitchen almost as speedily as Nina entered it, practically knocking her over in the process. 'Craig wanted to start a fight today, have you seen him?' Nina asks Scottie, before adding, 'Something smells good.'

Scottie and Monika are cooking aubergine parmigiana, wafts of basil, mozzarella, toasted pine nuts and tomatoes making my mouth water. He's also doing a ratatouille, and a veggie lemon courgette pasta, as there were so many aubergines and courgettes delivered this morning.

'Saw him on my fag break,' Scottie replies. 'Think he'd had a beer or two. I told him to go.'

Nina doesn't allow anyone to volunteer if they've been drinking. 'If he comes back, talk to him, see what's going on, but then send him packing.'

'Will do, don't worry.'

'Courgette and lime cake?' Nina says, approaching me.

'You should have seen Tom's face when I told him.' Tom had looked so crestfallen at the idea of a vegetable in his pudding.

'Try it, you'll love it. You can't really taste the courgette,' I'd promised him, but I might as well have been speaking another language. He moved off in a huff, pulling up the straps of his braces.

'Clever way to get rid of it,' Nina says. 'What's Angus doing now?'

We both look through the hatch to see him dancing as he lays the tables, singing along to Frank Sinatra's 'Come Fly with Me'. I smile, knowing *exactly* what he's doing. Lauren, Angus and I are having a step count competition. Tom is now on his feet, joining in.

Nina touches my shoulder. 'You're doing a good job, Holly, and not just here.' She knows about Angel, and I have to admit, even though we've only had six sessions so far, it's going far better than I expected, so much so that we've signed up to train with her for another four months, until Christmas. Angus and I also run together every Tuesday, Thursday and Sunday, but I know he's working out every day, on top of Angel's sessions. He's so determined. Once he sets his mind on something, he's like a terrier.

'Isn't she?' Scottie calls across the kitchen. 'Angus is applying for jobs. He's not going to the pub anymore, he's even out the door first thing to go for a run.' He turns to me, gratitude in his eyes. 'Whatever you've said, Holly, it's worked, and I can't thank you enough.'

My heart softens towards Scottie, who clearly cares deeply about his brother.

Lauren returns with the menus. 'Can you put them on each table?' I tell her.

'Yes, Holly,' she says, before checking herself. 'I mean yes, Chef!'

'I prefer Holly!' I call after her, watching as she leaves the room with an actual spring in her step. I watch her moving from one table to another with a speed I didn't know she possessed. I'm not sure she knew she had it in her either. If I have any chance of winning this competition, I need to step it up a gear, I think, pouring the sponge mixture into my loaf tins, before placing it in the oven, and deciding to do a quick run to the loo, not that I need to go, and then a quick run upstairs to the office, and a few star jumps by the printer, for good measure.

Finally, it's time to sit down and enjoy what's left over from lunch. The café was packed, about eighty people turned up today. Lauren and Angus were taking the step count competition to the extreme, serving up at any opportunity, encouraging visitors to have seconds, refilling water jugs constantly, and racing round tables, placing small silver jugs of cream on each. I, on the other hand, stayed in the kitchen and helped stack plates into the dishwasher. I also discovered that a four-pint bottle of semi-skimmed milk is an excellent substitute for a weight. Who knew serving up tea and coffee could be such a good way to tone my arms? I catch Angus's eye as Lauren tucks into a whole bowl of fresh fruit salad, refusing cream. She also tried some of Scottie's lemon courgette pasta, saying it wasn't as gross as she thought it might be.

'Thanks, I think,' Scottie had replied, enjoying the change in Lauren's healthy appetite.

'But I'm not trying your cake, Holly,' she says earnestly. 'Courgette and cake, they ain't friends, they're like cats and dogs.'

Everyone laughs.

'You should always try something once, Lauren,' Angus suggests, 'otherwise you never know.'

'Would you lie in a coffin full of snakes?' Lauren challenges him, before confiding that *I'm a Celebrity... Get Me Out of Here!* is one of her favourite programmes. I notice, as she speaks, she isn't tapping her leg up and down. Nor is she staring at the floor. She's looking at us.

'I'd probably only do that if I was paid *a lot* of money.'

'Hang on, didn't you say you should always try something once, Angus?' Lauren rebukes him.

I'm not the only person to notice she's a different person today. She's not only sitting round the table, she's found her own voice, and her place, with us.

Nina tells us we have a new volunteer coming today, Max. He's here to help us clear the tables and clean the floors. Soul Food has teamed up with a private school in west London; they've agreed to lend out some of their boys during the summer holidays. As their school is a charity, they have to do voluntary work for their status. 'Uh-oh, he's back.' Nina gestures to Craig, approaching the front door.

'I'm not drunk,' he says, holding up his hands as if he comes in peace. 'I went for a walk, blew away the cobwebs. But I'm still fucking angry.'

Nina grabs Craig by the arm and forces him to sit down and explain.

Craig is angry because a copper, someone new to the area, gave him a lecture about getting off the streets yesterday, thinking he was doing him a favour, but it came across as patronising. 'I like my life. I'm not doing anyone *any* harm,' he claims, and I can see his point, especially when he adds, 'Go and arrest the real criminals, the murderers and rapists. Who's this?'

Max walks in tentatively, tall and lanky, wearing jeans and a white crew neck T-shirt with the Ralph Lauren logo, fine blond hair and an angelic face.

'He's helping out,' Nina says, waving him over. 'Hi Max, come and meet everyone!'

'Max?'

'Don't make a scene, Craig,' Nina insists.

'You replacing me with *Max*?' Craig stands up and faces the teenager square on.

'No one's replacing you,' Angus calls through the hatch. Lauren stands close by his side.

The colour drains from Max's cheeks as he backs away from Craig, no doubt wondering what the hell his school have signed him up for.

'You're here to help, are you?' Craig says, his bad mood continuing to project on to this poor innocent kid.

'Max, ignore him, Craig, stop it,' Nina orders.

But Craig has no intention of stopping it. 'Well, go on then, make us a coffee, Max.'

Max stares at him blankly.

'Black, one sugar. There's a good boy.'

I turn to Nina. 'Max, I tell you what, while you are here,' she says, 'if you could make Craig a strong black coffee that would be great.

The kitchen's there,' she adds, gesturing to Angus and Lauren through the hatch. 'They'll show you where everything is.' He stands, limply, clearly unsure how to place one foot in front of the other, let alone make a cup of coffee.

'Too posh to make a cup of coffee, are you?' Craig says.

'I don't know how,' he murmurs, head down.

'You don't know how?' Craig repeats. 'Blimey. You've never made coffee before?'

Max shakes his head.

And then something extraordinary happens. Craig places an arm around Max's shoulder and leads him into the kitchen, saying he's going to teach him how to make the best cup of coffee in the world. 'The trick is not to pour boiling water into the mug, 'cos it scalds the coffee. You know how to boil a kettle don't you, or don't they teach you that at school either?'

As Nina and I clear the kitchen and sort the flowers, we watch, through the hatch, Angus, Lauren, Craig and Max folding up the tables and mopping the floor.

'Look at them,' Nina says, watching her volunteers as if they're her children, her family. In many ways they are. Lauren has seemingly taken Max under her wing. We overhear her telling him, with pride, that she's been at Soul Food for a few months now, she helps make the puddings.

'When Lauren first came here…' Nina doesn't have to go on.

I glance her way. There's no doubt Lauren's skin looks clearer, she's bothering to wash her hair, and when she talks, we're all getting to see her blue eyes. She even agreed, with Angel, to work on a food diary, to help her cut down on her sneak-eating, and to think about reducing the amount she smokes. 'Angus looks good too,' Nina adds. 'Mind you he's so handsome he can get away with a few extra stone, but he seems different, happier.'

I nod, resting my eyes on Angus. No hint of stubble, he's wearing a white shirt that shows off his tan, and his recent haircut, plus losing weight, have made the years fall away. I can't believe I haven't noticed how handsome he is. Until now. Perhaps I wasn't looking.

'His life was a car crash waiting to happen,' Nina confesses. 'I could see it. We all could. But I think he's turned a corner. Did he tell you we lived together at college? He was one of the most popular guys.'

'That doesn't surprise me.'

Suddenly we hear raucous laughter coming from Craig and Max, followed by Lauren and Angus. Nina turns to me. '*This* is why I do it,' she says. 'This work is like throwing things into a pan, hoping it won't overheat or burn. Sometimes it's delicious, other times it's a disaster. You've got to have the ingredients, but you've got to have the faith too.'

I agree, unable to take my eyes off them. Off him.

'He has no idea of the impact he has on others, does he?' Nina says, turning to me. 'I guess that's half his charm. He's broken many hearts.'

As I watch Angus, I realise how empty my life would be without him.

'Don't let him break yours,' Nina says quietly, following my gaze.

19

'Lauren?' I knock tentatively on her bedroom door. The manager let Angus and me into the building, after we'd explained how concerned we were. She told us Lauren hadn't eaten any breakfast or dinner last night, had missed her art therapy and had been feeling low for the past few days. Normally residents have to be out of the night-shelter from 8.30 in the morning, to 6.00 at night, except on a Sunday. But given how unwell Lauren seemed to be, she'd made an exception. I open the door. 'Lauren, are you asleep?'

'Yes. Go away.'

She's lying under the covers, clutching Ted. 'We're worried about you.'

'I'm asleep.'

'You don't sound asleep,' Angus says.

'Well, I am. Go away.'

'OK, well when you wake up give us a call. We're worried about you.' We wait. Silence.

As we admit defeat and leave, I can't help thinking it was too good to be true.

Angus and I have had our eighth session with Angel, and Lauren didn't show up.

It felt odd without our partner in crime. It was as if we were missing an arm or a leg; our group didn't feel complete. I sensed Angel felt it too, despite reassuring us that this happened all the time. Depression and anxiety don't give up easily, she said, especially when its victim is trying to make changes. They love to get their claws in deeper. 'But don't worry, she'll come back when she's ready.'

Yet that didn't reassure us. Lauren hasn't responded to any of our recent text messages, and she was withdrawn at the café last weekend, heavy on her feet, her back playing up again, and painfully shy in front of a different chef, as Scottie was away. It felt as if we were back to square one.

Angel promised she'd text Lauren later and suggest taking her out for a coffee and chat. But after we left the park, Angus and I decided to head straight to the night-shelter, in case there was something seriously wrong.

As Angus and I are about to part ways – I need to get to work and Angus has to prepare for a job interview this afternoon – we encounter Ian outside, leaning against the wall, smoking. He stubs out his cigarette and heads towards us. 'We don't want a fight,' Angus says, weary, walking straight past him.

'Nor do I. We're on the same side mate, Lauren's side.' He offers Angus a cigarette. For a moment Angus looks tempted before turning it down.

'I've got to go,' I say, glancing at my watch. It's 9.30. One perk of working with Harriet is our day begins at 10.00, though we're often still in the office late into the evening.

'Me too.' Angus follows. 'Send Lauren our love? We'll stop by later.'

'Wait!' Ian calls.

We turn round.

He approaches us. 'You guys aren't too bad.'

'Thanks,' Angus says.

'She likes you,' he concedes with a shrug, as if he can't understand why. 'Laurie's been better, and not 'cos of me,' he admits though I sense he wishes it was. 'She stayed in bed all day Sunday, eating crap, wouldn't come out of her room, and that's not like Laurie. She likes her routine, you know, she gets up, does a strip wash, makes her bed before breakfast, and knocks on my door. Lozza's the one usually getting *me* up. What are we going to do?'

'I don't think there's anything we can do,' I say, noticing how he calls Lauren *Laurie* and *Lozza*. They're even closer than I thought, so if anyone can get Laurie up, it's Ian. 'She knows we're here,' I tell him.

'But I'm worried about her,' Ian protests, 'there's got to be something you can think of.'

'You probably know better than us,' I assure him. 'What cheers her up?'

He scratches his head. 'She loves colouring-in, we do it together.' There is something incongruous, yet endearing about hearing an ex-prisoner with a six-pack confess to colouring-in. 'You got a phone?' Ian looks as if an idea is brewing.

Angus hands him his.

'She loves these.' He shows us a YouTube video clip.

'Really?' Angus watches a kitten fall off a bed, followed by a dog flying out of a window.

'Trust me. And she loves watching people unblock drains. Come on, I've got an idea.'

'It's so weird it must be true,' Angus mutters, as we follow Ian back inside, and down the corridor, towards Lauren's bedroom.

'You go in,' Angus suggests to Ian. 'We'll wait here.'

Gently Ian opens the door. Lauren is still under the covers. 'Not you again,' she moans. 'I'm asleep.'

He kneels by her side. 'Look at the little kitten licking ice cream.' She doesn't stir.

'I've got to say, that's not going to get me up anytime soon,' Angus whispers, his face close to mine as we peep through the door.

'Nor me.'

'Want to watch your favourite man unblock some drains?'

I turn to Angus, even more perplexed.

'Good to see your face, my friend,' Ian says.

'If I didn't know better, I'd say Ian's madly in love with Lauren, wouldn't you?' I whisper to Angus.

'He's definitely in love,' Angus agrees, catching my eye.

'I should go,' I say, certain I'm blushing. I move away from Angus. 'Need to, er, get to work.'

'Don't,' he whispers back, pressing a hand against my arm. 'Stay. Let's see if she wants to talk.'

Angus must pick up on the hesitation in my eyes.

'I can't do this without you, Holly,' he says, 'we're a team.'

Ian, Angus and I manage to encourage Lauren to get up and have a shower, before giving her breakfast, waffles and maple syrup, at the nearest café on the Chiswick High Road. She tells us her anxiety kicked in last week, and the voices inside her head got too loud, voices screaming at her that she's worth nothing.

'Lauren, why didn't you tell us?' Angus asks.

'I was worried for your safety,' she says.

'My safety?' he repeats, confused.

'Yes, with all your problems. He has loads of problems,' Lauren alerts Ian. 'So does Holly.'

'Yes, but—' I object.

'Her husband's dead,' she interrupts me. 'And Angus nearly killed his son.' Lauren makes us sound like murderers. Ian assesses us with new eyes. I think he's almost impressed. 'I didn't want to worry you,' Lauren continues. 'I thought it might upset you, with everything you're going through.'

Lauren hadn't said a word to us that day in the café, after I'd confessed how lonely I was, and Angus had told us about Benjie's near-death experience. She'd sat so quietly, listening, but it hadn't occurred to me that she might feel anxious for us.

'If you're ever worried about Angus and me—'

'Or the black cloud gets in your way,' Angus cuts in.

'You tell us,' Angus and I finish off at the same time.

She nods, tapping her foot up and down, up and down. 'I wanted to help but I didn't know how. Then I worried that if I spoke to you, you might want to talk to me about my stuff, you know.'

'You can talk to us, anytime,' Angus says.

'If you want to. When you're ready,' I add.

'Listen to you lot, too scared to upset one another,' Ian says, with a thin smile. 'My dad died of cancer when I was eight. Watched him die in pain. I loved that man. He was a decent bloke.'

'Oh Ian, I'm sorry,' I say, anticipating this isn't the half of it.

'Mum lost it. Couldn't cope, you know. Got home from school to find her on the couch, passed out. She didn't give a shit about me, what I got up to. She didn't notice, too high on drugs. As I got older, I got in with the wrong crowd, you know, and then I messed up the best relationship I'd ever had. She loved me, she did. I know it sounds weird. We all need love, but when it comes along it's as scary as hell, and you push it away 'cos you don't deserve it, or you're goin' to lose it anyway, so I chose heroin and prison over the love of my life.'

Lauren turns to him. 'You never told me that.'

He shrugs. 'You didn't ask. Do you know what I go round thinking, pretty much all the time?'

We wait.

'That it's all going to get fucked up again.' Ian's face clouds over. 'I still walk down the street sussing out a place to squat.'

'Don't do that,' insists Lauren.

'But then I tell myself I've got a roof over my head, a chance, that I've got you, Lozza, keeping me on the straight 'n' narrow. I don't want to be on the streets again, stealing for drugs.'

'Don't even think about it, mate. I never begged,' Lauren adds. 'Never took drugs.'

'You're wiser than me,' Ian says.

'How did you survive, Laurie?' I dare to ask. 'I mean Lauren.'

'You can call me Laurie, or Lozza, I don't mind,' she says. 'I prefer Laurie. Lozza sounds like a throat lozenge or something.'

'I like Lozza,' Ian protests.

'My nan used to call me Laurie, she was nice. She's dead now but when I'm called Laurie it reminds me of her.'

'What happened after your step-mum kicked you out?' Angus asks.

'Me and Teddy walked to the train station, I took my Harry

Potter cushion with us, bought a ticket to the first place we saw on the screen. Yeovil. Somerset. Didn't have a clue where it was, but bought my ticket with all my babysitting and paper-round money.' She stops, looks out of the window.

'Do you want to talk about it?' I ask, to make sure she's OK.

She shrugs again, as if to say it's fine. Turns back to us. 'I lived in the town centre first, near the cinema. Met a bloke, he took pity 'cos I was young. He gave me a cheese sandwich and a sleeping bag too, it was pink.'

'Sounds like a decent man,' I say, praying he was.

'There were plenty of bad ones…' She pauses '…And women out there, people who'd rob you for their next fix. He was good to me.'

There's a 'but'.

'He wanted sex,' Laurie admits finally. '"It's ain't happening mate," I said.'

We all glance at one another before smiling at the way she said it, with a defiance I'm beginning to notice and admire. With a defiance that helped her to survive.

'The girls used to say that a lot to me too,' Angus says.

Ian agrees. 'All the time.'

'He's already tried his luck with me,' Laurie says, gesturing to Ian, and my heart softens towards him when I see him blush. Nina was right. When you discover what 'happened' to people it humanises them. Ian might look tough, and no doubt he is in some situations. If I was walking down a dark alleyway, I'd feel safe in his company. But when it comes to human emotion he's as vulnerable as the rest of us. Somehow, we are all in it together. Every single one of us walks down the street with a story to tell, some more horrifying than others, but knowing what Ian went through makes me feel far less scared of him and his muscles. If he hadn't lost his dad, who knows how his life might have ended up?

'So this guy didn't hurt you, Laurie?' Angus wants to know.

'He was all right,' she reflects. 'But I wasn't having no man near me, ever again, not after…' She stops. 'You know.'

The thing is we don't know. I can't possibly know or understand what she's experienced. The mood around the table sobers again, from teasing Ian to now feeling sick to my stomach. I thought it was bad enough knowing Laurie had to step off a train and be in a strange place, alone and at risk. Yet she was safer on that train, and living in London, on the streets, than she was at home. I'm struggling not to hate Laurie's stepmother, and her dad – how could he have allowed her to treat his daughter so badly? Why didn't he love her? Protect her? I'm struggling not to feel bitter about people who can have children and then treat them like objects. Mothers and fathers who can't keep their children safe.

'I hate her,' Laurie says, as if she can read my mind. 'I hope she's dead. I know that might sound harsh—'

'No,' Ian, Angus and I cut in.

'No one's entitled to love,' Angus says. 'Not even a mother or father. You have to earn it.'

I still need to understand how she survived.

'I learned tricks,' she tells us. 'You get to know who's good and who's bad out there. Who will nick money off you. The days were OK. It was the nights I hated. It was cold in my sleeping bag. I used to wonder what the point was, maybe the world was better off without me?' She shrugs. 'I'd be lying there thinking no one would care if I was dead or alive. It's all right, everyone. Stop crying, mate,' she says to Ian. 'You're all looking at me like I'm dead or something.'

'I'm proud,' Angus exclaims.

Laurie scoffs at that.

'I can't believe you're sitting here, telling us what happened. You're so brave, Laurie,' Angus continues.

'I had no choice.'

'You did. You chose to survive,' I say.

Laurie shrugs again. She seems to distance herself from what she has experienced. Her voice isn't shaking, she isn't shedding any tears. She's telling us what happened, and while that must take courage, I also sense she has to stay removed from what she has lived through in order to get by. There is no way she is ready to tell us who abused her, and I'm not going to push her on it. She can tell us when and if she wants to. I know she sees a therapist at the shelter, so at least she has someone to talk to.

'Doesn't mean I like it though,' she admits. 'I can't watch any programmes with families in them, you ask Ian. When *EastEnders* comes on I'm out of there.'

'You've never seen her move so fast,' Ian says.

'They might shout and slap one another but they care about each other. They love their kids,' Laurie says.

Suddenly it dawns on me why Lauren responds to videos of people unclogging drains. These films are devoid of human emotion, something Lauren wants to avoid like the plague. It's too painful to watch programmes where mothers hug their children.

'Smoking helped,' Laurie continues. 'Rolling up kept my hands warm, the flame kept my face warm too. I got bad frostbite though, man that hurts. The worst time was when I got my period on the streets. That's when Pat took me in.'

'The one who made the chocolate sauce?' I ask.

She nods. 'Yeah, she gave me a cup of tea and a sausage roll and said I could go home with her, have a wash, stay the night if I wanted to. I hadn't washed for about two weeks, I must have stank. That bath was amazing. I stayed with her for a month. Sixteen Arlington Drive. Always remember her address 'cos I was sixteen at the time, plus I'm a bit autistic like that. Anyway, her daughter kicked me out,' she says, 'called me a sponger. I never asked for money, not once,' she reinforces, and from the steely look in her eyes I know she's telling the truth. 'She said if I ever went near her mum again, she'd call the cops. Pat didn't want me to go. She was in tears and everything. I still have nightmares about it. It wasn't Pat's fault. She's the only person who cared for me and I didn't get to say goodbye. I never thanked her. That kills me, it does.' Laurie stands up to leave. 'I want to go home,' she says, as if it's all too much for her now.

'Go,' Angus tells Ian, gesturing for him to look after Laurie, to take her home. Ian follows Laurie out of the café, leaving Angus and me alone in our thoughts, until finally Angus breaks the silence, saying, 'Sixteen Arlington Drive. Remember that address. We *have* to track Pat down.'

20

'Hang on, you and Angus knocked on some stranger's door?' says Milla, as she hands me a chopping board, knife and a brown paper bag filled with mushrooms. It's Friday night, and I'm having supper with Milla and Dave, but Dave isn't home from work yet, so we have the kitchen to ourselves. The children, who have started primary school after the long summer holidays, are watching television in the next-door room, before bedtime.

I describe to Milla how an eighty-something year old woman had appeared at the door, Angus asking if she was called Pat.

She'd shaken her head. As she was about to shut the door, he'd stepped forward and offered her his hand. Tentatively she shook it. She was dressed in a tracksuit, her grey hair in rollers, and was wearing dusty-pink-coloured slippers, finished off with a matching pompom on the front. 'I'm Angus and this is Holly.'

'Whatever it is you want,' she'd said, chewing gum, 'I'm not interested.'

'We're not Jehovah's Witnesses,' Angus had reassured her, 'or trying to sell you something you don't need, like a de-bobbler.'

'We're here on behalf of a friend, Laurie,' I said, 'who once stayed with Pat. It was about three years ago? Did you buy this house from a Pat or a Patricia?'

'Might have,' she replied, guarded.

'Is Pat still alive?' Angus asked.

'Touch 'n' go.'

'Touch 'n' go?' Angus and I repeated together.

'On her last legs. Like us all.'

'I'm sorry to hear that,' Angus said.

'I can't tell you where she lives. Against the law. Confidentiality and all that.'

'Yes, of course,' Angus conceded.

'But you look like a rule breaker to me,' I suggested with a smile. 'Sorry, I don't even know your name?'

'Mo. Short for Maureen.'

'My mother's name!' I exclaimed.

'Such a pretty name, it suits you,' Angus followed up.

Mo rolled her eyes. 'I'm never going to get rid of the pair of you, am I?'

'Can you hear us out?' Angus begged, deadly serious again.

He proceeded to explain, in depth, the reason for our visit.

'I hate to break this to you love,' Mo said, 'but I don't know where Pat lives anymore.'

'Oh.' Angus sighed. After all that.

'But Sheila does,' she said with a twinkle in her eye. With renewed hope, we followed Mo to another semi-detached house on the opposite side of the road. 'Sheila, it's Mo!' she called through the letterbox. Another eighty-something-year-old opened the door, a miniature wire-haired dachshund snapping at her heels. As Mo recounted why we were there, Sheila stopped her.

'I remember that girl,' she said. 'Pat always wondered what happened to her. She used to go to bed at night, scared to think of the wee thing out there, alone,' Sheila confided. 'She didn't speak to Rochelle, that's her daughter, for months. Don't for God's sake tell anyone I told you where she lives, especially not Rochelle. She's quite scary, she is.' She handed us a piece of paper. 'She's protective,' she warned us, explaining Pat was in a nursing home in West Bay, Dorset, 'where they filmed that good thriller, *Broadchurch* you know, with Olivia Colman and the Doctor Who man. I try and talk to her 'bout once a week. It's only forty minutes from here but I don't have a car so… but Pat likes to talk. Half the time I'm not sure she knows it's me. She's lost her marbles a bit, you know.'

'Like us all,' Mo had added.

'So the three of you are driving to West Bay this Sunday?' Milla asks.

'Yep.' I recall our car journey home, Angus and I on such a high.

'To see Pat?' Milla goes on.

I nod, detecting Milla isn't quite as excited about this trip as I am.

'What if she doesn't recognise Laurie?'

'She will,' I say, though realising Milla has a point. 'She's got to.'

'And can you just turn up? Don't you have to make an appointment?'

'Angus can get us in. All we have to do is call to let them know we're coming.'

'What if Rochelle shows up?' Milla seems determined to place obstacles in front of us.

'Well, she might, but we'll find a way.' With Angus, anything feels possible.

'I don't know. It could make things worse, especially if Pat doesn't recognise Laurie.' Milla takes another gulp of wine.

'Well, we think it's worth a shot,' I respond, noticing my defensive tone again, before caving in and pouring myself a glass. One isn't going to do me any harm.

Milla sits down next to me. 'Are you sure Laurie wants to meet her again?'

'Yes,' I insist.

'Are you sure you're not getting too involved?'

'Out with it, Milla,' I say, knowing something's bugging her, and I don't think this has anything to do with Laurie.

'It's Angus.'

'What about him?'

'You're spending a lot of time with him?'

'He's a friend.'

'It's the way you talk about him.'

'He's a friend, that's all.'

'Are you sure?'

'Positive.'

'I'm worried about you.'

'I'm fine. Meeting Angus and Laurie has been one of the best things I've ever done. Before we met, my life was so empty, Milla.'

'I know.' Her face softens. 'I know it's been great, and I love the sound of Soul Food, I'm longing to come and see it but I'm worried, OK?'

'I'm not falling for Angus, I promise.'

She's quiet.

'Milla, I'm not. We've become good friends, that's all.'

'It's…' She frowns. 'You're doing everything you can to help Laurie and Angus but…' She pauses, unsure how to continue. 'I'm scared you're the one who's going to get hurt. You two hang out practically all the time.'

'We're training together. I'm having fun!'

'But what if he gets back with his wife?'

'I'll be happy for him. I don't want to break up his family. I'm helping him get back with them,' I insist.

'Great, so he'll go back to his family and then what?'

'We'll stay in touch.' As I say it, I'm not sure I believe it.

Milla doesn't look convinced either.

'For the first time in months I'm happy, Milla.'

'I know and it's wonderful.'

'Angus has quit drinking, he's getting his life back on track, and Laurie is much more confident.'

'Exactly. You're solving all their problems, but what about you? What's in it for you?'

'You don't get it, do you? What's in it for me?' I repeat, unsure why I suddenly feel so angered by this question. 'I'm going out more, I'm cooking again, I've lost weight,' I say, noticing my jeans feel much more friendly these days.

'I know, and you look great.'

'I love Laurie, and I'm hanging out with this amazing guy.'

'Who's married.'

'Well, technically separated.'

'So you do like him?'

'No,' I stress again, though fear every time I say it, I believe it less. 'Yes. Maybe.' When I clock Milla's face clouding over with concern, I exclaim, 'I don't know! But even if I did, would that be so bad? You were the one who loved the sound of Angus, who—'

'Yes, but I didn't know the full story back then.' She stops. Runs a hand through her hair. 'I'm scared you'll get hurt.'

'Getting hurt is better than feeling nothing.'

'What do you mean?'

I look up at her, surprised at what I've just said. 'Since Jamie died, I've felt numb.'

'I know.'

I stand up, ready to leave. 'No, you don't know. You couldn't possibly know. How could you?' In that moment, I hate myself for being jealous, but I am. I feel jealous that Dave will be coming home in a minute, and will keep her bed warm tonight. Jealous that she has two beautiful girls in the room next door, a family I never had. I feel jealous that the world she lives in feels a million miles apart from mine right now, and that there is no bridge to bring us even close. 'You have no idea, Milla.'

'Sorry, don't go Holly, forget I said anything.'

But I can't. 'What do I get from being friends with Laurie and Angus?' I picture Laurie's stunned face when Angus and I had told her about our meeting with Mo, and how we'd like to drive her to West Bay. I hear Angel clapping during our last session in the park, when Laurie managed a whole training circuit in record time. Whenever I'm feeling low, all I have to do is recall Angus and Tom singing Frank Sinatra as they lay the tables. I feel the pain of hearing what Laurie has endured. I feel hope that one day she might move out of the night-shelter and find her 'forever home' with someone who will love her, unconditionally. I picture Angus's face as he dropped me back home, after our visit to Mo and Sheila. He'd turned off the car engine and swung round to face me. 'Do you have a mother called Maureen?' he'd asked, a smile creeping on to his face when I replied, 'What do you think?'

We'd stayed in the car talking, and planning our trip with Laurie. I was tempted to ask him inside for a coffee, but lost my nerve. *What do I get from being friends with Laurie and Angus?*

'I get to feel something,' I tell Milla tearfully, unsure now if I'm grieving purely for Jamie, as she takes me into her arms, and holds me.

21

'Benjie, how are you?' Angus asks, as we follow signs for the M3 South. He's talking to his son on the speakerphone as he drives Lauren and me to Pat's nursing home in Dorset. Lauren sits in the front, I'm in the back. It's a three-hour journey from London, we should be there by two in the afternoon.

'Not good, Dad.'

'Fuck, I mean, what's wrong?'

'I'm fine.'

'Don't tell your mother I said "fuck".'

'I've heard the word a million times, Dad,' he says, as if his father really is out-of-touch.

'Well don't say it in front of your mum. Anyway, what's up?' Angus asks him again.

'I don't want to go to Auntie Nell's for lunch.'

'Why not?' He mouths to Lauren 'she's seriously bossy'.

'She's so bossy!' Benjie exclaims. 'Always telling me to get off my phone.'

'Well, to be fair you shouldn't be on your phone.'

'You always are.'

'It's only lunch, and you'll see your cousins.'

'They can eat whatever they want.'

'I know it's frustrating, Benjie.'

'It's not fair.'

'I wish you didn't have to worry about any of this, Benjie. I wish I could take it all away.'

I can feel, in the silence, Benjie is close to tears.

'Did you have a bad night last night?' Angus asks.

There's another long silence.

'Benjie?'

'I want you to come home, Dad.'

I look out of the window, trying to appear as if I'm not listening to every single word.

'This isn't forever, Benjie.'

'Why can't you come home?'

'It's complicated.'

'Why? Mum's lonely, Dad. She misses you.'

'Did she say that?'

'I know she does.'

'You know your dad loves you, don't you?' Angus's voice is close to breaking. 'And I'm seeing you next weekend, OK? Not long.'

'Why can't you come home now?'

'Benjie, I can't.'

Benjie hangs up.

'But I love you,' Angus finishes.

'You miss him?' Laurie asks.

'All the time.'

'What's he like?' Laurie asks. 'Is he like you?'

'In some ways, but he's had more to deal with.'

'It's hard for you too though, Angus,' I say. 'Watching someone you love suffer is tough.'

'It's hard watching him try to keep up with his friends, he hates feeling different.'

Laurie sighs. 'It's not fair.'

'Life's unfair.' He turns to her briefly. 'You know that more than anyone else.' Angus goes on to tell Laurie that a few weeks after Benjie was born Soph was convinced something wasn't right, he wouldn't settle. 'I didn't notice it so much then, but at around three months, he developed this rash all over his face, so bad he couldn't sleep. Try telling a baby not to scratch. By the time Soph and I reached his cot, his face was a bleeding mess.'

'No way,' Laurie says. 'Scary.'

'People would stop and stare at us in the street. "Someone's had too much sun!" they'd say. Parents still tell their kids to stay away from Benjie because they think he's infectious. I've never wanted him to see how angry it makes me. I've always tried to give him as normal a life as possible. But it was hard when people assumed we were bad parents when we'd tried everything. God, you should have seen the things we did. We put him in Babygros with mittens, and silk pyjamas.'

'Silk pyjamas?' Laurie sounds confused.

'They're cooler. We'd cover his little body in wet bandages and smother him with cream and lotions to try and stop the itching. Soph even took the carpet out of his room, and replaced his curtains with blinds, but nothing helped. When he went to primary school Soph had to bandage his neck under his uniform. You want to stick out for being cool or being the funny one.' Angus draws in a deep breath. 'They went to Spain over the summer, Marbella. Soph's mother, Granny Heather, has a holiday home there. While I'm not exactly best son-in-law-of-the-year right now, we actually get on well. She knows exactly where to go in a medical crisis, and exactly what to cook for Benjie, so at least a couple of meals a day feels less like Russian roulette. We go there each year, it's our one safe holiday. I missed going this year, being with them all.'

'That sucks,' Laurie says generously, when we know she's never been up in the sky, that 'holiday' is a foreign word.

'It does, but listen, I've spent the summer with you. If I'm honest, there's a part of me that's relieved to have a break from the never-ending worry. I feel guilty saying that, but I can admit that with you two. It's not so easy talking to friends when Benjie's problems are day after day, week after week, year after year. Most of my mates assume he must be better now. Scottie doesn't get it, but don't tell him I said that.'

'I won't,' Laurie agrees. 'He's scary enough.'

Angus laughs lightly. 'I don't know what it is about you two, being with you is like taking a truth drug. To think we were strangers only three months ago.'

'What's Amy like?' I ask, wondering how she copes with it all.

'Brilliant at everything, especially sport. Mind you, Benjie's good at hockey. He was made vice captain last year, but in the last few months, after my massive stuff-up, he's struggled to keep up with his fitness again. Benjie's real passion is skiing. You should see him,' Angus says with pride, as if watching him on the slopes right now. 'He's so free.'

'Free?' Laurie repeats.

'The mountain air is great for his asthma.'

I notice Amy doesn't get much of a look-in. That can't be easy for her.

'Soph tells me he's still scared of being on his own at night,' Angus continues. 'He's anxious about falling asleep and not waking up. She's put a camp bed in our room, and he's seeing a counsellor. He's an amazing boy, the best, but the shit I've put him through…'

'Angus,' Laurie says with that defiance I'm getting used to, 'you're a good dad. Benjie's lucky to have you. You made one mistake.'

'A few, actually.'

'But you love him.'

'Yeah, I love him,' he says, understanding what Laurie is getting at.

'My dad died when I was ten. My step-mum woke me up in the middle of the night, said, "Your father's dead." Heart attack. She didn't let me go to his funeral.'

The things Laurie says don't shock me quite as much as they used to. But they still make me feel sad, and I tell her that. Her mum died giving birth to her, her dad died when she was aged ten, and she was left with a stepmother who didn't love her, abused her, kicked her out of the house. And that's probably only a fraction of it.

'The past is the past,' Laurie says, deflecting the attention away from herself as she says, 'I hope you can work things out with your family, Angus.'

He turns to her, one hand on the steering wheel. 'Thanks, Laurie, so do I. How are you in the back?' he calls out to me, glancing in his rear-view mirror. 'You've been quiet.'

'All good,' I say, wondering if I'm a bad person for thinking that while I want Angus to be happy, and for Benjie to have his family back together, equally I love what the three of us have, and I don't want anything to change.

'Bridport straight on,' Angus says, as we go straight over the roundabout. 'We're almost there, guys.' Thankfully no one has to navigate since Angus knows West Bay well. He told us it's a small fishing village with a harbour, on the Jurassic Coast, a coastline of beautiful golden cliffs that stretch for miles.

'Laurie, do you want us to come in with you, at least to begin with?' I ask.

She composes herself. 'What if she doesn't recognise me?'

'She might not,' Angus warns her. 'If you're in any doubt, we don't have to go through with this. We can turn round and go home.'

'We can't do that!' Laurie protests. 'That would be stupid.'

'Point is, this is your decision, Laurie,' he says.

'I'm seeing Pat, so let's get on with it.'

Angus glances in the rear-view mirror and catches my eye again. As he parks in a large pay and display carpark by the beach, I can tell he's thinking the same as me. That Laurie surprises him, that she's stronger than we give her credit for. She knows her own mind, far better than we do.

We press a buzzer and a nurse greets us at the door, asking who we're visiting and to sign our names in the visitors' book placed on the desk in the hallway. 'Could you show us the way to Pat's room?' Angus asks, explaining we haven't visited before. The nursing home is busy, staff bustling around. I can hear a television playing in the lounge, and take a quick peep inside. Half a dozen elderly folk are sitting side by side, a few have nodded off in front of the screen.

The nurse points to a passage on the right, telling us she's room number twenty-five. 'She's sitting up in her chair now, and I'm sure she'll be pleased to see you. She doesn't get many visitors, only her daughter. Are you related?'

'I'm an old friend,' Laurie says, crunching her knuckles.

'Oh, how lovely,' she replies, before she's needed somewhere else.

Laurie tells us she needs the toilet.

'There's a visitors' toilet by the entrance,' the nurse calls out, on her way upstairs.

Minutes later, Angus knocks on Pat's door. I squeeze Laurie's hand. She squeezes it back, before we go inside.

We find Pat sitting in a high-backed green armchair beside her bed, the television playing loudly in the background, though Pat seems completely disinterested in the cooking programme. On her bedside table is a book of wordsearch puzzles, a framed family photograph and a box of After Eight chocolates. Her room backs out on to a garden, with a view of the sea. Pat's wearing a navy cardigan over a blouse, and despite it only being a mild day in mid-September, she has a thick crochet blanket across her lap. Pat sits motionless, no hint of recognition in her watery blue eyes when Laurie says hello. Her hair is fine and light brown, tinged with grey, brushed flat with two plain clips on one side. She smells of sleep, rose talcum powder and that old people smell which is indefinable, yet unmistakable. 'Hello Pat, it's me, Laurie.'

Pat looks confused. 'Where's Rochelle?'

'It's Laurie, do you remember me? You looked after me.'

No response.

Laurie glances at Angus and me helplessly. We urge her to keep going.

'You took me in, Pat. When I was sleeping rough you brought me back to your place, do you remember?'

Pat shakes her head.

'You gave me a cup of tea and a sausage roll,' Laurie persists. 'We used to play Scrabble and cook.'

Something in Pat's eyes changes.

'You taught me how to make chocolate sauce and roast a chicken. I was amazed all you had to do was bung a bird in the oven, d'you remember! And we made an After Eight cheesecake! Can see you still like them chocs.'

Pat looks at Laurie more inquisitively now.

'It's Laurie, Laurie Rose you used to call me, because you loved my middle name.'

'Laurie Rose,' Pat repeats, as if allowing the name to sink in.

'We used to listen to music. You had an old record player in your lounge that used to belong to your hubby. You introduced me to Elvis, d'you remember?'

Pat clicks her fingers and sings, in a surprisingly good voice, Elvis's 'All Shook Up'. As Laurie sings along with her, Pat stops abruptly. 'I know you, don't I?'

'Yes! It's Laurie!'

'Laurie Rose.' She opens her arms and Laurie falls into them. Angus and I know we should leave, yet it's so tender and moving, I can't. 'Is it really you?' Pat asks again, as she strokes Laurie's hair. 'What happened to you?'

'I'm OK,' Laurie says, 'I'm good.'

'Are you happy? Are you safe?'

'Yeah, I live in London now.'

'You have a home?'

'I moved to the big smoke! And these are my friends, Angus and Holly,' Laurie says. 'We work in a café.'

Yet Pat only has eyes for Laurie. 'What happened to you, my darling little girl? I never believed I'd see you again.'

'Nothing bad happened,' Laurie reassures her, kneeling by her side, and taking Pat's hands into her own. 'If it wasn't for you, I wouldn't be here. I was fine.'

Angus and I remain so touched by the scene that we don't notice the door opening until we hear, 'What's going on?'

'Rochelle, it's Laurie Rose,' exclaims Pat joyfully to a grey-haired woman who can only be her daughter.

Rochelle seems to be suspicious. She looks at Laurie, as if she's beginning to piece together who she might be. 'Mum, do you want these people to leave?' She doesn't wait for her to reply. 'I think you should go. Mum's tired.'

Pat looks confused now.

Laurie looks at us, then back to Pat. 'But I've only just got here.'

A man enters the room next, possibly Rochelle's husband or brother, friend, partner, who knows. 'They won't leave,' she says to him. 'This is the girl who squatted with Mum, took her money—'

'To buy her stuff!' Laurie protests. 'I'd go down the shops for her 'cos her knees were bad.'

He swiftly walks across the room, yanks Laurie up by the arm, as if she's an animal.

'Hey,' Angus shouts.

Soon he's pushing her out of the room.

Angus intervenes, grabbing Laurie from this man's clutches.

'How dare you upset my wife,' the man says before the three of us are turfed out of the room like bad smells. He closes the door firmly behind us and moves us down the corridor, out of the way. 'Pat's old. Fragile. You can't turn up like this.'

'Hang on a minute,' Angus says, trying to keep a lid on his temper. 'If we could explain why we're here?' He looks over to Laurie.

'All I want to do is say thanks.'

'You stole from her.'

'I swear I didn't,' Laurie says, on the verge of tears.

'Pat trusts anyone. She did this all the time, opened her doors to the waifs and strays. It was a huge stress for Rochelle. What have you come back for? What do you want?'

'I didn't take anything from Pat,' Laurie says again. 'I don't want anything!'

'She was young,' I defend my friend. 'Homeless. She'd never been loved by anyone until she met Pat.'

'She wasn't Mum's responsibility,' Rochelle says, joining us, every inch of her body clenched and unforgiving.

'No, she wasn't,' Angus agrees.

'She lived there for weeks!'

'Well thank God there are some kind people out there,' I can't help saying.

Rochelle remains tight-lipped. 'She's been preyed upon for years by druggies and layabouts.'

'Do you have children?' Angus asks coolly.

She looks taken aback by the question. 'Yes.'

'Well imagine your little girl, out on the streets, alone at night.'

I can tell she doesn't want to.

'Unimaginable, isn't it?' he continues. 'There is so much kindness in this world,' he proceeds, impassioned, 'the kindness your mother showed Laurie, but then there is so much distrust. And sadly, it seems to me, nothing in between.' Neither Rochelle, nor her husband, can quite meet Angus's eyes.

'Is everything OK here?' asks a member of staff approaching us. Angus and I look at them both beseechingly, before we notice Laurie is missing. You go, Laurie, I think to myself. Rochelle rushes back to her mother's room, but Angus manages to stop her as she's about to open the door. 'Give them five minutes, *please*, and then we'll leave.'

She hesitates.

'I understand this is a bit of shock,' Angus goes on, loosening his grip around her arm, 'us turning up out the blue, but we're not here to cause trouble. Laurie's here to say thanks, that's all.'

'We volunteer together, at this Saturday place, a café,' I explain, thinking Rochelle must be wondering who the hell we are too. 'Pat was one of the first people she mentioned to us. She told us about your mum's famous chocolate sauce and After Eight cheesecake.'

Rochelle's face finally softens as she says, 'She did?'

I nod. 'She's never forgotten her.'

Her grip on the door handle loosens when she sees Pat and Laurie through the glass pane in the door. Pat cups Laurie's cheeks in both hands before we watch them embrace. 'I haven't seen her this happy in years,' she admits. She looks at Angus and me, before glancing at her mother again. She presses a hand to her forehead. 'Mum used to get taken advantage of all the time.' She bites her lip, close to tears now.

Her husband agrees. 'She didn't have it in her to say no to anyone. She's a golden person.'

'I understand,' I say, knowing how protective I'd be of my mother too, 'but Laurie's golden too, and look.' I follow Rochelle's gaze. 'They've found one another again.'

Somehow her anger is thawing. We're beginning to earn her trust, not enough for her to say she could be wrong, or that she's sorry she accused Laurie of stealing. 'Tell Mum we'll visit tomorrow,' she says, slowly walking away.

Laurie, Angus and I enjoy fish and chips on the beach. Laurie sits in the middle of us. It's close to five o'clock, the beach less crowded than when we arrived, but to be honest I'm not bothered about anyone else right now except my two favourite people next to me. Angus helps himself to another chip.

'What a day,' he says. 'Laurie, we didn't even notice you'd gone.'

'While you guys were busy arguing, I made a run for it,' she says, with a twinkle of pride in her eyes.

'Clever,' says Angus. 'It worked.'

'It's been the best day of my life,' she tells us. 'I can go to sleep tonight, knowing I said thank you. Pat said the same. She could go to sleep, knowing I was safe.'

'We did the right thing coming, didn't we?' I say, recalling Milla's warning.

Laurie nods. 'Oh yeah.' She turns to Angus and me. 'The way you spoke to them, no one's *ever* stood up for me like that before.'

'You're our friend,' Angus says, catching my eye.

Laurie blushes. 'I wasn't sure about you two when we met. Especially you, Holly.'

Angus and I exchange looks again. I love how Laurie says what she thinks, no beating around the bush. 'What was wrong with me?' I protest. 'Hang on, maybe I don't want to know.'

'We'll be here all night,' Angus adds.

'You were all posh like, "We'll have so much fun!"' Lauren mimics, making us laugh.

'But now you think we're not *too* bad,' Angus says, or hopes.

She breaks into a smile. 'You're not too bad. For oldies.'

The three of us sit, peacefully, listening to the sound of the waves, enjoying the end to this perfect day, until Angus says, reluctantly, 'We'd better make a move, I don't want to get a parking ticket.'

'Race you to the car,' I suggest, before we all scramble to our feet, laughing as we run across the beach, back to the carpark.

22

Laurie and I have been busy all morning making fig tarts, a plum and apple crumble, and a fruit salad. As I put the crumble and tarts into the oven and set the timer, I think about the past month, since we went to West Bay.

Laurie, Angus and I still meet Angel in the park twice a week. We're now doing burpees (guess who laughed at the name) which is basically a push-up followed by a leap in the air. Angel tells us this builds our strength and endurance, especially if we can do as many as possible, in a row, without stopping. There is no way Laurie could have done this in week one, nor me probably. We also have added into our circuit training pop squats, which are simply standing with our feet a hip-width apart, positioning ourselves in an elegant squat position, before jumping straight into the air and landing, supposedly softly, and gracefully, back in the squat position. Laurie once toppled over, but picked herself up and tried again, not seeming to care as much when passers-by stopped and stared, though Angel is always quick to move them on. Angel doesn't encourage us after every single exercise anymore, which I take as a compliment. In fact, she pushes us harder, living up to her name of the Smiling Assassin.

Angus and I still jog three times a week, on a Tuesday, Thursday and Sunday morning. He knocks on my door at 7.30, before we run five km, usually down the Chiswick Mall, towards Hammersmith Bridge, and back. Whereas I used to arrive at the office hungover and lethargic, and in desperate need of a second coffee, I now have more energy to face the barrage of unread emails and deal with clients. And whereas I used to dread the weekends, I now live for the café, my Saturday place as I've come to call it, and my runs with Angus. I haven't given up wine, life's too short to give up all the things I love, but I do feel healthier taking more exercise and bothering to cook a decent meal for myself in the evenings, instead of eating out of a cereal packet. Angus, however, is an all-or-nothing man. He is working out every day, religiously, and the weight is falling off him as he hasn't touched an alcoholic drink or a cigarette since we began our programme. 'Once I make up my mind about something, that's it,' he'd told me on one of our runs. 'I don't need nicotine patches, hypnotists, or any other bollocks like that.'

Laurie still smokes, but she smokes less. She's outside right now on a fag break with Ian. He wanted to put in an appearance at the café today, to finally suss out where she spends every Saturday, and to sample one of her puddings. No one would dare force Laurie to give up smoking. It's been her constant friend. Yes, people die of it, but at the same time, people die behind the wheel of a car, and we're not all about to stop driving.

Laurie has had one or two more dips in the past month, her anxiety returning like a toxic friend never getting the message. She confided to Angel that she still sneak-eats, once, sometimes twice, a week. Angel is good with her; she takes her out for a coffee and a chat, reminding her of the reason why she wants to get fit and make changes in her life. Angel receives no extra money taking Laurie out, and she still discounts our sessions. 'I can say this now,' she'd confided to Angus, Laurie and me, 'with my friend hat on, but when I first met you, I was daunted, and I mean *really* daunted. I had never trained three such different people. But I *so* wanted to help.'

'You took pity?' Angus suggested.

She tutted. 'I wanted to help. Seeing you improve, Laurie, and build your confidence, and seeing you wear tops that don't hide your figure, Holly, that gives me more pleasure than anything.'

'Me too,' Angus had agreed.

Angel tutted again, hands on hips. 'Quit flirting, Angus.'

'Hang on, what about me?' he'd then asked.

Angel laughed, asking Laurie and me how we put up with him, before adding, 'You were like a little old lady to begin with. "My feet hurt!"' she mimicked.

'Now you're a man, Angus,' I finished off.

'Exactly,' Angel agreed.

As I head out of the kitchen, I glance at Laurie through the glass doors, still talking and smoking with Ian outside. She does look different. I can't put my finger on what exactly has changed as she still wears the same T-shirt tucked into black trousers, she often doesn't bother to wash her hair and her skin remains pale. Since visiting Pat, we've returned to West Bay once more. Laurie is now friends with Rochelle. She has realised her mother loves Laurie, and perhaps, with hindsight, she did over-react. 'Pat would have given up her home to anyone if she'd been asked to,' she'd explained to us on our second visit. 'She used to give all her money to charity. You should have seen her bank statements. But I can see Laurie is different,' she'd admitted, finally.

Angus and I would have liked an apology, but we've settled on them being friends. I marvel at how Laurie holds no grudges, yet we believe this is what has enabled her to survive all these years. Aside from her stepmother, who could be dead or alive for all she cares, Laurie has the most forgiving nature. 'She could hold so much anger towards the world,' Angus had said, 'but where would that leave her?'

Angus, Laurie and I talked a lot in the car on the way to see Pat again. Jamie and I always used to say how car journeys were good places to chat because your audience was captive. Angus and I had wanted to know what had happened to Laurie after she'd been kicked out of Pat's. Laurie described how she'd returned to Yeovil town centre to find a place to squat. Returning home, to her step-mum's, wasn't an option. Being near her boyfriend was far more frightening than sleeping on the streets. 'When my dad died, she started going out with him pretty quick. She didn't waste no time. He used to come over most nights and enjoy more than a hot meal, if you know what I mean.'

Angus and I felt sick. Laurie, however, was somehow able to talk about it without tears or anger. Angus told me that had to be a protective mechanism. She was distancing herself, numbing herself, as much as she could from the horror of his abuse. At the same time, she'd taken a giant leap of faith by telling us what had happened to her. It made me feel even closer to Laurie.

She found herself a washing-up job in the Ritz Café in the town centre – 'Not so ritzy if you know what I mean, but they were good, gave me free lunches and hot drinks.' She worked at the café for over a year. She described how she met a guy there, almost ten years older. He'd come in for his beans and fried eggs on toast most mornings. She'd just turned seventeen and was on jobseeker's allowance; he was twenty-six. She moved in with him. 'He wasn't nice, didn't like me speaking to other men. I remember one time we were out of milk. I was standing at the door, with my coat on. He kicked off, pulling me back by the hair, asking why the fuck I hadn't bought the milk. One morning I woke up and knew I had to get out. I'd had enough of being his punchbag. I walked to the train station, Yeovil Junction, but he followed me, and I moved back, stayed there another year,' she told us. 'It got worse. I couldn't even have a conversation with another guy without getting a cut lip. In the end I knew if I stayed, he'd end up killing me, so in the middle of the night Teddy and I got on a train to London. Thought London is a big place, millions of people; he can't find me here. I came to Hammersmith, slept rough for a few weeks. On the street you get to know people and they have a few friends, so I sofa-surfed on and off for another six weeks, but I knew I wanted to find a proper home, I needed more support. I went to the council every day, and then Simon from the housing team called, saying he'd found me a place in the night-shelter.'

'Thank God for Simon,' Angus had said.

'I wasn't thanking anyone at the time. I was dead scared. I sat in the lounge thinking I don't know these weird men that live here, and I can't get away from them. The manager was kind, but I didn't trust anyone. Had panic attacks night and day. And then my support worker, Jane, asked me if I wanted to work at Soul Food. She knew I'd had experience working in a café before. That's when I met you guys,' she'd finished.

Laurie returns to the kitchen, breaking up my thoughts by informing me she's going to give Ian a guided tour. 'So, this is the kitchen, obviously, where Holly and I cook and Angus nicks the chips. Come and meet Scottie, our head chef. He's the bossy one, but actually he's a real softie.'

'Hi Ian,' Scottie says, shaking his hand, 'nice to meet you, but can you get out of my kitchen?'

'This is Monika, she's Polish,' Laurie adds.

'Ignore Scottie. Welcome,' she says to Ian.

As I watch Laurie introducing him to everyone, it dawns on me what it is about Laurie that has changed. It's the way she carries herself; it's as if, finally, she understands that she's worth something.

As for Angus, he's spending more time with his children. When he arrived at the café today, he told me he'd spent the previous night at home, on the sofa bed. 'The look on Benjie's face when he saw me this morning for breakfast,' he said, glowing. 'Even Amy looked happy I was there, though of course she wouldn't admit it. I don't want to raise their hopes, who knows what's going to happen between Soph and me, but it was good to have breakfast together, as a family. It felt almost normal, Holly. Whatever happens, our children come first. Soph and I are even talking now, without it descending into a row.'

I can't deny that as he was talking, I felt that fear again of losing us, our team of three, but I keep forcing myself to focus on the bigger picture: that I want him to get back together with Sophie and his family, that I want Angus to be happy. As for me, Milla's words kept haunting me. 'What if he gets back with his wife? He'll go back to his family and then what?' She had a point, so finally, I bit the bullet and spent last weekend signing up to an online dating agency. I need to prove to Milla, and to myself, that I'm not falling in love with Angus. So tonight, I'm going on a date, with Giles. I'm so anxious I need to keep busy. I decide to head upstairs to print the menus.

'Sorry,' I say, flustered when I see Angus in the office, semi-naked, about to put on a clean shirt. 'I should have knocked.'

'Holly?' He grins. 'It's only me.'

Head down, I walk over to the printer, before promptly dropping the menu sheets. Paper scatters on to the floor. Angus and I both reach down to pick up the sheets, heads bumping, hands touching. 'Sorry!' I say, staggering back. 'Sorry.'

'Holly, what's up?'

'I'm nervous.' I bite my lip.

'I can tell. Why? What's going on?'

'I've got a date tonight.'

'A date?'

I nod again.

'When?'

'Tonight,' I repeat.

There's a lengthy pause. 'Say something encouraging, Angus!' I break into a nervous smile.

'Who's the unlucky guy?'

'Funny,' I say, pushing him away.

'So who is he?'

'Want to see a pic?'

'Hmm. What if I don't think he's good enough for you?'

I reach into my apron pocket, dig out my mobile and show him a picture of Giles: forty-eight, divorced, three grown-up kids, hedge funder. I wait for Angus to say something, but he's unusually quiet. 'You don't *know* him do you?'

'No.'

'He looks OK, doesn't he? With any luck he won't argue over the bill.'

'You don't know hedge funders very well.'

Milla and I had wondered about this but forgave him since he was good-looking. Superficial, I know.

'You wouldn't quibble over the bill,' I say to him, 'would you?'

'He's good-looking,' Angus decides. There's a 'but'.

'Angus, I've got to get out there again,' I say, as I put my mobile back into my apron pocket and get the photocopying machine to work.

'Yeah. I know.'

'I haven't been on a date for over fifteen years,' I confess, already feeling my heart hammering in my chest. 'I don't know if I'm ready yet, but at the same time the longer I wait, the harder it's going to be, right?' I don't feel confident. The only thing I'm sure about is that I don't want to spend the rest of my life alone. I touch my hair, glance at my unmanicured fingernails. 'I should get my nails done at least.'

'Well, stop chewing them,' he says, taking my hand away from my mouth, before releasing it quickly. 'You don't need to get your nails done, Holly. Remember he's there to impress you just as much as the other way round. Try not to be nervous, I know easier said than done but remember, if you can work in Scottie's kitchen, you can have a few cocktails with a handsome stranger.'

I nod.

'If I can put up with you, I can go on a date,' I suggest. I wait for him to say something punchy back, but he's still looking at me, unnervingly.

Laurie bounds into the room with Ian. 'This is where I do the menus,' she tells him, before Angus and I move apart abruptly. 'Scottie needs you, Holly. What are you two doing in here?'

'Talking,' Angus says.

'The menus,' I say at the same time.

'Holly's going on a date,' Angus tells her, running a hand through his hair.

'Yeah, Angus was saying I didn't need to get my nails done.' I show Laurie and Ian my hands.

'Nah, don't bother,' Laurie agrees. 'You don't care what my nails are like, do you Ian?' She doesn't wait for him to answer. 'Ian loves me just the way I am,' she states, confiding they're an item now. 'We were in the supermarket, down the cheese aisle, and I said "Ian, you and I have been friends for a while now, how about it?" And he said, "Why not?"'

'That's great,' Angus and I say together, congratulating both Ian and Laurie.

'Right, enough chat you two, Scottie is getting stressed,' Laurie tells us. We head downstairs together, the dining room beginning to fill up.

Before I go into the kitchen, Angus grabs my arm. 'Don't bother with your nails, or your hair, be yourself. He's a lucky man, OK?'

I'm almost moved until he adds, 'But wear your hair down and wear a low-cut top.'

23

'Hi, I'm Holly, what do you get up to in your free time?' I say in my bedroom, after my shower, my hair washed and drying in a turban. I fling open the doors to my wardrobe. 'Any siblings?' I continue with my best date voice, before practising a pout. I look like an idiot! Deranged. Don't pout. I apply some lipstick, rub my lips together. Practise a sexy smouldering look. Stop it, Holly! I wipe the lipstick off. Jamie and I never went on a date. It was so easy, no contrived 'what do you do?' conversation. Earlier this evening I Googled successful strategies for a first date, but I've got to say asking my date if he has any pets doesn't sound like the most exciting opening question, though I guess I've got to start somewhere. One tip was to prepare some topics so I scanned my untouched copy of *The Week* magazine to get up-to-date with what was going on in the world. Another site had a whole list of questions designed to make sure the conversation flows. 'What's your biggest passion?' I practise. 'Your dream job? Your biggest fear? What would you do if you won the lottery?' Another tip was not to be too serious, keep the conversation light. 'Don't talk about me,' I can imagine Jamie advising. My mobile pings. It's a text message from Milla, wishing me luck. Call if you need rescuing but hopefully you won't ☺ It pings again, and this time it's from Angus. I know you'll be Googling questions to ask on a first date, Holly, so here's one from me. If he found a fifty quid note on the pavement, would he keep it? If he says no, he's a liar and run for your life.

Laurie sends me a message, saying have a nice time. My mobile then rings, my mother calling me to wish me luck. My phone has never been such a hot line. My date has turned into the most epic event of the year. It'll be broadcast on the ten o'clock news tonight. Turned into a movie. Hopefully Kate Winslet playing me.

'Darling! I hope you have a lovely time! Where's he taking you?'

'We're meeting in Covent Garden.' Mum still has the idea that men 'take' you out, that they open car doors and pay the bills.

'You're not wearing jeans, are you?'

Even if I was, I wouldn't tell her. 'No.'

'I hope you're wearing a dress. You look so pretty in red. Don't wear black.'

'Mum! You're making me even more nervous.'

'No need to be nervous, darling! All good things start with a date. Your father and I got on like a house on fire and we were engaged within three months. Now you go out and enjoy yourself, darling. You've got a whole new life ahead of you,' she says, before hanging up.

I stare at the clothes in my wardrobe, dresses I haven't worn in a long time. With renewed determination I take Mum's advice and pick out my red dress, before I spend the next half-hour applying makeup and drying my hair, resolute to do myself, and Jamie, plus all my friends, even my mother, proud tonight. I am going to have the best evening ever, I tell myself, beginning to feel excited as I slip on some heels. 'You look a million dollars,' I hear Jamie saying as I check myself out in the mirror, before my mobile pings again. It's another message from Angus. If he doesn't realise how special you are, he's not worth knowing.

As I lock up, I can't stop smiling.

As I sit in the Tube, I reread his message, realising I'm thinking far more about Angus's last text than meeting my date.

* * *

Giles and I arranged to meet outside Covent Garden Tube. I feel petrified now, my stomach churning with nerves. Come on Holly, you can do this. I've got to put myself out there again, take some chances, a few risks. I could turn round and go home? No one needs to know. I can tell everyone it went well. But then they'll be asking me when we're going on date number two. I could say that sadly he'd had to leave the country on business and follow it up with disappointment that he never called me again? He'd ghosted me.

'Any spare change?' says a scruffy-looking man slumped on the ground, his back against the wall, holding up a large piece of cardboard that claims it's his birthday. As I'm wondering whether to give him something or not, 'Hello!' greets a tall, suited man. 'You must be Holly, sorry I'm late. Thank God you look normal,' he adds as he kisses me on both cheeks, and up close I can smell his expensive aftershave. 'I've met *so* many women recently and they are *nothing* like their profile picture. Time hasn't been kind to them if you know what I mean.' He stands back, gives me an all over body scan. 'You're gorgeous. How come you're still single?'

'Any spare change?' the man says sullenly again.

Giles peers down at him. 'It's my birthday,' he reads out. 'And I'm twenty-one! Come on, Holly, I've booked us a table at this place just down the road, close to the opera house.'

As we leave the homeless man behind, I find myself turning round, aware of that same old guilt gnawing away.

Giles catches me looking at him. 'It was probably his birthday yesterday too, and the day before.' He rolls his eyes. 'And anyway, if you gave him money it would only go up his nose. Nearly there,' he says, striding on ahead of me. 'They're all addicts.'

No, they're not.

'Here we are.' Giles ushers me through the door of an American restaurant. He clearly knows this place well because the man behind the desk greets him personally, before taking our coats. 'I've booked us a table in the martini bar,' he shouts over the noise. The place is packed full with successful-looking thirty-somethings. 'More laid back than the dining room!' What I reckon he's saying is he can escape after a drink if we have nothing to talk about. Good tactic. I sense he's a pro at this dating game.

'Come and sit down.' He pulls out a bar stool for me. 'What can I get you to drink? Tell me about yourself, Holly,' he says, 'are you a white or red kind of girl? I'm white. Or we could have one of their famous martinis?'

'White's great, thanks.'

Giles grabs the waiter's attention. 'Bottle of Chablis, please, two glasses. So,' he says, returning his attention to me, 'I think it said on your profile you've been married before? Stupid husband, letting you go, if you don't mind me saying.'

'I'm widowed.'

'Oh shit, I'm sorry.'

'Don't worry. You weren't to know. My husband died almost two years ago now.'

'I'm so sorry, that's bloody hard. Cancer?'

'A car accident.'

'Oh crikey, even worse,' he says, as if he has a mental scoreboard in his head. A car accident is the bullseye on a dartboard. 'Do you have children?'

I take my drink gratefully. Despite the dating website saying don't drink too much I knock back a large gulp. And another. I shake my head.

'Lucky,' he sighs as if mentally calculating my predicament's not quite so bad anymore.

I follow the successful first date rules and move on, asking him about his family. 'I don't recommend divorce to anyone, this one was particularly bad.'

'This one?' How many has he had, exactly?

'I've been divorced twice.'

'I'm sorry. And this one was especially awful?'

'For my bank manager. She took me to the cleaners. Anyway,'

he says, as if he doesn't want to dwell on his baggage either, 'it's all in the past and I'm a free agent now.' He winks at me, as if his loss is my gain, before refilling my glass. 'So, what do you do, Holly? I seem to remember you work in advertising?'

'PR.'

'I've never fully understood what it is you do in PR? Is it a lot of schmoozing, taking journalists out for dinner?'

'If only,' I say, laughing since I can't remember the last time I did that. A breakfast meeting and a croissant is about as swanky as it gets. I also feel slightly patronised. If I knew him better, I might say something. If it was Angus, I'd never let him get away with that. Then again, Angus wouldn't... Stop thinking about Angus. 'How about you, you're a hedge funder, aren't you?'

'For my sins.'

'How long have you been doing that?'

'Far too long. Even if I wanted to get another job, I'm not sure I could now. Can't train an old dog new tricks!'

I smile, reminded of one of Angus's exes who spoke in clichés. 'Swings and roundabouts finally pushed me to breaking point,' he'd said on one of our runs.

'If I'm honest, I've never really understood what hedge funders do either,' I admit. 'All I know is it involves a lot of money.'

'And risk. It's not for the faint-hearted.' He touches his chest, as if feeling faint at the thought of all those risks he takes. 'But I love it, it makes me feel *alive*. Wow, you knock it back, Holly,' he says, impressed. As he refills my glass my eyes are drawn to his expensive watch. There is no doubt Giles is a catch for someone. But he's not for me. I can hear Angus saying there should be a TV programme called, '*I'm on a Date, Get Me Out of Here!*'

'So, what do you like doing in your spare time?' I say, feeling light-headed from the wine already.

Let me guess. Driving his fast car and going to the gym.

'Not that I have much spare time,' he chuckles.

He's far too important to have spare time, Holly!

'No, I'm sure not,' I say, wondering if I should go to the loo and ask Milla to call me? Urgently.

'I'm an exercise junkie,' he says, returning to my question. 'Cycling's my passion. In fact, I've invested in a racing bike.' He shows me an image of his recent purchase on his mobile. 'Set me back eight thousand seven hundred quid. Are you into sport?'

'Um, I run three times a week with a friend, and I have a personal trainer too.' I try not to laugh as I say it. If Giles could see Angus, Laurie and me in the park, our motley little team of three, along with our Smiling Assassin, doing burpees and pop squats and seeing who can hula-hula the longest with our pink hoops. Hah!

Giles tells me he has an apartment in Canary Wharf with its own private gym and indoor swimming pool. 'You should come, there's a jacuzzi. And how about you, Holly, what do you like doing when you're not schmoozing clients?'

I find myself telling him about Nina and Soul Food and how much I'm loving cooking again, even if baking is bad for my waistline.

'Doesn't look too bad to me,' he says, raising an eyebrow flirtatiously. 'I might have to swing by, try out one of your puddings.'

Angus whispers into my ear, 'I think he wants to swing by and try you out.'

'Every Christmas my mother used to invite the waifs and strays to our house,' he reflects. 'Got to be honest, I hated having to share my Chrimbo lunch with them, and you could tell some of them hadn't had a shower in weeks. But that's typical Mum. Open house. Caring.'

I wonder if he's adopted.

'Anyway, enough of that. Tell me, Holly, what do you look for in a man?'

As if someone has heard my prayer, my mobile rings. 'Sorry, I'd better take this,' I tell him. On my screen is a number I don't recognise. It's probably Scottish Power. It's a scam, someone trying to sell me broadband. 'Hi Mum,' I pretend. 'What's wrong? Oh no, is he OK? I'll be right there.' I hang up. 'Giles, it's my father, he's fallen down the stairs, I'm so sorry, I must fly.'

'Yes,' he says. There's a pause, as if he's assessing if I'm telling the truth or not. 'Of course. Yes, you must go,' he insists, emphatically patting the front of his jacket and searching the pockets, before apologising profusely for forgetting his wallet.

24

I ring Angus. 'Where are you?' I ask, heading briskly for the Tube station.

'Home,' he replies, before adjusting it to 'At Sophie's.'

My heart sinks.

'Aren't you supposed to be on a date?'

'Disastrous.'

'That bad?'

'Worse.'

'I'm heading back to Scottie's in twenty. Want to come over?'

I stop when I see the homeless man, slumped outside the station. 'Happy birthday,' I say, emptying all the change in my wallet and handing it to him with a fiver. It's Christmas and his birthday.

Scottie and his family are out for dinner with friends, they took the children with them, leaving Angus and me alone. Scottie's kitchen could have been designed and made by Jamie. It's how you'd imagine a professional chef's kitchen to be: open-plan with a white quartz countertop island in the middle, a hanging pots rack above. It's a far cry from Soul Food, though that does have a certain charm now, maybe because I've grown to love the people who work in it.

'Fallen down the stairs?' Angus bursts out laughing.

'I know!' I laugh with him.

'How is your poor dad?'

'Miraculously he's fully recovered from his two broken legs. I shouldn't have lied, should I?'

'He sounds like an arsehole, Holly. I'm surprised you lasted that long.'

I cradle the mug of tea in my hands, relieved to be back in Angus's company, where I belong.

'Do you think he believed you?'

'Probably not.'

'I bet it's probably happened to him before.'

'I ended up paying for our drinks.'

'It's definitely happened to him before.'

'He forgot his wallet.'

'He didn't believe you,' Angus stated, and the more I think about it, the more I agree. That was his payback. 'No sex, so you can foot the bill,' he says.

'To be fair, why should he pay? I'm an independent woman.' I laugh again, not sure why that sounds so funny, but it does. 'At least it was good wine. And at least I drank most of it.' I press my head into my hands. 'Oh Angus, don't *ever* let me go on a date again, what was I thinking?' *Tell me, Holly, what do you look for in a man?* Someone who makes me laugh. Someone who listens. Someone who is generous. Fun. Someone I can trust. Be myself with. Someone I feel safe with. I tear my eyes away from Angus. 'Anyway, how was your evening?'

'It went surprisingly well. Soph and I had a civilised supper.'

'Oh good,' I say, wishing I didn't feel the opposite.

'I think Benjie feels more secure knowing we can be in the same room together.'

'And what about you and Sophie?'

'We haven't spoken about "us" yet. I don't want to push it. She mentioned I could have Benjie and Amy for a whole weekend if I wanted to. She's going on a spa break towards Christmas with a few of her girlfriends. She'd never have asked me a few months ago, so that's got to be positive, right?'

'Definitely.'

'I need to find a job. I mean, whether Soph and I get back together or not, I need to provide for them, and claw back my pride. And more than anything I need something to do. As much as I love watching *Homes Under the Hammer*.'

'No luck then?'

'More rejections. I tell you, it's not easy finding a job at the best of times let alone at our age…'

'Or going on a decent date.'

'Exactly. It's even harder after being sacked. I'm hardly an enticing option.'

'Maybe you should look for something different? You've always said your heart isn't in finance? Maybe your applications are screaming out that you don't want the job?'

'Maybe,' he says, as if he hadn't thought of that. 'I mean banking is death by numbers, but I don't know what I'd do instead.'

'Can't teach an old dog new tricks!'

Angus raises an eyebrow.

'Don't worry. Just mimicking Giles.'

'Well, don't.' He smiles. 'But he's got a point. What I'd love to do is act or work in film again.'

'Well, do it.'

'Don't be daft. That's like saying I want to be a popstar. It's never going to happen.'

'Says who?'

'Says an old man who needs to get real.'

'Come on, life's too short. And you're not old. Well, you're not *that* old.'

'Listen, Holly, the time to take risks is when you're young. I should have listened to my mother before I lost my nerve. She told me to pursue acting, be different, but all I could think was I'd never be good enough or earn a decent salary. I remember meeting a theatre director who helpfully told me ninety-nine per cent of actors don't make it. I panicked. But I should have followed my gut back then,

205

when I had no ties, no family, no Benjie to worry about, no Amy to fund through school, no marriage to fix. I can't follow that pipe dream now. I need to get a job that pays the bills. We have some savings set aside, and Soph works, but I can't be unemployed forever.'

I nod, accepting this with reluctance. 'I didn't know you loved acting?'

His face lights up. 'I remember this one time, at school, reading *Great Expectations* aloud. It was a passage with Joe and Pip and the teacher said, "All of you, keep that in your head. That's how you read a book." That comment always stuck with me. It's why I find banking so soulless. What I'd love is to be on stage, or writing plays or books. I sound like a pretentious loser, don't I?' He laughs at himself.

'No,' I say, thinking this is why I love being with Angus. I always discover something new about him.

'I used to love drumming too, used to whack pots and pans in the kitchen. I was in a band at school, played 80s alternative rock. I always had dreams about us reuniting.'

'Angus, your life isn't over.'

'Yeah, but time isn't exactly on my side. I mean, I don't have time to buy unripe bananas.'

'Oh stop it! You're young enough to still have dreams, and do the things you love, and buy green bananas.'

He looks sheepish.

'I get what you're saying,' I continue. 'You have a responsibility towards your family, but what's the point of going into another soulless job that will only drive you to drinking and smoking again, and feeling miserable? You'll undo all the hard work we've done. We at least owe it to ourselves to be happy, or happier, don't we, when life is short?'

'I'm sorry. You're right. Life is short.'

'So stop acting like yours is almost over.'

He nudges me. 'You OK? You have that serious look, Holly.' He furrows his own brow.

'I feel blue,' I admit, 'and it's nothing to do with Giles.'

'Jamie?'

'I don't know,' I say, confused and cross with Milla for sowing seeds in my head. I don't have feelings for Angus. I can't have feelings for him. It's a road I cannot turn into, let alone go down. Yet he was in my head for half the date. He might as well have been sitting beside me.

'Do you want to talk about it?' he asks. 'God knows you've counselled me enough.'

'Grief is weird,' I tell him. 'It makes me feel like I live this double life. There are still things I enjoy. I mean, I'm here with you and you always make me laugh. I don't go around feeling miserable, but I feel Jamie's absence all the time. When anything happens, like my date tonight, I want to tell him. I miss the way we used to talk. I miss how we did nothing together. There aren't that many people you can do nothing with, are there?'

'I guess not.'

'Jamie was my nothing and everything person. And as much as I long for a new life, a new chapter,' I say, thinking about what Mum had said to me earlier this evening, 'I dread everything I'll have to do without him. That's why I didn't want to be on my own this evening. I couldn't face returning to an empty flat.' Whenever I step inside my home, Jamie's presence is all around me, in the shape of our photographs, his art on the walls, his art and design books on the shelf, the kitchen he made for us, even the chipped mug with his initial in the cupboard. I feel choked with emotion. 'I know it sounds pathetic.'

'It doesn't sound pathetic. I'm sorry your date didn't go well, but honestly, Holly, you'll meet someone else. You'll find a new life. I know you will, because you're gorgeous, funny, wise, headstrong, beautiful and any man in his right mind would be lucky to have you. I'd be—' He stops.

I wait, pleading with my eyes for him to carry on.

'You won't be on your own forever,' he ends up saying.

'Sometimes it's hard, Angus.'

He edges closer to me. 'I can't imagine, Holly. I wish there was something I could do, or say, to make it better.'

'Hold me?' I ask, craving his touch.

'I can do that,' he says, allowing me to rest my head against his chest. He puts an arm around me and rubs my shoulder gently with his thumb, telling me it's going to be all right. It scares me that Angus was the first person I wanted to call after my date. That throughout the entire evening I kept on fantasising that he was with me instead. That somehow, over the past five months, he has become one of the most important people in my life. But what scares me most is hearing the sound of Scottie's keys in the front door, and realising how much I don't want Angus to let me go.

25

Six weeks later

As winter darkens the sky, Angel's classes now take place either under the arches at Ravenscourt Park, Angel bringing her lamp, or occasionally during my lunch hour too. 'How's your Saturday place going?' Harriet asks me, as I put my trainers on and brush my hair. Harriet knows all about Sander and his cinnamon buns, she loves hearing about Tom's endless marriage proposals, she wants to buy Craig a decent tent, but perhaps the people she's interested in most, unsurprisingly, are Angus and Laurie. I tell Harriet about Scottie getting in a terrible state last weekend because we had a new volunteer in the kitchen, a middle-aged gentleman called Peter who didn't know what he was doing, despite telling Nina in his interview that he was a brilliant cook, a modern man who threw regular last-minute dinner parties so knew how to cook under stress. The pressure for Scottie to produce a meal by 12.30 does build throughout the morning, and it only takes one person not to follow his instructions, thinking they know how to do it better, to make him explode. '"You do it like that, do you?" I could hear him say, standing dangerously too close. I thought Scottie was going to whack him over the head with his saucepan.'

Harriet tuts. 'Poor Peter. I can shout at you. I *pay* you.'

'You don't shout at me.'

'Wouldn't dream of it. I'm a gentlewoman. But I could, if I wanted to. Scottie sounds more frightening than Clarissa Pope.' Harriet and I look at one another, before both shaking our heads adamantly, saying 'no' and laughing. She peers at me from behind her glasses. 'And how's Angus?'

I think about our morning together, about three weeks ago. He came over for coffee and we brainstormed ideas, Googled jobs on the Internet, scrolled through social media sites, including LinkedIn. We bought a heap of weekend papers and scrutinised their Employment section. I helped him liven up his CV. All it needed was a few tweaks here and there. 'Tell them your passion is acting, and drumming,' I said, 'makes you sound cool.'

'Cool? How old are you?'

'Twenty-one. Makes you sound human.'

I discovered a small local theatre in Shepherd's Bush was advertising for a finance director. That was the job that excited him the most. It's a drop in his salary but we agreed that he should apply for jobs that make him want to get out of bed. To be honest, he needs a job now, *any* job, to give him structure and purpose. The only thing keeping him sane is running every day, and Angel's classes, plus he's joined an amateur dramatics club.

'He's lucky to have you, Holly,' Harriet says.

'He'd do the same for me.'

'You've become close, haven't you?'

'He's a good friend. Right,' I say, grabbing my bag before any further interrogation can begin.

'Any luck on the dating front?'

I've been on two more since my fateful evening with Giles, and I have one tonight, not that I'm madly looking forward to it. I know I've got to snap out of my mood. Mr Right could be sitting opposite me and I'm not even noticing him.

'No luck, yet,' I say. 'Right, better go, want me to get you a coffee or anything?'

'I was involved once with a married man,' she says.

I stop dead by the door, my heart beating fast. 'Harriet, I'm not involved, not like that.'

She either didn't hear, or she doesn't believe me. I'm guessing which one it is when she says, 'Be careful. It rarely ends well.'

'Three, two, one,' counts Angel. 'OK, from here you're going to come into a full plank, and hold,' she instructs, as Laurie, Angus and I lie on our mats, contorting ourselves into awkward shapes and poses. 'For twenty seconds.' She starts to count down to one. 'Bring yourself into a plank again, this time on your forearms. That's *so* good, Laurie.'

'Teacher's pet,' Angus calls out.

'Shut up and hold,' Angel tells him. 'Twenty seconds.'

'You said twenty seconds five seconds ago,' he argues.

'Twenty-five now!'

'Cruel!' I shout out breathlessly, still trying to forget what Harriet said. How did she know? I haven't said a word to her. I mean, I talk about the café, it's a huge part of my life, but why does everyone think I'm falling in love with Angus? Being close doesn't mean being involved or in love, does it? At the same time, I'm certain Angus feels something for me. I can feel it. Maybe his marriage is over? Being married doesn't mean you own that person. Am I bad wanting his marriage to be over? Do I? I can't. I don't.

Holly, *stop!* This has got to stop. Snap. Out. Of. It.

I am not, categorically not, falling for Angus. I care for him deeply. Oh fuck. I have feelings. But these feelings are feelings, that's all, and I can control them. I don't want them to get in the way of our friendship, or his marriage. I won't let them. He has a family that need him. Benjie needs his father. And so does Amy, even if she doesn't know it, or think it.

Oh fuck. Calm down, Holly. What was it my therapist, Susan, used to say to me? It's human to have feelings, it's what you do with them that counts.

'Holly, you are on fire!' Angel says, as I complete another circuit of press-ups, pop squats, lunges, planks, burpees and skipping in record time, determined to banish Angus from my thoughts. 'Go, Laurie,' Angel encourages, watching her jogging towards us after doing a lap around the park, to the tennis courts and back. 'Quick water break,' Angel suggests, 'then I want you on your mats again. It's time for some downward dog. Angus, get off your phone!'

'Yes, get off your phone,' Laurie mimics.

'I got it,' he says, eyes widening in disbelief. He turns to Laurie and me. 'I got it!'

'Got what?' Laurie asks.

My smile mirrors his. 'You got it?'

He nods.

'Oh my God, he got it!' I shout to Angel and Laurie.

Angel places her hands on her hips. 'Have you got any idea what they're on about, Laurie?'

'None,' she replies. They laugh, watching Angus and me jump up and down together, hugging like excited children. 'Whatever he got, I want it too,' Angel says.

'Me too,' Laurie agrees.

After we say goodbye to Laurie at the shelter, Angus walks me back to the office. 'Thank you,' he says.

'You don't need to thank me.'

'You gave me the shove I needed. You were the one who saw this job opening. I wouldn't have got it if it weren't for you, Holly. I wouldn't be here, if it wasn't for you.'

'Oh, stop it, my head's getting big,' I say. 'Carry on,' I add, nudging him.

'Let's go out tonight. Let me take you out, my shout, to celebrate? And I promise you I won't forget my wallet.'

I smile. 'You don't need to do that.'

'I know, but I want to.'

My head tells me to say no but my heart is in the lead. 'Oh.' I place a hand over my mouth. 'I forgot. I have a date.'

'Cancel it. Get your dad to fall down the stairs again. He needs to be more careful, your dad. Cut down on the sherry.'

'Whisky. I don't know.' Maybe I should say no?

'Let's go dancing,' Angus continues.

'I haven't done that for years.'

'Precisely.'

'OK.' I'm still unsure. Part of me is thinking I should go on my date.

'We can ask Laurie and Ian,' Angus says, his mind racing on ahead as he sends Laurie a text, and I notice I feel disappointed, unsure I want them to crash our date. But then it's not a date, Holly. I feel torn. Maybe I shouldn't cancel my original plans? I can celebrate Angus's new job another time. He can go out with the others. Though maybe it would be more fun to go out dancing with everyone? Let's face it, the next date is bound to be as disappointing as the last one, and then I'll be sitting at home, alone, wishing I'd made a better choice.

'I'm going to call Scottie and Nina too,' he says, before sensing my hesitation. 'Weren't you the one who said life is too short? Come on, Holly, we deserve some fun, don't we?'

26

'Hope the date goes well,' Milla says as I'm getting ready to go to an 80s-inspired nightclub in Fulham. I'm wearing a raspberry pink and orange-coloured retro print halter-neck dress which I wore at Milla's fortieth birthday party almost five years ago, which I haven't worn since, along with my knee-high black leather boots.

'I'm not going,' I tell Milla, trying to sound casual. 'I'm going out with Angus.'

'Oh right. How come?' she asks, trying to sound equally as casual.

'He got the job. We're going out to celebrate.'

'Oh my God, that's great news. But what about the date?'

'Next week. He was cool about it.'

'OK. Good. That's great about Angus. I must meet him one of these days.'

'Yeah, definitely.'

'Well, have fun,' she says, her voice stilted.

'Thanks. Should be a laugh. There's a group of us going.'

'Great.'

'Send my love to Dave and the children.'

'Will do.'

'Love you.'

'Love you too,' says Milla, before hanging up.

She might not say she's worried about me, but she doesn't have to. That's the trouble with a best friend. We can read each other like books. She knows I'm trying too hard to make it sound casual. She knows, deep down, that I am lying as much to myself as I am to her.

The guy behind the brightly lit bar does Tom Cruise proud, making and shaking our cocktails. Angus is still off alcohol, and Laurie and Ian don't drink as they don't fancy failing the breathalyser test at the night-shelter and sleeping rough tonight. Thankfully Scottie and Nina join me, ordering pina coladas. As I hand Laurie her Diet Coke, I think how much she has grown in confidence. Never in a million years could I have imagined the Laurie I initially met at Soul Food standing in a crowded nightclub. She still wears baggy T-shirts tucked into men's trousers and tonight is no exception: no makeup, and she's cut her hair as short as Angus's. I get the impression Laurie's clothes and her boyish hairstyle serve to stop people, especially men, looking at her in *that* way. Perhaps it helps her to feel safer? But she told me the exercise has helped her back pain, and sleeping on a bed isn't nearly so uncomfortable as it used to be. I've also noticed she doesn't breathe as heavily when she's standing beside me. 'Cheers,' I say, raising my glass to Laurie's, adding, 'This place is amazing, isn't it?'

'I like ABBA,' she says.

We have travelled back to the 80s, with its Rubik's cube and cassette tape tables, animal-print seating, and a giant retro fish tank. Angus had wanted to relive our youth by taking us to a club where we could dance to music we knew the words to. Angus joins us. 'Come on you two, and Ian.'

'I've never been to a nightclub,' she tells Angus, staying firmly put. 'I can't dance.'

'Nor can I,' I say.

'By the end of the evening I promise you you'll be able to dance as badly as me,' Angus tells Laurie, taking her hand and leading her on to the dance floor. Whatever Angus says, it always seems to do the trick. Because Laurie is dancing with us. He should work in sales, not finance.

* * *

It's eleven o'clock and the dance floor is heaving. Nina, Scottie, Ian and I are chatting round our table. Scottie is saying something about Angus's new job, Nina's discussing plans for Soul Food's Christmas party, and Ian told me on the quiet that he's moving out of the night-shelter into a joint living space, but he hasn't had the courage to tell Laurie yet. He needs to find the right time. I'm feeling steadily tipsier, the words floating around me as I watch Angus dance with Laurie to ABBA's "Dancing Queen". Laurie isn't the only one who has changed. I look back to meeting Angus at the café, wearing clothes he'd worn the night before, smelling like he'd crawled out of a dustbin.

As if reading my mind, Nina shouts across the table, 'Got to hand it to him, he's pulled himself together. So has Laurie. She could barely look us in the eye.'

'She's a legend,' says Ian, getting up and joining her on the dance floor.

Nina turns to me. 'So have you, Holly. You've changed.'

'Have I?' I take another gulp of my drink before leaning towards her, intrigued. 'How?'

'The day I interviewed you, I knew there was something you weren't telling me. I've interviewed enough people to sense things like that. I could see it. Feel it. Some people volunteer at the café to show off their cooking.'

'Never works,' calls out Scottie. 'Nina's giving Pete the boot.'

'I thought maybe you were going through an unhappy marriage, or a divorce. Angus wondered that too. We had a quick word over lunch, he told me if I didn't hire you, he'd quit. I told him I'd hire you if he had a shower and shaved.'

A smile spreads across my face.

'You're happier, Holly,' Nina continues, 'well, you seem it.'

'Who's happier?' Angus asks, joining us at our table, before grabbing my hand. 'Your turn, Holly.'

'Time for my bed.' Nina yawns, getting up from the table.

'Me too. Don't be late,' Scottie calls out to his brother.

Ian also says he and Laurie need to get home, back before their midnight curfew.

'Lightweights,' Angus calls back, before returning his attention to me. 'We don't need to go yet, do we?' he asks, like a child not wanting to leave the party.

'No,' I decide, reasoning my bed can wait.

Angus and I dance until the early hours of the morning. We dance our hearts out to Madonna, David Bowie, Blondie and George Michael. With Angus, just as I did with Jamie, we dance as if no one's watching us, because no one is. I look around, people throwing their heads back, singing, flinging their arms, forgetting all about their problems, for one night. And it feels great. I feel alive.

Angus and I walk home, hand in hand. It doesn't feel weird. It feels right.

'That was one of the best nights I've had in ages,' I tell him, still hearing the music playing in my ears. Still feeling our bodies pressed close to one another. Angus's breath on mine. Seeing his smile. Hearing his laugh. Feeling young again. Watching him make a fool out of himself. I realise, in this moment, that I love everything about him.

'Think how many calories we burned. Angel would be proud,' Angus replies.

'I wasn't thinking about that,' I say quietly.

'Nor was I.' We reach my front door. Angus doesn't let go of my hand.

'Angus,' I say, looking at him as if he needs to go home, but at the same time, not wanting him to. *Do you want to come in?* is playing on my lips as his grip tightens. Neither one of us asks the question. Angus simply follows me inside, kicking the door shut, before he takes my face in his hands, and we kiss, urgently, as if this is our only chance to be together. There is no hesitation in my mind or body.

I'm too tired to wonder if it's right or wrong, or if it will ruin our friendship. The truth is, our friendship crossed a line some time ago. The only thing my body tells me, right now, is how much I crave Angus's touch, and that I don't want to wake up tomorrow, alone.

27

'You know what?' Angus says, as we approach a table by the window. We're in a café in Hammersmith, located on the corner of the Goldhawk and Chiswick High Road. It's busy at this time of morning, people drinking coffee and working on their laptops. 'We deserve a day off the diet.'

'We deserve a mega fry-up. After all, it *is* Christmas,' says Laurie, sitting down opposite him, 'and I've just been paid.' Laurie means she has received her benefits.

'Well in that case,' I say, picking up the menu, 'I'm ordering everything.' Though I'm not hungry. I haven't eaten properly for days.

'I'm not paying then,' Laurie says with a small smile.

The three of us have been on one of our morning runs. Laurie recently asked Angus and me if she could join in, she wanted to get fitter, faster. Angus and I picked her up from the night-shelter at ten to eight, before getting a telling-off for being five minutes late. Rich, we felt, given we used to have to drag her out of bed and into a tracksuit.

As I order at the bar, I glance over my shoulder and see Angus talking to Laurie. I sense he's trying as hard as I am to appear normal in front of her. But at some point, we need to talk about the other night. Clear the air. Though the idea fills me with dread.

'Thinking of Christmas,' Angus says to Laurie, as I return to the table, 'any plans?'

'Chocolate,' Laurie replies. 'Me and Mr Cadbury will be hanging out a lot.'

'Does the night-shelter do Christmas?' I ask Laurie.

'Oh yeah, turkey and all the trimmings, but I can't eat turkey, it gives me wind.' Laurie's deadpan tone always makes things sound funnier than they should be. 'I prefer gammon. And we do presents and everything.'

'What do you want, Laurie?' Angus asks. 'If you could have anything?'

'The boys said they were going to club together and get me something nice. Maybe my own place?' she whispers, as if she shouldn't dare ask for it. 'I had a meeting with my support worker yesterday. They want to move me into independent living soon.'

'That sounds good,' I say, noticing Laurie tap her foot against the floor, 'but scary?'

'Dead scary. I've never lived by myself. Even when I was homeless there were always other people about. It was lonely, but I had no responsibilities except feeding myself. And I'll miss Ian.'

'Your bodyguard,' Angus says.

'Yeah, my bodyguard. He's moving out too. He wants us to move in together some day. Mind you that's probably 'cos I do all his washing and mend the holes in his jumpers. He had a job interview the other day, and guess what fool was ironing his shirt?' She points to herself. 'Moi. "Laurie, can you do this, Laurie, can you mend that?" Anyone would think I was his bloody mother, not his girlfriend.'

'He loves you, Laurie,' Angus says.

She laughs, secretly delighted. 'He's the first guy I've ever trusted. Apart from you, Angus, but you don't count.'

'Thanks,' he says, before reflecting, 'Hang on, why don't I count?'

''Cos you're like a dad to me.' I catch Angus's eye, close to tears. Mind you, everything right now is making me want to cry. 'I know I've got to leave,' Laurie goes on, 'but the shelter's been my first real home.' She bites her lip as she thinks. 'But I do want to find my forever home. Since I was a little girl, I dreamed about having my own house, no rules, no grown-ups. I could get up when I want, keep my bedroom door unlocked at night, no set days to do the washing, have the TV remote to myself. I could drink juice out of the carton,' she says, as if imagining herself in her own kitchen now. 'And fill the fridge with all the things I want to eat, like veggies and fruit. I'd have cats and dogs. And I'd have a kid, a little girl, maybe in a couple of years. We'd go on picnics and I'd read her bedtime stories, all the things I never got.' She stops, breathless. 'One day,' she sighs.

'One day, Laurie,' I agree, hoping with all my heart that that day will come.

'One day,' Angus says too, 'and that little girl will be lucky to have you.'

'Shut up,' Laurie says, 'or you'll make me cry and I don't want to cry in public. Anyway, how about you, Angus?' she asks, moving on. 'What do you want for Chrimbo?'

'If you'd asked me that six months ago—' He stops in his tracks. Clears his throat. 'I'd have said I wanted my old life back.'

'And now?' Laurie asks.

'I still want my old life back, but it's complicated.'

'You're talking in riddles, mate.' Laurie rolls her eyes. 'What's complicated?'

Angus puts down his knife and fork. 'Sophie's asked me to stay for Christmas.'

'That's great!' she exclaims. 'Isn't it?'

I tell myself there was never any doubt he'd be spending Christmas with his family.

Laurie frowns. 'What's the problem? You look like someone's poked you in the eye with a dirty stick.' I'm grateful for her being here, to fill the space that I can't.

'No problem, it's all good,' he says, still avoiding eye contact with me.

'How about you, Holly?' Laurie asks.

'Um, well I'll be staying with my parents.' *Don't cry.*

'That'll be nice,' Laurie says.

221

'Lovely,' I agree, reminding myself to feel grateful for my parents; I have a home to go to. Yet, my gratefulness doesn't negate the dread. Christmas or any anniversary is hard.

'Sophie's asked me back,' Angus says to Laurie and me.

'Back?' Laurie waits. 'For good?'

Angus nods.

'Why d'you look so sad then?' She waits. 'Holly, what's *up* with him?'

'No idea,' I say, feeling the colour drain from my face.

Laurie notices I've barely touched my food. 'You haven't eaten your bacon? What's wrong with you? You two are freaking me out.'

I feel sleep-deprived and close to tears. 'Listen, I need to make a move,' I say, heading to the counter to pay, anything to get away, adding over my shoulder, 'I'll do this.' Alone, I can breathe. It's going to be OK. This was always going to happen.

Yet the idea of Angus not knocking on my door before we go out for our runs, the idea of not seeing him each Saturday at the café, makes me feel indescribably sad. I wish he hadn't told me like this, with no warning. Not after the way things were left between us.

'Let me,' he says, distracting my thoughts, gesturing to his credit card.

There's yet another awkward silence until we both say, at the same time, 'About the other night…'

'I wanted to tell you earlier,' Angus claims.

'I wish you had.'

'I didn't know how.'

'It's good news,' I insist, willing myself to stay strong until I get out of here.

'Is it? I'm all over the place.' He taps his credit card against the machine. 'Can we meet tonight?'

'I don't know.'

'To talk things through?' he urges, as we head back to join Laurie.

I shake my head. 'I can't do this anymore. It's not fair. Be with your family, Angus.'

'Holly?'

'Angus, don't.' Out of the corner of my eye I see a little girl, about four years old, in a duffle coat and boots, running down the Goldhawk Road, heading towards the traffic lights at the Chiswick High Road junction. 'Chloe!' I hear someone calling.

'She's going to stop, isn't she?' I say out loud. 'Where's her mum?'

She's precariously close to Chiswick High Road now, early morning traffic moving in both directions. It's clear she's too young to have any road or traffic sense. She's running, escaping from Mum. Angus's pace quickens. 'What the fuck?' he says as he races out of the café. Everything happens in a split second. Angus rushing out into the main road. A mother running, screaming now, 'Chloe! Stop! Come back!' Angus grabbing the little girl from behind, pulling her back. Mum racing to Chloe, taking her arm, pulling her off the road. The sound of a car horn. Angus flung in the air. His body slams against the bonnet before he crashes to the ground. More screaming. And this time, I realise the screaming is coming from me.

Laurie and I rush outside and kneel beside him. He's lying motionless, blood smeared across his forehead. 'Angus, Angus, talk to me, are you all right?' Laurie asks, prodding his arm.

My hand shakes as I call for an ambulance.

'Is the patient breathing?' the woman asks on the other end of the phone.

When Angus groans, I am overwhelmed with relief that he is alive. 'Yes, yes he is.'

'Tell me where you are and what happened,' she asks, her tone calm.

I tell her, quickly. 'He's been hit by a car. He can't speak or move and his leg, his foot, it's pointing out at a weird angle.'

'Someone will be with you straightaway.'

'Hurry, please,' I urge.

'It's already dispatched. Don't move him, keep him as still as possible, just talk to him and keep him warm.'

Disorientated, Angus tries to sit up, but he's paralysed with pain and confusion. 'Don't move,' I tell him, squeezing his hand, as Laurie takes off her baggy jumper and places it over him, like a rug.

* * *

Never before have I been so relieved to see an ambulance, followed by two men in bottle-green jumpsuits rushing towards Angus. I watch as one of them approaches Angus from behind, and places both his hands on either side of Angus's head, to make sure he can't move a fraction of an inch. 'Hi there, Angus, I need you to keep as still as you can for me,' he says. For all we know, Angus could have a neck fracture, and be at risk of never walking again.

'He's going to be all right, isn't he?' the mother asks, Chloe sobbing beside her.

'Angus, can you tell me what happened?' the paramedic asks, catching my eye and nodding reassuringly.

Angus groans in agony again.

'Don't worry, hang on in there,' he says as another paramedic is now checking his pulse, his breathing. Quickly and efficiently, he examines his body, feeling and applying pressure against his stomach, hip and pelvis area. They check for bruising and if he's losing any more blood. They take his blood pressure. They slide a gadget on to his finger which I know is to check his oxygen. 'You're doing well,' the paramedic says to him. 'How's the pain?'

The panic and pain in Angus's eyes say it all. They give him some gas and air.

Give me some too.

'What are you doing now?' Laurie asks as one of them touches Angus's foot again. 'Is he going to lose it?'

'What happened?' another passer-by asks me, but I'm too anxious to respond to anyone. I overhear one of the team saying something about a displaced fracture. Clearly, they're worried about Angus's right foot, and so am I. It looks as if it's dislocated from his leg, and from what I can make out they're struggling to feel a pulse. I watch one of them pressing a finger against his foot once more. 'Would everyone mind giving us a bit of space?' says one of the ambulance crew. Traffic has piled up. People are getting out of their cars. Walkers stop, distracted by the drama. The mother and child are still here, Chloe now locked in her mother's arms. Angus has quite an audience. I know, if he could, he'd make a joke even now, saying it wasn't exactly his idea of a leading role. But he'll take it as it might be the only chance he'll have. And he'd better be awarded an Oscar for his bravery.

It feels as if there is no time to lose now, they've got to get Angus to the hospital urgently. I watch as he's carefully scooped up off the ground with minimal movement, and is now lying on a stiff yellow board. His neck is in a collar, his head protected on either side by two orange blocks and he's strapped on to this board. I watch as they lift him into the back of the ambulance. I put an arm around Laurie, telling her it's going to be OK. Angus is a fighter; he's not going to give up. I rush forward, asking one of the team if I can come with him.

'Of course, but probably best if only one of you comes,' he says when Laurie approaches.

'I'll call the moment I have news,' I promise.

'I ain't waiting for a call,' she says, 'I'll get a bus. Where we going?'

The doors shut and the siren blasts as we head, at full speed, towards St Mary's Hospital in Paddington.

As the ambulance careers towards the hospital, I look down at Angus, less alert now and so vulnerable, his life in their hands. At least he's been given some morphine for the pain. Never before have I felt this powerless, and it's terrifying. All I'm good for is keeping his belongings safe. I have his jacket, his wallet, his mobile. I pick up the mobile and search in his contacts to find her name. The most painful call I've ever had to make was ringing Jamie's mother to tell her that her son had died. This comes a close second. I hear the ringing tone, my heart thumping in my chest. To think that only a couple of hours ago I thought my biggest problem was untangling the mess Angus and I created last week. She picks up instantly. 'Angus?'

'Sophie, this is Holly.'

'Holly?'

'I'm Angus's friend, I'm calling from his phone.'

'What's going on?'

'Angus has had an accident.'

'What?'

'I'm in an ambulance with him.'

'Is he OK?'

'I don't know.'

'You don't know?'

'He was hit by a car.'

'How bad is it? Where are you?'

'They're taking him to St Mary's Emergency department.'

'Is he going to be all right?' Her tone is frantic. 'I'm on my way. What happened?'

'He was knocked unconscious, and he's hurt his leg, his foot, but they've given him some morphine.' I hear her running. It sounds as if she's racing down a flight of stairs.

'How did this happen?'

Briefly I explain.

Her voice softens. 'Oh Angus.'

'I'm so sorry, Sophie.'

'Thanks for letting me know and being with him…' She trails off. 'Sorry, who are you again?'

'Holly.'

'Holly. Right.' I hear her slamming a door, turning on an engine. She must be in her car.

I feel an overwhelming wave of guilt. 'We met at Soul Food. I'm a volunteer,' I say, as if that somehow makes our friendship more innocent. Then I feel even more guilty for feeling put out that Angus hasn't mentioned me to Sophie. It sounded as if she had no idea who I was.

Upon arrival at the resuscitation area, a whole team of doctors and nurses gather round Angus. There must be about ten of them. Clearly, they were expecting him.

'Patient is a forty-eight-year-old male,' says one of the doctors, 'struck by a car travelling at approximately 20mph – bullseye damage to windscreen. C-spine immobilised. Spontaneously breathing but with reduced level of consciousness with a GCS of 12.'

Again, I feel so helpless, useless, as I hear them discussing Angus in a language that's difficult to understand.

'Bruising over the right side of his chest. Tachycardic at 120 with a blood pressure of 110 over 60. He has a dislocated ankle with poorly palpable pulses.'

'Can I stay with him?' I ask.

They either don't hear me or are understandably too distracted to answer, but as they haven't said no…

'I'm sorry, but we need to look after him now,' says one of the doctors, taking me to one side as Angus is wheeled away into resus, which I know from Milla is where the sickest patients in an emergency department go. Doctors and nurses are rushing around in scrubs and all I can see is endless monitoring equipment attached to the wall, beds and patients and beeping noises coming from machines presumably keeping them alive. 'There's a waiting room for relatives and family on this floor, round the corner. When I have any news, I'll come and find you.'

'He's going to be all right, isn't he?' I can't help asking yet again, but please, *please* give me hope.

'We'll do our very best for him,' he says, which isn't anywhere near enough for me.

Yet the frightening truth is he probably doesn't know.

28

'After you'd gone the coppers arrived,' Laurie tells me, flustered when she finds me in the relatives' waiting room. She pulls out her earphones. 'They want to speak to you.'

I hadn't even thought about the police, or the driver, and how desperate they must feel. None of this was anybody's fault. Laurie paces the room. 'You heard anything from his wife?' she asks, twisting a strand of her short hair round and round.

'She's on her way,' I say, as the doctor I spoke to previously enters the room. He glances at Laurie.

'We're together, it's fine,' I explain, before urging Laurie to sit down next to me. 'Is there any news?'

'We've done an initial assessment.'

'Is he all right?' Laurie asks, tapping her foot up and down, up and down.

I can tell from his grave expression, and from the heaviness in the room, that Angus is far from all right. 'We're worried about some of Angus's injuries, and need to do a full scan, top to toe.'

'What do you mean? What are you worried about?' I continue, dreading the answer.

'The pain in his neck and spine,' he replies, confirming my fear that Angus might never walk again. 'We need to do further tests to see if there is damage to the spinal cord. I'm not saying there is,' he's quick to reassure us, 'but we need to be certain. He also has severe bruising in his chest and he's having trouble breathing.'

'Poor Angus,' Laurie says, breathing heavily herself.

'He's also not fully responsive, but let's face it, he's had a knock to the head, and morphine for the pain so it might just be concussion, but we do need to rule out any other possibility. We also suspect he has a fractured and displaced ankle.'

'What can you do about that?' I ask, not even knowing what it is, but it sounds bad.

'Surgery may be required, and we need to realign the ankle, which basically means pulling it straight.'

'Ouch.' Laurie inhales deeply, wincing with me.

'If we're happy with the position, and there's no break, we'll put his ankle in a cast and let it heal naturally. But we can't do any of this until we know exactly what's going on.'

I know the doctor is being so reasonable and patient with my questions, but I want more specifics. As if he can read my mind, he says, 'I'm afraid, at this stage, we don't know the extent of his injuries.'

I nod. 'How long will it take?'

'The scan doesn't take long, ten or so minutes, and someone will look at the results immediately. He's a priority patient. We'll come and let you know as soon as we can.'

'You promise?' Laurie blurts out.

'I promise,' he says. We are left alone, imagining the worst.

While Laurie sits on the sofa flicking through a magazine, I call Scottie. I try to keep calm and positive, telling myself that one day Angus and I will go on a run again, or we'll all be in the kitchen at Soul Food, and this nightmare of a morning will be a story to tell, not a terrifying reality. I wish I felt as positive as I sound when I explain what happened and what the doctor told us. It's not easy to keep calm when Scottie is upset. The truth is I feel sick to my stomach, as I try to reassure him everything will be OK, that he mustn't feel guilty for being so hard on Angus, and that he will get the chance to tell his brother he loves him. Angus is going to wake up, I tell him, trying to convince myself too. He's going to come round. He will walk again. Yet wherever I look, I see Angus lying on the road. I hear him in pain. I see his foot. See the blood. After finishing my call with Scottie, I tell Laurie I'm going to call Milla, my doctor friend. I need to hear her voice. If there's one person who can reassure me…

'Try not to panic until Angus has had the scan,' she advises.

'What's a displaced ankle fracture?'

'It's where the bone snaps into two or more parts.'

'Oh fuck,' I say, thinking that's going to hurt. Laurie throws the magazine back on to the table and paces the small bare room again.

'It's treatable, Holly. They'll relocate it, stabilise him. They'll be doing everything they can. The scan is ruling out options, not confirming them. He's in the best possible hands, I promise.'

I take in another deep breath. I feel guilty wishing Laurie wasn't here. Her restlessness and anxiety aren't helping.

'I'm sorry, Holly, it must have been such a shock,' Milla says, jolting my thoughts.

I don't think I've processed it yet.

'How are you?' she asks, softly.

There's a part of me that feels proud Angus rushed to the rescue. It would have been against his nature to do nothing. He acted on instinct and saved that little girl's life. Yet, right now, there is another part of me that wishes it had been someone else who'd dived in front of that car. Why didn't we leave the café a few minutes earlier? Why did we have to go on a run this morning? If we hadn't, none of this would have happened. Why had the mother let her child run away from her? Why couldn't she control her? Why, why, WHY? I want to scream.

'Holly? Are you there?'

'Yes,' I say, on the verge of tears.

'They'll let you know as soon as they can. He'll be a priority case.'

I picture Angus again, visualising him attached to every single kind of drip, fighting for his life. I imagine his heartbeat slowing down until it flatlines.

Just as Jamie's had.

'I can't lose him, Milla.'

I realise in that moment that I can't lose another person I love.

'You won't,' Milla says, before promising to call me later.

Laurie stops pacing when I hang up. She stares at me. 'You think he's going to die?' I can see the fear and panic in Laurie's eyes. That she, too, can't lose somebody she loves. Maybe the first person she has *ever* loved.

I shake my head, but I can't speak. No words will come out.

'What if he never walks again?' Laurie persists.

I see images of us dancing that night. Returning home together, hand in hand.

I see Angus racing out into the road.

I hear his body smash against the car.

'Or he can't come to the café, Holly?'

Stop it, Laurie. I can't hear you.

I see his blood.

'Holly!'

I feel sick. I'm going to be sick. I can't breathe.

Laurie rushes over to me. 'Why don't we get something to drink? A cup of tea,' she suggests. 'It's horrible being stuck in here. Holly? We've got to stay positive. Come on,' she beseeches, tugging at my arm. 'Let's go.'

As I get up and follow her out of the room my legs give way and I'm struggling to breathe. Laurie guides me back on to the chair, helps me sit down. 'Breathe in, in through your nose,' she says, kneeling beside me, 'and out through your mouth. In through nose, out through mouth.' She reaches into my handbag for my bottle of water, hands it to me, encouraging me to take sips.

I grip her hand as I try to regulate my breathing. 'I'm here,' she says, squeezing my hand back. 'I'm here. I ain't going anywhere. Keep breathing, Holly. Breathe. In. Out. Here.' She hands me the bottle of water again. 'Angus is going to be OK. He's a survivor. We're *all* survivors, right? We're a team.'

When I look at Laurie, I no longer see a little girl, frightened and alone, clutching Teddy. I realise then that Angus isn't the only one I love. 'You're safe,' she promises, 'safe with me.'

'They ain't nice, are they?' Laurie says.

'They're horrible. I forgot how frightening they are.'

'When was your last attack?'

'The night after Jamie's funeral. I came home to an empty house.' I close my eyes, remembering the chilling silence as I walked through the front door. 'The loneliness can be suffocating, Laurie. I go to bed, lie in the darkness. Everything feels so much worse and scarier in the darkness and if I think about how scared I am, I panic, and can't breathe. It's frightening.'

She nods. 'They're awful, so bad I sometimes think I'm gonna die. They're hard to explain, right?'

I nod.

'I tell Ian to think of someone walking behind me on a street, right, someone like him, six-foot, built like a brick shithouse, and this man puts his arms around me, from behind, and he squeezes me. It's a little squeeze at first, but then it gets tighter and tighter, Holly, and I'm begging him to let go, but it's too late, I can't breathe. I try to get away from him, but my legs are like jelly. I can't walk, can't see, it's like I've got this blurry cap or something over my eyes.'

'It's exactly like that,' I agree. 'How many times do you have them, Laurie?'

'Used to be 'bout twice, three times a week.' She shrugs. 'Now less. Maybe once a week.'

'I didn't know it was that bad.'

She shrugs. 'I'm good at pretending things are better. I had one before I met Angel,' she admits, 'and I had a massive one before my interview at the café.'

'I thought I might have one before mine too.'

Laurie looks surprised.

'Before I started volunteering, I was a recluse,' I tell her. 'Went to work, went to bed. I lost all my confidence. I'm good at pretending things are fine, but the truth is I shut myself off from the world. Volunteering, doing something different, was frightening. Change terrifies me.'

She nods. 'I have them when I'm doing anything new or if I don't know someone.'

I picture Laurie running across the park on that grey drizzly morning. Her effort to turn up to Angel's class feels even more courageous now.

'Thank you,' I say, 'for being with me. I don't know what I'd have done without you, Nurse Laurie.'

'Nurse Laurie,' she repeats. 'I like that.' There's a long silence which Laurie finally breaks. 'I don't want to lose him either, Holly. He's awesome, one of the best people I know.' She nudges me. 'But don't tell him that. Don't want him to get a big head.'

I nudge her back. 'I won't. The moment he's better *you* tell him.'

'He's like a dad to me. And you're like the mother I never had.'

Laurie reaches for the box of tissues on the table. Hands them to me. 'Stop crying!' she says, thrusting a tissue my way. 'I was saying something nice!'

'That's why I'm crying!'

And soon we're both laughing and crying. 'We've had a shit day, haven't we?' she says.

'Not the best.'

'There's shit, right, and then there's *shit*.'

We laugh again, and it feels good, like such a relief. I compose myself, before glancing at my watch. It's been forty minutes since the doctor spoke to us. They must have done the scan by now? He must have news soon? And Sophie is surely going to arrive any minute now? I'm anxious about meeting her, not knowing what

I'll say or how long Laurie and I should stick around, but I figure we'll work it out along the way. The only thing that matters, right now, is Angus.

The doctor returns.

'How is he?' we both ask when he's barely stepped inside the room.

'He's lucky.'

'He's going to be OK?' Laurie asks.

'He's going to be fine.'

'I told you, Holly!'

'Nothing major showed up on the scan,' the doctor reports, 'except for several cracked ribs, concussion, bruising on the lung, a dislocated ankle, but no fracture. We've pulled it straight, and we're happy with the position but it's going to need to go into a cast and then it's two weeks' rest and Angus is looking at four to six weeks on crutches.'

'That's amazing,' I say, never believing in a million years I'd think cracked ribs, a dislocated ankle, bruising on the lung and concussion would be worth celebrating. Without thinking I hug him. And so does Laurie.

He blushes before stepping back and smiling nervously. 'Just doing my job.'

'Is Angus aware of what's happening?' I ask.

The doctor shakes his head. 'He's disorientated and confused, but he's beginning slowly to come round. He's been calling out your name.'

'My name?'

'Yes, he's been asking for Sophie, so I told him he'd see you before too long.'

'She's not Sophie,' Laurie says.

'Oh. Are you Sophie?' The doctor looks at Laurie, clearly confused.

'No. I'm *Laurie*. Sophie is Angus's *wife*,' she puts him straight as a woman rushes into the room, dressed in a navy and white hospital uniform. She looks at me, and then at Laurie, before focusing all her attention on the doctor. 'I heard my name. How is he?'

I stand, crushed, as the doctor repeats to Sophie what he said to us, relief flooding her face when he tells her Angus will only have to endure rest and crutches. 'We'd still like to keep him in for a few days though.'

'Of course,' Sophie replies. 'When can I see him?'

'Soon. We'll be moving him up to the trauma ward shortly, where you can all visit.'

'I'd better go. Thank you for all your help,' I say to the doctor again, before awkwardly shaking Sophie's hand.

'Thanks Holly,' she says, 'for being with him.'

'Laurie's the one you should be thanking,' I say, avoiding eye contact, feeling guilty she's thanking me for anything. *If only she knew. I don't deserve her gratitude.*

As Sophie thanks Laurie, I catch her looking at me curiously, trying to join up the dots of our friendship. I wonder how much Angus has told her about us, if anything. I don't want to hang around to find out. Laurie follows me, tired and keen to go home.

'Wait!' Sophie says as I'm halfway out the door. 'Before you both go… how did this happen again?' I stop, turn to her. Notice how beautiful she is, even when she's distressed, with her long, layered dark blonde hair, and I'm drawn to her vivid green eyes, filled with love, kindness and concern. I recall Angus telling me how much he'd fallen in love with those eyes.

'The three of us had been on a run,' I explain. 'We've been training for a few months now.'

'We met at the café,' adds Laurie.

Sophie nods as if it's beginning to make sense now. 'Ah yes, with Scottie. Angus has mentioned you.'

I continue to tell Sophie what happened, keeping it brief. 'He was unbelievably lucky.'

She sighs. 'He has nine lives, that man.'

I agree. 'Tell him I'll visit tomorrow,' I say, not sure I will or can.

'Me too,' Laurie says.

'Thank you,' she calls after us once again.

As Laurie and I leave, all I can think about is Angus calling out Sophie's name.

I fight the tears, overcome with exhaustion and emotion.

It's over.

Over before it even began.

29

Milla wraps her arms around me. We're alone in her kitchen, Dave is upstairs bathing the twins. I haven't stopped crying since the moment I arrived, the shock of the day finally catching up with me, like a storm that was brewing.

After I left St Mary's, Laurie and I returned by cab to the night-shelter, where Ian was waiting outside, his loyalty touching. While she said she was fine, I was relieved to know she wouldn't be spending the rest of the day alone. As for me, Harriet insisted I take the afternoon off. I spent most of it at home, in a daze.

Empty is how I felt. Relieved for Angus, but empty inside.

When Milla called to see if I wanted to spend the evening with her, I didn't hesitate. I needed someone to talk to, to make sense of my scrambled thoughts. I needed my best friend.

'It's been a shocking day, it's not surprising you feel like this,' she says, the smell of her perfume familiar, her touch comforting. 'But the main thing is Angus is going to be OK.'

'Milla,' I say, withdrawing from her touch.

'What is it?' she asks, recognising from my tone there's something else playing on my mind.

'It's Angus.'

'What about him?' she asks, pulling up a stool and sitting next to me.

I cover my face with my hands. 'Don't hate me.'

'I could never hate you. Did something happen between you?'

'Yes.'

Milla holds my hand as she waits. I inhale deeply, before reminding her about the night we went out dancing, to celebrate Angus's new job. She nods, encouraging me to go on. I pick up my glass of wine, take a sip, before returning to that night.

'You were right. I am in love with him,' I confess. 'I am hopelessly in love with him.'

'Oh, Holly,' Milla says, taking me into her arms.

I knew it when I heard him standing up for Laurie at Pat's nursing home. I knew it when I called the ambulance, praying so hard that Angus wouldn't die. I knew how much I loved him when the doctor told me he'd said Sophie's name because my heart died, for the second time.

'We kissed,' I tell Milla. 'The night we went out, he came back to my place.'

I recall every cell in my body wanting him as he'd unzipped the back of my dress. His phone rang. I was relieved when he ignored it. We kissed once more; his phone rang again. It was as if we were competing against one another for Angus's attention.

The phone won. 'It's Sophie,' Angus said, sobering me up instantly.

'We didn't sleep together,' I tell Milla. 'We probably would have done, but the moment she called Angus left.'

'Why had she called?' Milla asks.

'She'd been trying all night. The music was loud, he hadn't heard, hadn't even looked at his phone. Benjie had spent the day in hospital. She wanted him to come over. He was at home, crying for his dad. She couldn't do it on her own anymore. She needed him.'

That call killed the mood, bringing us both back to reality. I can see Angus now, putting his coat on as he rushed towards the front door. The look in his eye when he apologised was humiliating. 'Go,' I said, unable to maintain eye contact. After he'd left, I locked the door behind him, before sinking to the floor, and crying, hating myself for wishing he'd stayed.

'I should have listened to you, Milla. I guess I was on a high. Being with Angus was like a drug. I loved the way he made me feel. In so many ways being with him reminded me of being with Jamie. I got caught up in the moment, in the idea of us.'

'I get it,' Milla says. 'I'd have felt the same.'

Yet nothing could be more sobering than his wife calling, saying their son needed their dad. Nothing could be more sobering than seeing him run out of the door to be with them. And then today, hearing Angus had called out her name. The truth tends to come out in a crisis. When Angus thought he might die, it was Sophie he wanted. I realise now, I was always playing a game that I was never going to win. I shouldn't have even been competing. 'I feel so stupid,' I confess to Milla, telling her how small I'd felt when the doctor assumed I was his wife. 'I'm such an idiot.'

'No you're not, you had feelings for him, and he obviously had feelings for you too. You're human, that's all. Oh Holly, why didn't you tell me all this before?'

'I felt guilty. Ashamed. I knew you would have said I needed to stop seeing him, to protect myself from being hurt.'

She nods, acknowledging I'm right. That's exactly what she would have said.

'I didn't want to stop seeing him. But when I saw Sophie…' I sigh, still feeling guilty. 'Why does he have to be married?'

'It's sod's law.'

I smile at that.

'Life is messy,' she continues.

'But yours is so neat,' I can't help saying.

'Not all the time.' She refills our wine glasses.

'What do you mean?'

'Dave once had feelings for someone else,' she whispers.

'No? Who?'

'One of his colleagues. I'd had the twins, all my time and energy was taken up with them, he felt rejected and confused and turned to her. They slept together.'

'Oh my God! You never said.'

'Shh. Keep your voice down.'

'Sorry.'

'He made me promise not to, and to be honest, we felt guilty. We knew how much you and Jamie wanted a family. How could we burden you with our problems when you longed for everything we had? I couldn't, Holly. He swore it meant nothing, that it would never happen again. All I wanted to do was put it behind us, move on.'

This is typical Milla; so self-sufficient. She keeps her feelings contained in a box, and very few people, if any, get to unlock it. I always feel like I need her far more than she needs me. 'You forgave him, just like that.'

'Holly, Dave isn't perfect. He was struggling with his depression and didn't know how to handle it or how to talk to me. It's a real cliché, but he was feeling low and unloved, so he turned to someone else.'

'How did you find out?'

'He came home one night, after a conference, and was acting weird. Then it all came out. You know what he's like, he can't lie or pretend to save his life. You should have seen him. He was in tears, begging me not to leave him. I couldn't forgive him, not straightaway. I felt angry, disappointed, but in a way, over time, it brought us closer together. I always trusted he'd never do it again, but it was messy for a while.'

'What was messy?' Dave asks, coming downstairs with Emily and Kate, dressed in their matching flowery pyjamas, their faces pink and glowing, their hair washed and smelling of fresh coconut. How I long to have their innocence and youth. 'They wanted to say goodnight to Auntie Holly.'

'You need to give Auntie Holly an extra big hug and kiss tonight,' Milla says, 'because she's had a hard day.'

'My life's a bit messy at the moment,' I explain to them. 'I'm a little sad.'

Kate and Emily open their arms wide and I find myself holding on to them tightly, breathing them in. How I love the fact they ask no questions; they simply love me unconditionally. And I love them back. Dave also gives me a hug, a man who for so many years, I've placed on a pedestal. Their relationship always appeared untouchable. Invincible. In many ways it's comforting to know we all have flaws and vulnerabilities, that we all create mess. As Dave takes them up to bed to read them a story, I turn to Milla. 'I need to let him go, don't I?'

'Angus?'

'No, Jamie. It's time,' I say tearfully, 'time to scatter his ashes. Will you do it with me?'

30

The following morning, when I wake up, the sun streaming through my bedroom window, I know that not only do I have to say goodbye to Jamie, but to Angus too. I know Laurie will want the three of us to hang out and continue working at the café, but I can't. It's too painful. Because the truth is I do love him. Perhaps I love him most for helping me see a point to life again. For helping me believe in love again.

As I said to Laurie, before I began volunteering, I was stuck in a rut. As a child, routine made me feel safe. After Jamie died, I stuck rigidly to one. There weren't many, if any, shocks or surprises thrown into the mix, and that suited me fine because I couldn't cope with any more. So long as I knew what was coming next, I felt in control. So, I did all the things I was programmed to do: wake up, coffee, work, home, supper washed down with a bottle of wine, or occasionally an evening out with friends, bed. But slowly this routine made my life shrink. It felt as if I was drowning in my loneliness. Angus entered my world and gave me a life jacket. He shook it up, exploding into my life like fireworks.

And then along came Laurie. Our mission to help her wasn't entirely altruistic on my part. Both her friendship, and Angus's, saved me. Before we met, I was dying of loneliness. Angus, too, was on a mission to self-destruct. I guess, in different ways, we all needed each other.

If someone had told me I'd fall in love with a man who reeked of smoke, burped and told me bad knitting jokes, I'd have thought them mad. Never in my wildest dreams did I think I'd fall for him; that wasn't part of the plan. Yet even if I can't have my happy ever after with Angus, he allowed me to reconnect with an old part of myself. He enabled me to see I don't want to live alone for the rest of my life and how I still have a lot to give, and yearn to be loved. He made me see how much I want to fall in love again, only this time with someone who is free to fall in love with me.

As I get out of bed and take a shower, I wish things could be different. I don't want to say goodbye to him at the hospital today; I don't want to let our friendship go. It's like dropping something so precious, so valuable, on to the floor and watching it shatter into tiny pieces. Yet equally I can't pretend nothing happened. I can't switch my feelings on and off like a tap. If only I could.

Angus lies in bed, his ankle in a cast, his face bruised. 'About time I had some attention,' he says with a small smile, when I sit down in the blue plastic chair beside his bed. He gestures to the grapes and homemade ginger biscuits. 'Scottie has never been so nice. Want to see something?'

'Go on.'

He lifts up his T-shirt, and reveals his chest, a lovely deep dark shade of purple.

'Show-off,' I say, sensing he's as nervous as I am. 'How's the ankle?'

'Sore, and it's going to drive me insane being an invalid for six weeks. What am I going to do with myself? I spilt my lunch over my lap today. A baked potato and cottage cheese. That was exciting.'

'But you were lucky.'

He nods, slowing down as he says, 'I was so lucky, Holly.'

We end up talking about yesterday. I get the feeling Angus needs to let it all out, process the trauma of the accident. 'Can't have been easy for you either,' he says finally. 'I was blissfully unaware of pretty much everything going on around me, pumped full of morphine, while you were left to pick up the pieces.'

'It wasn't much fun,' I admit, though don't tell him about my panic attack. 'Don't ever scare us like that again.'

'I'll try not to. How's Laurie?' he asks, and I get the sense he wants to talk about anything but us.

'She's fine. She said she'd come and visit you later. When will they let you out?'

He tells me he'll be going home on Monday, once the physio is happy with him walking up and down stairs on crutches. By home, I assume he means back to Sophie.

I steal one of his grapes, along with a ginger biscuit, trying to build up the courage to talk to him about that night.

'How's the little girl?' he asks.

'Chloe. You saved her life.'

'At least I've done something right,' he says, unable to meet my eye.

'Angus.'

'Holly. I'm sorry things are awkward between us.' He looks at me. 'I care, I really care about you.'

'You said her name,' I say, knowing if I don't bring it up now, I never will. 'The doctor told me you were calling out for Sophie.'

I can't bear the look of sympathy in his eyes again. I don't want it.

'I'm so sorry, I never meant to hurt you. My feelings for you, they were real. They *are* real.'

'I know.' I never doubted that.

'You've been there for me, through so much. I was a sad old excuse of a man before I met you, drowning my sorrows in booze and feeling like the world was against me. Poor old Angus. I was pathetic. You made me see that life is short, that I needed to get a grip and fight for my family. Meeting you, Holly, it's been—'

'Angus, don't,' I say, on the verge of tears.

'I never meant to hurt you,' he repeats, reaching for my hand. 'What can I do? How can I make it up to you?'

'You can't. That's the problem. It's not just your fault, Angus. I shouldn't have let myself get so close to you.' I shrug helplessly. 'You're married.'

'I should tell Sophie.'

'Tell her?'

'About us.'

'Why?'

'I think I need to be honest, don't you?'

'Angus, don't.'

'If our marriage stands a chance?'

'Then don't tell her. Maybe if we'd slept together.'

'But I wanted to, Holly.'

'I know. So did I.'

'When Soph called, I panicked. I raced out that door. I couldn't let them down again, I couldn't, not after what happened last time.'

'I know. Don't tell her,' I say, realising how strongly I feel about this now. 'Look, we need time apart. I can't see you right now.'

He nods. 'I'll drop out of the café. And Angel's classes. I have to anyway, not up to much exercise in this state.'

It's hard to imagine Soul Food without Angus. Or Angel's classes. Nothing will be the same without him. 'What good will it do telling Sophie? It might ease *your* conscience, but what about me? And Laurie?'

'What do you mean?'

'If Sophie knows about me, she'd hate me and never want us to see one another, and I wouldn't blame her for that. But how could I explain it to Laurie? If she knew what happened between us, she'd only worry, get upset that we might stop seeing her too. She sees us like her parents, Angus. We're the first two people who have cared for her, who have actually given a damn. I know we won't be able to spend as much time together, not with your new job and being at home, and you and I need time apart, but we can't abandon Laurie.'

'I wouldn't. I love that girl.'

'Exactly. We kissed, but nothing more,' I say. 'We had feelings for one another, life got messy, but we're going to deal with those feelings by taking some time out and letting them go. But if you tell Sophie about me, the café, then everything blows up in our faces and everyone is a loser. Haven't Sophie, Benjie and Amy been through enough? Hasn't Laurie been through enough?' I realise I've barely drawn breath. 'I mean, do what you need to do, Angus. If you have to tell her, then tell her, but please think about what I've said.'

'I'm going to miss you, Holly.'

'Me too.'

'Whoever said you can only have one soulmate in life was wrong.'

'Don't, Angus.'

'They didn't meet you. If things were different…'

'Don't make this even harder.'

'I have to try and make things work for my family.'

I put on a brave smile. 'You have the chance to be with your family again. Don't screw it up this time.'

'Yeah. Don't go and fall in love with someone else,' he tells himself. 'Especially not with someone as lovely as Holly, someone who doesn't deserve to be hurt again.'

'I'll be fine.' I wipe my eyes. 'I'll buy some cats or something.'

He smiles, before wincing in pain and adjusting his position on the bed.

'Or take up knitting,' I suggest. 'Or maybe I'll give Giles a call? Go and hang out in his jacuzzi.'

'Stop making me laugh, Holly.'

I laugh with him. 'It's better than crying.'

'You're one of the best people I know,' he says. 'You deserve to be happy. I don't.'

'Yes you do.' I rest my head against his arm because I don't want him to see me cry now. Because I know this will be the last time I see him for a while. Gently he strokes my hair. I don't want him to stop. When I'm close to Angus I feel like I'm home. I could stay here forever. He's right. I used to believe in soulmates, that there was only one person out there who could make me happy, but I'm not so certain anymore. Loving Angus doesn't diminish my love for Jamie. It's made me realise there are many people out there who are right for us. If things were different, Angus and I could be together.

We might have stood a chance. We met at the wrong time. Right person, wrong time. If I don't go now… I force myself to get up and leave. 'Be a good patient.'

'Holly?'

'I'll see you around,' I say, knowing I won't.

'Holly?'

I can't turn round.

'Holly,' he repeats.

I keep walking through the ward, towards the nurses' station. I don't want him to see the tears streaming down my face now. As I'm about to leave, a dark-haired boy, about Benjie's age, charges past me. It can't be anyone else.

'Wait, Benjie!' says a harassed-looking Sophie, rushing after him, a sullen teenage girl, with dyed blond hair, ripped jeans, glued to her mobile, lagging behind. I see them approaching Angus's bed, at the end of the ward, by the window.

'Dad!' the boy says, throwing his arms around his father.

'Be gentle, Benjie!' Sophie demands.

'It's all right,' says Angus, hugging him back. 'How's my boy?'

'I'm nearly thirteen Dad, I'm not a boy.'

'Gentle, Benjie. Your father doesn't need another cracked rib,' Sophie says, kissing Angus on the cheek. 'Are you comfortable? Do you need anything?'

I watch Sophie adjust the pillows behind Angus before Amy approaches her dad and he persuades her to give him a proper hug. 'No one's looking,' he says. I know I should leave, but letting him go is one of the hardest things I've ever had to do. I catch Angus's eye, and without words, we say our final goodbye.

31

Milla and I stand at the top of the steps, looking down towards the wide open landscape, the endless miles of golden sand. We spent last night with Jamie's parents before driving to Holkham beach this morning. Over dinner we talked about Jamie. His mother recalled that when he was four, he'd said, 'Now that I'm four, I'm not going to speak to any three-year-olds again.' She'd wiped away a tear. 'He was always grown up before his time.'

'When he met you, Holly,' his father said, 'he said he'd met his match. He'd found his soulmate.'

'Let's go,' Milla says gently, waking me up from my thoughts as we walk towards the sea, wrapped in our coats and scarves, the fresh air bracing, the sky a crystal blue. It's a perfect winter's day, and I swear I can feel Jamie with us. He's by my side.

'It's quiet here, peaceful.'

'I never tire of this view. When I die, I want my ashes scattered here.'

'Stop it.'

'I mean it. When I go.'

'Don't you dare.'

'I want to rest here.'

'Jamie, stop being so morbid.'

'Promise me, Holly.'

I realise now why Jamie wanted his ashes scattered here. It's magical, remote and secluded. Right now, it feels as if there is no one here except Milla and me, and the only sounds I can hear are the sounds of my footsteps across the sand, the gentle waves, and the birds.

'Here,' I say to Milla, when finally we reach the place where Jamie and I went for a swim that Sunday afternoon. I close my eyes, remembering that day, as if it were yesterday. I don't want to let him go yet. I can't. Give me a few more minutes. I see him wading into the water effortlessly. I remember cursing, the water was freezing. But Jamie had urged me to follow him. 'It gets better,' he'd promised. I trusted him. I kept going, and began to feel different, less cold, less inhibited. I felt free. In a way it reminds me of grief. Somehow the pain does recede. The sadness will never go, the grief won't disappear; it gives way to something new.

I look at the sea, and see us so vividly that day.

'This is where he asked me to marry him,' I tell Milla, tears filling my eyes.

'I know it's only been six months, but why wait when you know?' Jamie had said.

'It's the perfect spot then,' Milla says.

I thought I'd be anxious, terrified, to finally let him go, but all I want to do now that we're here is to make Jamie proud. I feel a certain peace. Perhaps it's knowing it's the right time. I picture Jamie, the first time we met in Milla's kitchen. I see us getting married. We chose to exchange our vows in a registry office a year after we met. Neither one of us needed anything fancy. We wanted to save up for our first home together. I recall us discussing if we were unwise to buy a two-bedroom house in west London, would it be big enough for our family? 'Let's cross that bridge when we get there,' he'd said. That bridge never came, but we didn't let the sadness of no children wrench us apart. We were lucky in many other ways. We had ten years of marriage, and while it was cruelly cut short, I only want to hold on to the happy memories now. I see us playing tennis in the park, Jamie laughing, telling me the whole idea is to move towards the ball, not run away from it. I see us in our kitchen, enjoying a meal, telling each other about our day. I see us here, on this beach, racing each other towards the sea. 'Last one in pays for lunch!' he'd called out, knowing it would be me. It was the simple things that made us happy.

The day he proposed was the happiest day of my life.

I look to Milla, who nods, as if to say I can do it. I release the water urn into the sea, and we watch as it floats away. Our song, 'Live Your Life Be Free', comes into my head. I sing it to him now, picturing him so impressed that I could sing that badly. I encourage Milla to join in, and the two of us sing our song until I can no longer see the urn. Yet Jamie hasn't gone, because whenever I hear that song, or return to this beach, or to our old haunts, I can feel him close to me.

32

Six months later

'No Angus today?' Dr Stratton says as we follow her into her office. It's a Monday morning, officially my least favourite day of the week, and it's ten past nine, and Laurie's come in for her regular follow-up appointment. Angus, Laurie and I saw Dr Stratton about six months ago, just before Angus's accident last year and clearly, she was expecting the three of us again. That's why I couldn't say no to coming here with Laurie today. While Angus can't be as involved in Laurie's life anymore, I can. Though in many ways, I feel she'd be more than capable of seeing Dr Stratton on her own now.

'He's at work, he has a new job, in the theatre,' Laurie replies, taking a seat next to Dr Stratton's desk. She seems calm this morning, less fidgety. Now that she knows Dr Stratton and what to expect, her anxiety is under control. I feel that familiar ache in my heart when I see the empty chair by my side. Angus's absence in this room, in my life, still hurts. I haven't seen him, nor have we communicated, since we said goodbye at the hospital before Christmas. I miss him, more than I should, probably more than I'd dare to admit. Even if it has to be this way, life is greyer without him. But I have a new man in my life: Bruno. It's unconditional love. Finally, I decided to get that dog Jamie and I had always longed for. He's a rescue, from Battersea, a Jack Russell mixed with a Beagle. He comes with me almost everywhere. Harriet dotes on him. It was love at first sight. Laurie spotted him first. 'That's the one,' she'd said, pointing to a small sturdy dog lying down at the back of his cage, 'the one with the cute little brown patch over his eye.' Meanwhile, Angus and Laurie are still in touch. They send one another texts and funny videos. I told Laurie a white lie, that Angus and I do occasionally catch up on the phone. Deep down, I believe she realises we became more than friends, that perhaps our relationship was more complicated than we let on. After all, it was Laurie who noticed we had feelings for each other months ago. Yet she's kind enough not to quiz me on it. I sense she doesn't want to upset anyone, including Angus, so she lets it be. And I love her even more for that. I always want us to be remembered as a team of three.

'So, how is the exercise and food diary going?' During Laurie's last appointment Dr Stratton had helped her set up some personal goals. She wondered if Laurie might find a food diary helpful, to identify habits she was unaware of, things like sugar in her tea, habits that Laurie could change. While it all sounds fairly simple, nothing ground-breaking, what mattered was Dr Stratton was taking an interest in Laurie, and asking her to come back regularly to see how she was getting on.

'I've quit smoking,' Laurie announces with pride, as if she never believed she'd utter those words. 'Haven't touched a ciggie for three weeks and I'm noticing the difference already. I'm not nearly so wheezy. The other day I walked from my flat to the park, without stopping.'

Dr Stratton looks delighted. 'Laurie, that's *wonderful*. It takes a lot of willpower to stop.'

'Yeah, I miss it, but now I've got my own place, I don't want the walls in my lounge and kitchen to go yellow.'

'It must feel good to have your own space,' Dr Stratton says, 'to be more independent?'

'Yeah, frightening as hell too,' admits Laurie. 'You know change and me don't get on that well.'

'It must feel like a big step, a lot of responsibility?' asks Dr Stratton.

Laurie crosses her arms. 'Yeah, a lot of responsibility. Too much sometimes.'

After Christmas Laurie moved out of the night-shelter to a house shared with four others. At the time she didn't want to, especially because they were four blokes, but she had no choice. This was a step she had to take before her support worker could find her a place of her own. She had to prove she could live independently. It was also made easier by the fact that Ian had moved out of the shelter. So far, she seems to be managing with her bills. She told me that every month she receives an allowance that helps her put twenty pounds on gas, twenty on electric. She also gets council tax and housing benefits that cover her rent. She sets aside another twenty pounds a week for food and twenty-five for her phone and the Internet. All she needs now is a job. Nina wants to employ her to help with the community workshops and cooking lessons.

'Holly's going to help me paint the house.' Laurie turns to me. 'Aren't you?'

I nod. Laurie now lives in a block of council flats in Shepherds Bush, close to Westfield, the large shopping centre in White City. Her flat is on the fourth floor, it's small, it's basic, but she can sleep with her bedroom door open, fill the fridge with whatever she wants, and drink orange juice out of the carton with no one telling her off – it's *hers*. 'Not that you'd think it, Ian has practically moved in too,' she told me, but I knew, from the way she said it, this was a good thing.

'We've chosen an off-white for the lounge and my bedroom's purple,' Laurie continues, 'and Holly's given me a sofa, and Nina's given me a kitchen table with a set of chairs. We also picked up a fluffy rug, a set of mugs and a teapot at a car boot sale.'

Jamie had kept some of his furniture, from his old home, in storage. We didn't want to throw anything away in case we needed it when we moved out of London. I figured how pleased he'd be to know his old sofa had found a home with Laurie. As for the mugs and teapot, and the fluffy rug, I love going to car boot sales. It reminds me of my childhood.

'It sounds like you're settling in well, and Holly's helping you make it feel like home,' Dr Stratton says, catching my eye.

'Yeah, and Angus bought me a fridge off eBay, a bright pink SMEG one for sixty quid,' Laurie continues in full swing, not that I'm sure Dr Stratton has the time to hear about every single donated item in her flat. 'Angus had an accident, nearly died,' she states in her trademark matter-of-fact way.

'How terrible, I'm sorry to hear that.'

'No need to look so sad, Dr Stratton, 'cos it got him back with his wife and kids. His wife realised how much she loved him, and he loved her, so a happy ending for everyone, right Holly?'

I look down at my hands, trying not to give anything away. My happy ending is nowhere in sight.

'The only thing is we don't get to see him so much, but I understand.' Laurie shrugs. 'We went to the cinema the other night though. Holly couldn't make it. After the film we had a pizza. A veggie one. Healthy.'

Dr Stratton holds back a smile. I wonder if she's used to her patients sharing all the gossip. It also makes me realise that when Laurie feels safe in front of people, nothing shuts her up. Though I don't sense Dr Stratton minds. I think she's encouraged by how much has changed for Laurie in the last six months. During our previous appointment, Laurie was adamant she was never going to quit smoking. 'Everyone smokes at the shelter,' she'd insisted, 'even the staff. It's social to have a smoke in the garden, and it helps my anxiety.' Dr Stratton hadn't pushed it, since it was clear Laurie was making significant changes to her diet alongside exercising with Angel, Angus and me. Plus, she was having counselling at the night-shelter, art therapy. Laurie had told me she wasn't comfortable sitting in a chair staring into space, with too many silences. She felt more relaxed drawing. Instead, Dr Stratton had suggested Laurie try slowly to reduce smoking, since the health benefits would be huge. 'And think of the money you'd save,' Angus had chipped in.

'I could go to Hawaii,' Laurie had suggested.

'Exactly, wearing your little grass skirt sipping your virgin cocktail on the beach,' Angus replied.

'One day,' the three of us had said together, much to the bemusement of Dr Stratton, before Laurie had said, 'I'd still rather smoke than go to Hawaii.'

Dr Stratton makes a note that Laurie has given up smoking. 'It's one of the best things you can do for your health, but I know it can be hard, so if you need any support down the line, do let me know.'

Laurie shakes her head. 'Nah. I don't need support. I'm like Angus, an all-or-nothing guy. What would help is if Ian stopped.'

If Angus were here, he'd be sure to say something like, 'Suggest no hanky-panky unless he quits.'

Dr Stratton empathises. 'That must be tempting when he smokes in front of you. But keep up the good work. And how's the back pain?'

She nods. 'Better. Holly and I still go to Angel's classes, Angus can't join in now 'cos he's working. She makes me do all these boring stretches, but they do help. It actually feels good when I don't have to stop to breathe or rub my back all the time. Sometimes I even forget about the pain. It's my birthday soon, gonna be twenty, and I'm not looking forward to that, but other than that, it's all good, Dr Stratton.'

What Laurie doesn't confide to Dr Stratton is something she told me a few days ago, at the café, when I'd asked if she'd like any clothes for her upcoming birthday, this coming weekend, on Saturday. 'Maybe a nice dress or something?' I'd dared to ask. I'm longing for her to stop hiding behind her baggy tops and tracksuits. I don't think Laurie ever looks in a mirror. 'When I feel better 'bout myself, Holly, I might wear a dress, but it's a long way off. Maybe five years. I'm not putting a time on it.'

I understood, and besides, why should she change? Why should she dress to look pretty and conform? While I felt sad that Laurie remained so threatened by the thought of being 'seen', especially by men, at the same time I was relieved she could tell me how she felt. 'Maybe at some point I won't have to think about what's safe and not safe,' she'd continued, 'but not yet. Buy me a bar of soap or something.'

'Or some veggie straws,' I'd suggested, making us both laugh.

What Laurie does admit to Dr Stratton is that she still sneak-eats when she's anxious, about once a week, but she's keeping her food diary, and her favourite meal now is boiled chicken with sweetcorn, carrots and garden peas. 'The only thing I won't eat is lettuce, makes me feel like a rabbit.'

Dr Stratton and I smile at that.

'And I have to be in the mood to eat celery. It's like string. It needs a nice creamy dip.'

Dr Stratton couldn't agree more. 'Yes, a nice hummus wouldn't go amiss. Well, it sounds like you're going in the right direction, Laurie. There are no quick fixes, and giving up smoking takes a lot of determination, which you have in spades, but please don't forget there is support if you need it. Right, is there anything else we need to discuss today?'

Laurie crosses her arms. 'Nope, don't think so.'

'Why don't we book you in for another appointment in about six months? I'd like to keep an eye on you.'

I suspect Dr Stratton can't do this for all her patients. I sense she's taken Laurie to heart, and I love her for it.

'Keep up the good work,' Dr Stratton says again before exchanging a brief look my way, as if to say keep up the good work too. She stands up and opens the door, but she's not quite ready for us to leave yet. 'Laurie, if we're ever in a position for you to come back and talk to other patients, would you consider it?'

'Me?'

'Yes, you. I think you'd inspire a lot of people.'

She nods. 'All right then. Why not.'

Again, I wish Angus were here to see us all smiling. It still feels wrong without him, as if the centrepiece of the jigsaw puzzle is missing.

33

Laurie and I have been busy since ten this morning making straw-berry fool, vanilla-flavoured shortbread, meringues and a passion-fruit pavlova. Scottie, Monika and a couple of his prep chefs have made enough coronation chicken to feed the entire borough of Hammersmith and Fulham, along with a couple of trays of rice and potato salad. Scottie is also making his homemade burgers, espe-cially for Laurie, with fresh herbs and onion. The smell is making me ravenous.

'Feeling any older and wiser?' I ask Laurie as I spoon meringue mixture on to the baking trays and Laurie makes a passionfruit syrup for our pavlova, and for anyone who wants strawberries with a sauce. I've come to realise what a good cook Laurie is now. The syrup was her idea, as was the shortbread. No longer do I have to tell her what to do. She comes up with her own ideas and teaches me new recipes.

'Shh.' She nudges me hard in the ribs. 'Don't tell anyone.'

'I haven't,' I whisper, which is technically true.

Laurie doesn't want anyone to find out she is twenty today. The trouble is Nina knows, and so does Scottie and Monika, along with our new Jamaican volunteer, Chandice, who replaced Angus. I feel disloyal not telling Laurie that Nina has something up her sleeve but Nina made me promise not to say a word too.

'I hate my birthday,' she murmurs. 'Growing up I never got nothing, only cards and the odd present from friends and teachers, but even if I did get something nice, as soon as I got home my step-mum would take my presents off me.'

I still find it hard to believe the cruelty.

'Why would I want to celebrate my birthday?' Laurie continues quietly. 'Mum died giving birth to me, and evil step-mum didn't want me the moment Dad died. She was only after his house and money. Oh well,' she adds with a laugh, not allowing herself to feel angry, 'that's life, hey ho. Try this sauce, Holly, it's good.'

'How's the flat looking?' I ask, before tasting her sauce, which is delicious. Harriet donated some curtains for Laurie's bedroom. 'I want to do *my* bit,' she'd said, longing to contribute something towards Laurie's new home, before telling me she'd also like to come to the café for Laurie's birthday. 'I'd love to see the café, if that's OK,' she'd said. The only thing left now to buy is a decent mattress for Laurie's bed, but we want to find one that supports her back and that's at least two hundred pounds that she doesn't have. 'Did Ian help you put up the curtains?' I ask.

'I'd be grey and old if I waited for Ian. I did it,' she says, reminding me how capable she is. 'They look nice. A bit flowery, but nice.'

'When are you going to have a house-warming, Laurie?' asks Scottie.

'Never,' she says, her face clouding over once more.

'Laurie, are you all right?' I ask.

'Sorry, hate my birthday,' she mutters again, making me wonder whether Nina should abandon any idea of celebrating it. But then again, Laurie's flat was supposed to mark the beginning of something positive, it was a giant step away from her past. From her childhood and teenage years. 'New home, new me,' she'd said when we were painting her kitchen. I've noticed Laurie's moods are still up and down, like a rollercoaster. When I'm with her, sometimes she's full of chat and doesn't stop talking. Other times she's withdrawn, and pays even less attention to her appearance than normal. Like today. If I'm honest, she looks awful, as if she has just rolled out of bed and bunged on any old clothes, and her hair is greasy. Does she do it to make the hurt of not being loved feel less? I'm not loved because, well, look at me! I can't even be bothered to wash my hair! I'm a mess! Who'd want to love me? She also told me recently that she'd ended her art therapy sessions. 'She kept on asking me deep questions and stuff,' Laurie had said. I imagine what she needs to do is truly grieve for the life she's had, grieve for her past, for the family she never had, and then possibly she could heal. Yet, at the moment, she's keeping me, and the counsellor, at a certain distance so she can stay in survival mode. And that's fine. I don't blame her. Sometimes that's all we can do to get through; going any deeper than that is terrifying. Therapy was daunting for me because I had to talk about Jamie, I had to process my feelings and work through the pain. At times I wanted to leave the room and head straight home to bed. Therapy could unearth so much trauma for Laurie, so maybe it's safer to keep it at bay. Stay in survival mode. Still, when I look back to a year ago, Laurie is a different person, and that's what Nina and I, and all the gang here, want to celebrate today. We want to show her she's accepted and loved. Ignoring her birthday would allow her past to win.

'What I'd like is to see Angus,' she says, bringing me back to reality. 'I miss seeing him through the hatch.'

'I don't,' Scottie calls. 'It's bliss having the house back to myself.'

'I miss him too, Laurie,' Monika remarks. 'He always made me smile.'

'I miss Angus,' calls out Tom, who's in the dining room, preparing the cutlery with Chandice. 'But I like you too,' he tells her, patting her on the arm with affection. 'You're very nice.'

'I wish I'd met Angus,' Chandice remarks. 'He sounds fun.'

'I miss him too,' I confess. I still hear his voice inside my head. Hear his laugh. When I go out for a run it's not half the fun it used to be. Instinctively I turn, as if about to say something to him, and he's not there. Often, I think of him, and wonder how he is. Occasionally I'm tempted to call him, longing to hear his voice. But I never do. I wish I knew how to stop missing him. Because most of all I miss him as a friend.

'Can everyone stop missing Angus and cook?' Scottie snaps.

Monika frowns. 'Miserable sod.'

'You didn't have to put up with him twenty-four-seven.' Scottie turns to us, wiping his hands on his apron, before conceding with a smile, 'I miss him too, all right? But in the meantime, you're going to have to put up with me.'

'I've put up with worse I suppose,' Monika teases, touching Scottie on the arm.

Nina rushes in and grabs me by the arm, before marching me out of the kitchen. 'I've done the balloons, they're in the office, so don't let Laurie go up there. Has everyone signed her card?'

'Yep.'

'Good. Listen, I completely forgot about the candles.' Nina has made Laurie a carrot cake. 'Quick.' She shoves a fiver in my apron pocket.

'Laurie's feeling low today,' I warn her.

'Well, this will cheer her up.'

'She hates her birthday.'

'That was before she met *us*. Have faith.' Nina pushes me away. 'Go. I promise you it'll be fine.'

'Where are you going, Holly?' Laurie asks, joining us.

'Nowhere.'

'She's getting me a coffee,' Nina says, giving me a final shove out of the door.

It's half past one and the dining room is packed, with some eighty or ninety people. There isn't a spare seat to be seen. Craig is here, looking as tired and ravaged as ever, and yet he always turns up at the café, every Saturday. It's his one decent meal of the week, plus it's a chance to see people and talk. He's talking to Harriet, Sander and Lady Sarah. I introduced them. I overheard Harriet saying she'd heard all about Sander's cinnamon buns. This is why Nina set up this place. No matter how tough life is Soul Food is always here, every Saturday, like a faithful friend, with delicious food and human connection to feed the soul. As I refill Craig's water jug and give him a second helping of chicken, he tells Harriet, Lady Sarah and Sander he's thinking, finally, about applying to get some accommodation. That he's getting too old to sleep outside shops and under archways, but he doesn't have much faith in the system. 'I'm going to say it straight,' Harriet says to him. 'I have no idea how hard it must be, no idea at all and I'm not going to pretend I do. But what I do know is life is unfair. Life sucks. I hope the system doesn't let you down, Craig, because I imagine you've been let down far too many times in your life already.'

'She's all right, your boss,' Craig says to me, clearly impressed by Harriet's honesty.

'She's not too bad,' I agree, touched Harriet is here.

'Oh, I bought Laurie some bath stuff, hope she likes it,' he whispers. 'Thanks for the tip. Not often I buy presents for girls.' He winks at Harriet and me.

Laurie doesn't stop to chat to the visitors today. She simply plants plates of food down, before moving away as quickly as she can. I still have a nasty feeling this birthday celebration could be a disaster. As I watch Nina head out of the kitchen and stand outside the hatch, tapping a spoon against a glass, I feel as if I'm watching a film, dreading the next scene to come. It's a car crash waiting to happen. This is when I miss Angus standing by my side. If he were here, what would he say? I think he'd want to celebrate Laurie's birthday, instead of letting it slip by, unnoticed.

'Everyone, listen up!' Nina shouts. People quieten down and turn towards her. 'Sorry to interrupt,' she says, still talking over a few voices. 'Shh! Everyone, quiet! I've got an important announcement!'

'What's she doing?' Laurie says to me in the kitchen, gripping my arm. 'It's the middle of service.'

'I wanted to let you know,' Nina continues, 'it's our volunteer Laurie's birthday today.'

'Oh no,' says Laurie, 'no, no, no.' She turns to me, cross. 'Did you know about this?'

'Laurie, can you come out to the front?' Nina calls.

Laurie grips my arm even tighter.

'Come on,' I say, 'we can do this, together.'

'People haven't had their puddings yet,' Laurie says to me, firmly rooted to the spot.

'Come on,' I encourage once more.

'Their dinner will get cold.'

'Laurie, for once in your life can you allow yourself to be loved?'

'No.'

Somehow, I manage to walk her out of the kitchen and into the dining room. 'Here she is,' Nina says, everyone cheering and clapping as we stand alongside Nina, and all the other volunteers, including Tom, Chandice, Scottie, Monika, Craig and Ian. Nina makes space for Laurie. She stands, stiff as a piece of cardboard. 'Can everyone start singing to our baby of the group, Laurie! Twenty today!'

Laurie holds my hand, her palm sweaty, as we all sing. She looks like she wants the ground to swallow her up.

I'm certain I'm singing the loudest.

'You're *so* flat,' Laurie tells me, her grip finally relaxing, and I do my best to sing the last line even more loudly.

'Isn't she?' someone says as everyone cheers.

My heart stops, before we both turn round to see Angus walking towards us. I feel many different emotions, but the overriding one is how happy I am to see him. I watch as he high-fives Laurie, the two of them laughing. Angus and I still don't hug her, mindful of how she reacts to touch. And then he turns to me and it's as if someone has pressed 'pause'. I don't know how long we look at one another, wanting to say so much and yet there are no words left. 'Come here,' I say, before we throw our arms around one another like long-lost friends.

'Angus!' Nina breaks us up. 'I hope you're staying for lunch? I thought your family were coming?'

'They'll be here any minute,' he says as we part. 'Soph's parking the car.'

Perhaps it helps me that today is all about Laurie's birthday and marking the beginning of something new for her. It's only right Angus is here, with us. Laurie's birthday would not have been complete without him. No matter how little time we spend together now, we will always be a team of three. He came into my life when I needed him most, they both did, and nothing will shatter the precious memories I have of the three of us hanging out together. I grab my mobile from my apron pocket and take a picture of Laurie looking up at him, as if he is the best birthday present ever. 'Didn't I tell you she'd love this?' Nina whispers to me.

I'm only too thrilled to acknowledge Nina was right. Laurie hated birthdays before us, but now that she's standing in a room filled with love, admiration and acceptance, perhaps she might hate them that little bit less. 'I'm sorry I didn't tell you about Angus,' Nina says quietly. 'I wasn't sure he'd come, and I know things have been awkward.'

'It's fine, all good,' I promise, truly meaning it.

Nina runs a hand through her hair. 'I miss him not being here, but don't you dare leave us, Holly.'

'Don't worry, you can't get rid of me that easily,' I reply, thinking my Saturday place is my home. It's my family.

Angus beckons his children to come forward and meet everyone. 'Laurie, this is Benjie, Amy, and I think you've met Sophie,' he says, as they all hand her presents, which join the various other gifts on the table.

Laurie isn't the only one who has changed in a year. Angus is looking a different man, so healthy and fit, but it's more than that. He seems happy. And being happy isn't just about working out and quitting booze. He is a father and a husband again. Isn't that ultimately what we all crave? To belong to something or someone?

There will always be a space in my heart that misses him. How I'd love to spend the afternoon with him, whiling away the hours as we used to. Maybe, in time, we can be friends again, but what I do know is I can't keep on pining for what could have been. My life is too short to be in love with someone who cannot love me back. I take in a deep breath.

At last, I feel free.

* * *

After all the visitors have left, including Harriet who told me she now understands why the café means so much to me, Nina brings out the party balloons and presents for Laurie. It's the usual bunch of suspects: me, Scottie, Monika, Ian, Craig, Laurie, and Angus. Angus's family left shortly after they arrived, but Angus had always planned to stay on at the café to celebrate Laurie's birthday.

So far, Laurie has unwrapped soap bombs, coconut shampoo and conditioner, body cream, sparkly hair accessories that I'm not sure she'll ever wear, and Prosecco that I'm not sure she'll ever drink, though I can help her out there, but it's the thought that counts. Laurie opens another card. This one's from Pat, the handwriting wobbly. *Come and see me soon, have a happy birthday dear Laurie. God bless you.*

She opens a card from Angel, who calls Laurie her star pupil.

'Teacher's pet,' says Angus, as we pass the card round.

'How are you?' I ask Laurie, aware she's been quiet for the past few minutes.

'Scared,' she confides to everyone. 'I've never had this.'

'Well, it's about time you did,' claims Nina, encouraging her to keep opening her presents. Laurie unwraps a collection of Harry Potter books and DVDs from Scottie, a gym bag from Nina, a Moleskine journal from Monika, and Lady Sarah has given her a purple fluffy bedspread. Bruno, being looked after today by Milla and the twins, gives Laurie a water flask, pair of running socks and a box of Maltesers. Angus hands her a badly wrapped present. 'I was in a hurry,' he says. Inside is a framed photograph, taken by Angel, of Angus, Laurie and me after an exercise class in Ravenscourt Park. I recall the day so vividly. It was after we'd been fooling around with the hoops Angel had bought us. Laurie leaves my boxed present to the end. Inside is a pair of Nike trainers that Laurie has coveted more than once, but that's not it. There's a message in the box too, I point out. It's a message asking Laurie if she will run 5 km with me. When she doesn't respond I tell her we can research what runs to do on the Internet, there are so many in London, and we can think about who we want to raise money for, maybe the night-shelter? But it will motivate us to keep fit. 'What do you think?' I ask, aware she hasn't said a word.

'I say, oh yeah!' she says, close to tears, before she gets up and walks over to me, and for the first time ever she places her arms around mine. I can't hold back my tears. Laurie allowing me to hold her, to love her, makes me feel like it's my birthday too. 'Can we raise money for the night-shelter and for Soul Food?'

Everyone claps, especially Nina.

'I love you, Holly,' Laurie says, finally letting go.

'I love you too.'

'We've got one more present!' says Nina, jumping up from her chair, and shortly returning with a carrot cake, decorated with a thick orange and cream icing, and twenty lit candles.

'Wow,' Laurie says, 'that's one massive cake.'

We all clap and cheer again as Laurie blows out the candles.

'Make a wish,' Angus tells her, immediately asking, 'what did you wish for?'

She stares at him. 'If I tell you, it won't come true.'

'For Holly to go to singing lessons?' Angus suggests.

'Or Angus to stop telling jokes?' I follow.

'Amen to that,' says Scottie.

'For Scottie to stop throwing tantrums in the kitchen?' Angus fires back.

'That would be a miracle,' Monika joins in.

'Be let off the washing-up,' jokes Craig.

'Or your boyfriend quits smoking,' Ian says.

Laurie laughs. 'Nah, just that my birthday next year is as good as this one.'

As Laurie cuts the cake into generous slices for us all, I find myself making a wish for better things to come for her. Maybe one day a holiday in Hawaii. Maybe one day a family of her own and her forever home, with her two ginger cats. Maybe one day she'll feel safe enough to wear a dress, if she wants to.

I make a wish for Angus and his family to be happy. For Benjie to keep well and out of hospital. For Angus never to darken the doors of St Mary's emergency department ever again. Or darken Scottie's door ever again, for that matter.

I make a wish for Craig to find some accommodation. For Nina to keep Soul Food going, because this café makes the world a better place.

And while I'm at it, I make a wish for myself too, that Jamie is happy and at peace, wherever he may be. And that maybe one day, I will find someone to love, again.

I will find the right person, at the right time.

34

It's been a month since Laurie's birthday, and here I am, still working for Harriet, still heading to the shops on a Friday, like I always do, to grab us some lunch. On a Friday Harriet and I allow ourselves a special treat in the office; chocolate, or custard tarts are a favourite. This evening I'm going on another online date, and this time my friends and mother won't be sending good luck texts as if it's the event of the year. I'm not about to broadcast to everyone that I'm going out for one drink with a stranger. I feel far less anxious about online dating now. I tell myself that it's one drink after work with someone I don't know, and if we don't click, I'll survive. I'll go home to Bruno, who is always happy to see me. My father doesn't need to fall down the stairs again. Milla doesn't need to invent a crisis. But while I don't broadcast my dates to friends, I do find myself making a wish, as I did on Laurie's birthday, that I might find my somebody to love. That *this* date might be different.

Tomorrow I'll be going to the café, and when I arrive, I'll enjoy my usual cup of strong coffee and a warm cinnamon bun with Laurie. And then, in the evening, I am heading over to see Milla and Dave. Kate and Emily are used to seeing me now on a Saturday night. The moment I arrive they are waiting up for me, with Bruno, whom they look after every Saturday now, while I'm at Soul Food. Bruno loves them almost as much as me. They argue over whose turn it is to feed him, or who gets to hold the lead. I tell Milla I don't want them ever to grow up, 'especially not into teens'. Milla agrees.

I smile, knowing Jamie and I will always feel different about routine. Routine keeps me going. It helps me feel grounded. Safe, even. Yet when I think about the past year, before I worked at Soul Food, I realise that my routine, and I, have changed. I have new friends. My love of cooking has been revived. No longer am I so scared of being alone. No longer do I feel as lonely. This morning, when I woke up with the sun shining through my bedroom window, I felt alive. I felt more myself than I have done in years.

And it's all thanks to Soul Food. 'I want to help others,' I'd said to Nina, when she'd asked me during my interview why I wanted to be a volunteer. I now understand why that response fell flat. I can see her face now, unimpressed by that old chestnut. Of course, volunteering helps others, but the truth is working in the café has filled a deep void in my life. Before I met Lauren and Angus my life was empty. Before I met everyone at the café, my world was small. I'd forgotten who I was. During that interview, I was crying out for help, desperately seeking connection to others, and to myself.

I never expected to make such important friends in the past year. Firstly, there's Laurie, someone whom I cannot imagine not being in my life now. Then there's Nina, Monika, Tom; even Scottie and I have become close. During these past few months, really ever since Angus moved out, Monika and I have noticed he has been far less vile in the kitchen. Clearly having his home back to himself, and not having to worry about his brother's drinking, job and marriage, is a burden lifted off his shoulders. 'I hope Angus doesn't separate from his wife *ever* again,' Monika said to me last weekend, when Scottie thanked us all for our help. Monika and I had nearly fainted at those two words.

Monika is unaware I had feelings for Angus. Nina is the only one who knows he stole a piece of my heart. And possibly Scottie, but he's kind enough not to mention a word. I still look through the hatch and expect to see Angus talking and playing the fool with Tom. I still expect him to walk into the kitchen and nick a chip from the roasting tin. I miss him coming over to the pudding station and keeping me company. Often, I find myself smiling, recalling a funny story he told us. When I'm out walking along the river, towards Hammersmith Bridge, I picture us dancing that night to Belinda Carlisle's 'Live Your Life Be Free'.

Occasionally I ask Nina how he is. When she mentioned he was thinking about moving out of London, to the country, perhaps near the coast, that he and Sophie wanted a new start for their family, I'd be lying if I didn't say I felt sad. While I don't see Angus anymore, that piece of news somehow felt like the final goodbye. I know Milla feels protective; he goes back to his family, and what am I left with? But I don't feel that way, at least not anymore. I will never regret our friendship. Before we met my life was grey. He came into it when I needed him, and he needed me. I realise now, so clearly, that Angus helped me to fall in love with life again. Angus, Laurie, and Soul Food showed me a way back to love, a way back to myself.

''Scuse me, you couldn't buy me some porridge could you, doll?' says a woman, breaking my thoughts. I look down to see her sitting outside the front entrance of Waitrose in Chiswick. She looks about sixty, with straggly hair and a greyish tinge to her skin. She's wearing a navy tracksuit finished off by odd shoes, one blue, the other black.

I'm about to walk on by, but something stops me. I recognise her. She's the woman I saw outside Turnham Green Tube last year. 'Sure,' I say, thinking porridge is an odd request in the summer, but if that's what she wants, then why not? I tell her I'll be about ten minutes or so, that I'll bring the porridge out to her, but she staggers to her feet, as if she can't believe her luck that someone has spoken to her, let alone said 'yes'. She follows me inside the supermarket, sticking uncomfortably close to my side, her beady eyes fixed on mine. I can hear the sound of her heavy breathing, the rattling wheeze in her chest that suggests she's a heavy smoker. I think of Laurie, who still hasn't caved in and had a cigarette. We're training together this weekend, on Sunday morning. She's the one that decides the routes now and where to reward ourselves with breakfast afterwards. She's also working part-time for Nina, helping out with the cooking workshops Nina runs, teaching adults with complex mental health needs, people who don't want to get out of bed, let alone chop an onion, how to prepare healthy meals. 'They like her,' Nina had confided in me. 'Unlike me, they don't mind Laurie bossing them about and telling them to get into the kitchen! "If *I* can do it, so can *you*," she says to them,' Nina recounted.

Self-consciously I pick up a packet of sesame seed bagels, the ones Harriet likes, which I'll fill with some mozzarella, tomato and basil, aware I'm being watched.

'Honestly, I'll bring it out to you,' I say, hoping she'll go away, but she's not going to let me out of her sight now.

I might buy us some custard slices as a treat too. It is Friday after all. She nudges me in the stomach, her elbow sharp and bony. 'You couldn't grab me a loaf of bread, could you, pet?'

I reach for the nearest one.

'Not the white sliced,' she says, grabbing the packet from me and shoving it back on the shelf. 'Tastes of nothing! I like the posh bread with seeds too. They get stuck in your teeth, mind, but better for you.' She nods my way and I can't help but notice she is severely lacking in the tooth department.

Anyway, I place a loaf of brown seeded bread into my basket, thinking she's got some cheek, but admiring her for it.

'No! I like the individual sachets,' she says when we reach the cereal section. 'The organic porridge. Better for you,' she adds as if I should know. Shame on you, Holly.

And three times as expensive! Seriously!

Despite myself I shove the box of organic porridge into the basket, keen to leave now, before it costs me a week's pay. 'Right, that's it,' I say to her, something my mother used to say to me at the super-market if I was making too many demands for chocolate and crisps. Unfortunately, we join a rather long Friday afternoon queue, giving my homeless friend plenty of time to eye the various treats sitting seductively on the shelves close to the checkout. I catch her looking at the selection of spirits and cigarettes on offer behind the till.

'Be a doll.' She points to a bottle of vodka.

'No,' I say, though I can't stop smiling. 'Quit while you're ahead. Besides, I don't have enough cash on me.'

She eyes my handbag. 'But you lot,' she says, as if 'us lot' come from another planet, 'pay with plastic.'

I turn to her. 'Stop pushing your luck.'

She shrugs, as if to say fair enough. 'Can't blame me for trying though. Most people don't give me the time of day.' We shuffle forward in the queue.

'People spit on my shoes,' she goes on, 'or tell me to get off my arse and get a job. Like I haven't tried!' She tugs at the sleeve of my shirt. 'But it's hard when you have no address, no nothing.'

I nod, recalling Laurie telling me the same thing, how she'd often go for weeks without a shower. 'Who's going to employ someone who stinks? Anyhow, I'm fifty-eight, no spring chicken.'

'It must be hard,' I say to my companion.

'It is! Who's gonna take me on? Would you employ me?' She looks intently into my eyes, her stare disarming. 'I used to work in a bank, can you believe it? Counting money and giving advice! Hah!' She wags a finger at me. 'Me! Giving advice! It's no joke. I used to have a home, one hundred per cent. And a man. Nicholas. He put me high up on a pedestal. He died, you know. The love of my life. A lot of bad things happened to me. Bad things happen to *good* people, you know.'

I nod, telling her I do know, and how sorry I am again, tempted to give in and buy her the vodka. I mean, what's the harm? Why shouldn't she have a drink? I'll have one with her too. 'Do you know about Soul Food?' I ask her instead.

She shakes her head. 'What's that, pet?'

I tell her about the café, giving Nina's enthusiasm a run for its money. 'It's every Saturday, half past twelve.' I tell her the address, though fear she won't remember it. 'It's by the church, you can't miss it. We put banners and signs out on the street. They do charge a little, but we never turn people away if they don't have enough money.'

'Sounds too good to be true,' she says, swinging round and nudging the man behind us. 'Doesn't it? Do you know 'bout this Soul Food place? You been?'

'No.' He catches my eye and smiles. 'But it sounds wonderful. I might come along too?'

'Yes!' I say, rather too enthusiastically.

She nods at him. 'The more the merrier! I'll see you there, pet. Blow me down, you're a good-looking chap. Isn't he, doll?'

I try not to laugh again as we reach the front of the queue. But yes. Yes, he is. I actually noticed him when we were in the cereal aisle. From the amused look on his face, he'd clearly overheard my friend asking for organic porridge. He's tall, slim build, light brown hair, black-rimmed glasses which made him look like a thinker, and a wide, open smile that could surely make anyone feel that life is worth living, even on the greyest of days.

I begin to unpack, noticing the odd look coming from the cashier, as if my new friend and I are unlikely companions.

My companion swings round and peers nosily into the stranger's basket again. 'A lasagne for one,' she says. 'Shame. No one special in your life then?'

It's a good excuse to turn round and look at him again, trying to communicate with no words that I'm sorry about this invasion into his love life. But he doesn't seem put out at all. 'No, no one special at the moment. Unfortunately.'

'Oh, shame! Isn't that a shame, doll?' she repeats to me as I pay for our food, distracted, flustered, wondering if I should ask him out for a coffee, or would that be weird, spook him out? Would it be too forward? Yet I asked Jamie first, and look how that turned out.

'You're an angel,' she says to me when I hand her the shopping outside. A scruffy-looking man wearing a cap and carrying a guitar approaches us. He looks familiar. I'm sure he's someone I've previously ignored on the street. She shows him the food I bought for her as if she still can't believe her luck.

Just before I paid, I saw her looking longingly at the packets of Dairy Milk and couldn't help myself. Besides, it kept me in close proximity to the stranger for that little bit longer. 'Right, I must be off,' I tell her, knowing Harriet will be wondering why I've taken so long to get our lunch. 'It was lovely to meet you. Take care. And don't forget about Soul Food. We'd love to see you there.' I glance at her friend. 'You'd both be welcome.'

She takes my hand and holds it firmly in hers. 'What goes around comes around, doll,' she says. 'I'm Cindy by the way. God bless you.'

As I head back to the office, I catch myself looking over my shoulder. I see Cindy and her friend walking the other way, their arms linked. It's only then I notice how pronounced her limp is. What I wish I could have done is buy Cindy a pair of comfy, matching shoes. Maybe, if she comes to the café, I can find out more about her, which doorway she sleeps under, or where she lives, but most importantly, what size feet she has. It wouldn't surprise me if Craig knew her. It's a small world out there on the streets.

My mind then drifts to the man in the supermarket. I wonder how many times we encounter strangers in a shop, on the Tube or in the park, strangers who could become so much more if we got over our fear and struck up a conversation. Instead, I walked away. Why didn't I have the courage to ask his name? Or even ask him out for a coffee? I mean, what did I have to lose? The worst thing he could have said was 'no'. Why wasn't I brave like Laurie, who asked Ian out when they were in the supermarket, walking down the cheese aisle? 'Holly, if I'd waited for Ian to ask me, I'd be half dead! Sometimes you've got to grab the bull by the horns, right?' Laurie will be disappointed in me. Maybe he will come to the café? Or was he only saying that to be polite?

'Excuse me,' someone says, interrupting my thoughts with a tap on my shoulder. 'I think these are yours?' I turn. It's him. Breathless, as if he's been running for his life, he holds up my house keys with the Waitrose loyalty card attached to the keyring. After the cashier had scanned my loyalty card, I must have put my keys down to pay. But that's not the point! My scattiness has finally done me the most gigantic favour. Don't let him go again, don't let this stranger walk away. The universe is giving me another chance. The universe is trying to tell me something.

'I'm Marcus,' he says, offering his hand.

'Holly,' I reply, my hand remaining in his. 'Would you like to have a coffee with me sometime?'

Why can't we stop smiling at one another? Why do I feel as if we've met before?

Someone was listening when I made that wish.

Acknowledgements

Writing *The Saturday Place* has been a story in itself. It began with a friend and neighbour of my parents in Winchester, Sarah Chester, asking if I'd like to join her for lunch at a café called FirstBite. FirstBite was a community-focussed social enterprise using surplus food to fight food waste. The moment I arrived, enjoyed some delicious food, and asked the people sitting at my table why they came every week, I knew I had to write about this amazing place. FirstBite wasn't just about food. It was about friendship and community, and providing meals people could afford. All thanks to Sarah, for introducing me to FirstBite, knowing it was a place I'd fall in love with.

The next step was to ask Debbie Lockett, who ran the café, if I could create a story inspired by her venture. Within days, she handed me an apron, and introduced me to the other volunteers who worked in the kitchen, warning them I had a notepad and pen in my apron pocket. I loved meeting and greeting the regulars, and talking to the volunteers who told me what volunteering meant to them. They include Simon, Fergus, Caroline, Toby, Paul, Richard, Laura, Thea and finally Tracey. Tracey was in charge of looking after me, and she and I became good buddies. She told me how FirstBite had transformed her life. When she was interviewed by Debbie, she was scared to be around people and crowds. She told me what it was like to be homeless, and to live with severe anxiety. She also prided herself on not being a quitter. FirstBite and her friendship with Debbie was her chance of a new beginning. While Lauren, Holly and Angus's story is complete fiction, Tracey's spirit, kind heart, and fierce determination to survive have inspired this novel. I also want to thank Debbie, so much, for her encouragement, trust and all the support she gave me while I was writing *The Saturday Place*. I couldn't have done it without her.

Thank you to Michele Price from the former Winchester Churches Nightshelter (WCNS) for her insight into night-shelters. To Andy, Charli, Gill, Hugh and Matthew (who has sadly died since this book was written), who all told me about their life experiences. I found each story thought-provoking, moving and inspiring.

Thank you to Sue Thorne, Caroline and Kitty who each gave me a taste of working in the PR world. To my doctor friends, Anna and Ben, who came to the rescue when my characters needed expert medical attention. To Sarah, a personal trainer, who I met in the hydro-therapy swimming pool. Together, we devised a fitness programme for my characters. To Sylvia, also a personal trainer, who runs fitness bootcamps in west London and allowed me to watch her classes in action. I had great fun talking to you all.

Thanks to Felicity and her son, Eddie, who told me what it is like to live with anaphylaxis. Anaphylaxis is a severe and potentially life-threatening reaction to an allergic reaction which can be caused by food, medicine or insect stings. Felicity described the impact it had on their family. What came across strongly for me was the constant care, love and vigilance needed by parents to keep their child safe from an anaphylactic reaction, along with the courage and sheer frustration for children like Eddie who don't want to be held back, who long to eat whatever they like, and be carefree children. I was deeply touched by their story, which is why I wanted to raise aware-ness of something so hidden, and how it affects families.

To my friend Tom, for his humour, charisma, and support with this book. Tom, you have the best laugh in the world.

To all my friends and family who cheer me on from the side-lines when I'm writing. To Mum and Dad, I love you. To my best buddy, Mr Darcy, who gives me loads of ideas as I walk him round the park.

All thanks to my editor Carolyn Mays and the team at Bedford Square Publishers, for loving my story as much as I do, and creating such a beautiful book. I have felt in such safe hands, and been inspired by the new direction you have taken me in.

Thank you to all my loyal readers, and the bloggers who continue to support me. I cannot wait to hear what you think of *The Saturday Place*.

And finally, to my agent, Diana Beaumont at Marjacq Script. Diana and I have worked together for over 20 years, and she has never lost her faith in me as a writer, even when I've lost faith in myself. Thank you, Diana, for all your guidance, friendship and support. You are the best.

Photo credit: Alicia Clarke

Alice has published two non-fiction books, and ten novels, including the critically acclaimed *A Song for Tomorrow*, and the No. 1 Kindle bestselling title, *Monday to Friday Man*. Her writing is funny, romantic, powerful and emotional. At the heart of each novel is a love story but Alice always includes hard-hitting and thought-provoking themes within her storylines, based on her own experience of a professional tennis career cut short at the age of 18 when diagnosed with rheumatoid arthritis.

Alice is currently living in west London, and training to be a psychotherapist. Her favourite thing in the world is walking her beloved Lucas Terrier, Mr Darcy, in the park.

alicepeterson.co.uk
🐦 **@alicepeterson1**
📷 **@alicepeterson39**
❶ **facebook.com/AlicePetersonAuthor**